THINGS WE SHOULD HAVE SAID

PEACE SUMMERTON SERIES

EVIE HILL

BLACKROCK BOOKS

Publisher: *Blackrock Books*, 2024

Created with Vellum

PROLOGUE

Dear Reader,

Peace Summerton is a small, honey coloured, stone village, nestled amongst the rolling green hills of the English countryside. It has a pub - as all good villages do - a small supermarket, a post office, and a community village hall. It is quintessentially English. But it is not perfect. Nowhere is.

The people of Peace Summerton have problems, like us. They are sometimes good, sometimes bad, but mostly they are somewhere in between. And they make mistakes, like we all do, then try to make amends. If they're lucky, they succeed. Peace Summerton is a place of community, of friendship and kindness. It is also a place where mistakes are allowed and forgiveness, if sought sincerely, is given.

This is the first story in Peace Summerton, a story of loss and love and a realisation that home is where the heart is. It is also a story about honesty and seizing the moment to tell the truth. There is too much regret in *the things we should have said*.

Happy Reading, Evie.

ONE

WILLA

Oh great, a padlocked gate. Just what I need. I'd seen romantic pictures of Peace Summerton Lodge, but I'd never actually been here before and if the reality of the overgrown driveway and the ramshackle house up ahead weren't enough of a surprise, I was also locked out!

I banged my gloved hands together, slipped the mitten off my right hand and tried my luck with the combination lock. God bless Maud for helping us escape, but this place was in the middle of nowhere, I had no signal on my phone, and she certainly hadn't given me any numbers to memorise. I was stumped and I wasn't prepared for doing battle with a frozen padlock at 5am in the icy cold. Not after the night I'd just had!

I fiddled a bit with the numbers, blew on them, tried to lick them warm, and got my tongue stuck on the ice.

"Ouch! Shit!"

I looked behind me to check no-one was listening.

"Lord Willa, of course no-one is listening! GET A

GRIP! You're miles from civilisation, it's just after daybreak, it's dark and cold and miserable and..."

I stopped.

"And you must stop talking to yourself. It's really weird."

I went back to the van. The engine was still running, and I couldn't see any heads popping up which was a good sign. I leant in and took the envelope Maud had sent me off the passenger seat and looked at it. 'Don't forget my birthday' was written on the outside of it in thick green pen with a lopsided smiley face underneath. Typical Maud - loves attention. I shook the envelope out and stared at the house keys and the random sheets of paper on the seat. No codes, no numbers, just a reminder to send her a card on the thirteenth of August.

"Ahhh! Willa, you twit! Of course!" The code was 1308. Maud's birthday! I hurried back to the lock, rubbed it several times to defrost it and twirled the numbers.

"Tahdah!" We were in.

THE VAN heater was thankfully still churning out warm air, a welcome respite as I had got quite a chill out there. I climbed in and a fug of fetid, sleepy breath and coffee dregs enveloped me. It had been a long night, and I was pretty much fraying at the edges. Hell, I'd frayed halfway down to the seam to be honest and I desperately needed caffeine, a wee and an hour or two of sleep. I revved the engine and drove through the gates and on towards Peace Summerton Lodge, our new home.

Ha! New home it may have been, but it was one I now couldn't get into! If I thought that the padlock on the main gate was my only challenge then I was wrong, with a capital

R. The key for the front door didn't work - didn't even fit – there was something prickly nesting in the wood basket under a pile of old jumpers and a jackdaw had made a nest behind the lintel over the door. She was watching me with an expression that said, 'I wonder when she's gonna blow...'

"I'm not," I told her, "Well not yet anyhow..." I had a plan.

Checking still no heads popping up in the van, I surveyed the façade and reckoned that I could climb up the front of the house, using the front porch to the right as a foothold and prize open the window closest to it. Peace Summerton Lodge was a long, low roofed, rickety house made of honey coloured stone. It must have been over a hundred years old and the small crooked, cottage style window frames were painted the colour of clotted cream to match the stone. There was a chimney at one end of the roof, which seemed to sag in the middle, and the stone porch had a front door that was painted bright pink. That was a Maud-ism; it had to be. I crossed the frosty lawn, leaving footprints in the white icicles, and hitched my skirt up, tucking it into my knickers. I started to climb. Thank God for DMs, they had excellent grip.

I got my foot onto the brickwork and pushed myself up, reaching with my fingertips to just below the window. I found a small hold and heaved, my legs and feet scrambling underneath me to find purchase. I got it and dragged my lower body towards my arms and the window. I was almost there when...

"Got you! Oh no you don't! You get down here now!!"

Someone had hold of my legs and was pulling me down, gripping my thighs in an arm lock. I kicked and held onto the window.

"Get off me!" I shouted, "Get off me, you madman!!"

My legs began to flail, and my fingers were slipping. "Get the devil off me! I'm going to fall! Get..." I let go and suddenly my body dropped like a stone, right on top of whoever still had hold of my thighs. He broke my fall as he landed smack into the hard, frozen ground. I kicked loose and jumped to my feet.

"What the hell are you doing?" I shouted. He was winded, he couldn't speak. "I have every right to be here, I've been driving all night and I..."

He'd got onto all fours and amid my apoplectic rage, I couldn't help noticing that he had the peachiest of butts, muscular and tight. Christ Willa, focus on the fury, will you?

He got to his feet and began moving towards me. It was just light, and I could make out a wall of muscle under his shirt. Wait, was that his pyjama shirt? I brushed my hair out of my face, put my hands on my hips and took up a fighting position... or as close to a fighting position as I could muster, having never been in an actual fight.

"Now listen here," I said again, "I have every right to be here, I..."

He continued to advance, and I had visions of him placing his hands either side of my arms and lifting me up to move me like a forklift truck. By the look of his biceps, he'd be able to do that easily.

"I don't care what rights you think you have young lady, but this is not a place for squatters so you can take your tin can of a van and whoever else you've got sleeping in there and get the hell off this property!"

Tin can of a van?! Young lady? Squatters? I sucked in a breath. How dare he? The van wasn't top of the range admittedly, but it was mine, and all paid for, and it slept four, which was lucky as Basil took up a whole bunk to himself. And young lady? How old was I, twelve? Sooo patronising.

"I am not a squatter!" I shouted, "And that is my camper van, which, for your information, is vintage and home to my..."

"Willa?"

We both turned and Esme stood on the drive, in bare feet and nightie, Basil by her side, baring his teeth in what looked like a Scooby-Doo grin, you know, the one where Scooby's eaten all the snacks?

"Willa, are we there yet?" Esme said. "I really need a poo."

TWO

TYE

Oh, fucking great! A kid! And a dog! This was gonna be a whole lot worse than I thought. It was all very well evicting squatters, but squatters with kids and dogs, well, that was a whole different ball game. Kids I could do without, but I was a sucker for dogs. Hell, I cried so much during Marley and Me I had to lie down after the movie.

But admittedly this kid was quite cute, and, if I'm honest, so was her mum. All wild hair, DMs and scowling offence. Gorgeous eyes. Intense. Come on Tye, focus on what's gotta be done.

"Right!" I said loudly, "Kid or no kid, you can't squat here! I'm sorry, but I must ask you to leave. NOW. I know it's early, but if you head towards town, there's a tea and coffee van on the lay-by just before you get to the petrol station and here..."

I dug in my jeans pocket for my wallet. I always keep an emergency twenty in there. "Take this and buy your daughter a bit of breakfast. There's a good library in town, they'll give you lots of advice on where to go." I shuddered.

It was bloody cold this morning and the thought of the kid on the side of the road eating a bacon bap was a dismal one.

"Oh nice, thanks. And I'm guessing Esme can poo there too, right?"

Esme. Nice name, sort of old fashioned. Oh God, yes, the poo.

"Erm..."

Wild-hair-DMs stared at me.

"Erm?" she queried. "Is that an erm, no? Of course, she can't poo in a lay-by on the side of the road. Or a yes, let her poo wherever she likes?"

"Yes! I mean, no, yes, it's a no." I was NOT usually tongue tied but I spied Esme shuffling from foot to foot and sensed an air of urgency. "It's no and look... I live up the road, well, across the fields. So, if you want, Esme can use the toilet in my house. My Land Rover's parked...." I didn't want to open up the Lodge, I might never get them out again.

Esme's face changed, sort of crumpled up and Wild-hair-DMs strode towards the van yanked the back door open and bent inside. She scooped up a Paw Patrol duvet and turned.

"Look, you can use the toilet, I didn't say you could move..." The duvet wriggled.

Oh, fucking great. Another kid. Or another even larger dog!

Esme began to whimper.

"Where's the jeep?"

I pointed.

"Let's go!"

"Right! This way."

We cut through the small, wooded area at the side of the house to the fields behind and I opened the doors of the

Land Rover. Wild-hair-DMs scuttled onto the back seat with the duvet, which wriggled a bit more and was moaning and Esme shuffled in after her, then the dog. I jumped in, started the engine and revved. This *was* a farm vehicle, but nevertheless, I really didn't want a child's crap in the footwell!

We got to the house faster than I've ever done it before. Admittedly, it is only two fields away, but I was impressed with my driving. So obviously was the dog, as he had his head on my shoulder the whole way, licking my ear to encourage me. I yanked on the handbrake and leapt out.

"This way!" I shouted. Esme jumped down and sort of ran, half waddled behind me, trying to squeeze her butt together.

In the kitchen we made it past Eadie, who looked up from the lump of dough she was kneading as if she'd just seen a rat run through the kitchen. I flung the door of the downstairs loo open. "Lav – there - GO!" I shouted and made a swift exit.

In the kitchen, the duvet was sitting on a chair whilst Wild-hair-DMs made a quick dart towards the toilet. Eadie slapped the dough down on the table with a thwack and stared hard at me.

"Dear Lord in Heaven, Tyler Malloy, do not tell me that this is Maud's niece and her two children?!" She stared at the dog, who looked to be a Heinz 57 - a bit of this and a bit of that, and quite a lot of Labrador. "And a dog. Sit!" The dog did what we all do with Eadie and sat down immediately.

"What? Maud's niece? What the devil are you talking about Eadie, who the hell is..." I stopped and looked at the small head that had just emerged from the duvet. It was sleepy, creased and on the verge of tears. It had bright red hair, freckles and was the kind of mischievous face that inspired cartoons. I had a horrible feeling that I had missed something.

"Maud sent a card, a few days ago," Eadie went on. "Said her niece was having trouble. Lived in... where was it now? somewhere in the north..."

"Newcastle," Wild-hair-DMs said from the doorway. She was holding Esme's hand and she stared challengingly at me. "It's up north, in case you've never heard of it. About eight hours drive away, in a camper van."

I sat down. Christ, I felt a chump. I'd seen the card, ignored it and waited for Eadie to tell me what it was all about - which she had and which I'd then promptly forgotten.

Eadie wiped her hands on a tea towel. "You poor loves," she cooed, moving towards Wild-hair-DMs, "Maud said you'd got into a bit of a pickle and had to make a quick exit. Have you been driving all night?" Eadie had gone into full commando-caring mode. "Come and sit down my darlings, you must be exhausted." Eadie held out her arms and Esme gravitated towards her. Wild-hair-DMs watched Eadie hug Esme, who seemed perfectly happy by the way, but something must have triggered her tears because her bottom lip had begun to quiver. "Thank you," Wild-hair-DMs said, her voice tremulous. God, I felt abso-fucking-lutely terrible. There was something killing about tears, but tears from a woman as beautiful as this made me want to double over.

"Sit!" Eadie instructed, looking at Wild-hair-DMs. "Tye, put the kettle on and make yourself useful. You can go and get some fresh eggs while it's boiling and grab me a bag of cookie dough from the freezer in the shed on your way back."

I stood. "So, you're not squatters then?" I asked lamely.

"No."

Eadie threw me a look.

"*What?!*" I shrugged. "It was an easy mistake to make." I looked at Wild-hair-DMs. "You *were* trying to climb in the window, weren't you?"

"Maud sent me the wrong keys," she said defiantly.

Eadie tutted loudly. She glared at me. "Did she now?"

Oh fuck.

"I couldn't open the front door."

"Well, trying the window seems like the obvious thing to do to me, seeing as you couldn't get in the front door..." Eadie said, glaring at me even harder.

Oh, double fuck.

"Is there something you might want to give... erm,"

"Willa," Wild-hair-DMs said, "Willa Hart. And this is Esme, Teddy in the duvet there and that's Basil, our dog."

"Is there something you might want to give Willa? The new keys for the new locks in Maud's house perhaps?" Eadie prompted.

"New locks?" Willa's defiance had swollen to a sort of constrained rage. I could feel it bubbling, just beneath the surface.

"Someone had tried to get into the house", I said, "last week, so I thought it would be best to change the locks and..."

"And not let Maud know?"

Willa – great name, even more old fashioned than Esme, so fucking cute – narrowed her eyes and she had a flush of anger that swept across the top of her cheeks. If I'd been even one iota interested in finding a woman at that point in my life, she'd have been so fucking perfect. But I wasn't. Thank God. A woman was the last thing I needed.

"No." I said.

"So you attack me..."

"It was hardly an attack..."

"And wrestle me to me to the ground..."

"I don't think I wrestled you, I think it was more of a gentle tug..."

"And you didn't even think to ask me what I was doing there, you assumed, ASSUMED, that I was a squatter, A SQUATTER! And all that time it was you! You had gone and changed the locks and not thought to tell anyone, especially not the person who rents the house!" Willa crossed to me and pointed her finger at my chest. Basil growled at me. "You," she said, tapping my pecs, "Are not a very nice person. AT ALL!"

I stared down at her hand and resisted the urge to take hold of it. '*Not a very nice person?*' Was that the best she could do? Lame. I shrugged. Then I turned and hotfooted it across the yard to the hen house to find our new tenants some breakfast.

THREE

WILLA

Good God! The nerve of it. It was lucky he scurried away because I was likely to do something that I rarely do - I'd been tempted to kick him hard, in the shins. I was so mad, so tired, so desperately in need of a cup of coffee that I had completely forgotten that a pee had been top of my list nearly an hour ago.

"Could I use the bathroom myself please... erm..."

"Eadie. Eadie Flood. Very pleased to make your acquaintance Willa, Esme, Basil, and Teddy." Eadie looked down at the duvet.

"Teddy," I said, "Is a force of nature, with a heart of gold." Teddy kept his head buried. "Ted? Say hello please." Teddy popped his eyes above the edge. "Hello please," he mumbled.

"Haha, very funny. Ted?"

Teddy put his whole head out and smiled. "Hello Eadie Flood." Teddy had been blessed with a melt your heart kind of smile, which was pretty lucky considering the amount of calamitous trouble he got himself into.

Eadie grinned back. "Well, nice to meet you, Teddy. I'm guessing that you're a boiled egg and soldiers' kind of chap, am I right? Shall we get some toast on for you while we wait for fresh eggs? And how about a hot chocolate?" She looked at me. "Go on, he's fine, leave them with me. Third door on the right."

I glanced round the large, warm kitchen. Eadie stood at a long pine table which took up the centre of the room, there was an Aga in an alcove and an eclectic selection of cupboards. This was the sort of kitchen where families were raised, comfortable and easy, with a dresser full of small clay figures made in year 2 and chairs that held old feather cushions to ease your back. Yup, safe to leave the kids here for a few moments. I excused myself and headed for the toilet. I was sure Teddy could be left for five minutes, at least I hoped he could. Now that I'd remembered, I was suddenly desperate to go.

THE THIRD DOOR on the right was a Victorian cloakroom, all black and white tiles, the size of a single bedroom, with a throne-like pan, complete with polished wooden seat and stained-glass window behind it. Blimey, this family really knew how to elevate the ordinary.

I peed, flushed - pulling a porcelain knob on the end of a chain that released a symphony of gurgles and whooshes - and went to wash my hands in the sink. I glanced in the mirror above it, an old, faded affair with mottled silver but even that didn't hide the pale tension in the face that stared back at me. I dried my hands and twisted my dishevelled hair up into a top knot, securing it with a pin from the pocket of my skirt.

"Willa," I said aloud, "What on earth are you doing?" I

stared hard at my reflection, but I honestly didn't have any answers. I'd had to run - I didn't have any choice - but what on earth was Syd going to say when she found out? And what would she do? I dug in my pocket and checked my phone. It was too early for messages, just past 6am, but they'd come, as soon as she realised. I turned the damn thing off and did what Harry had suggested. I blocked her number. Best not to know, I thought.

I straightened my skirt and left the bathroom. Shit. Now, where? I'd found it easily enough, but standing in the dark passageway, I had no idea what door led back to the kitchen. I guessed - I had a 25% chance of getting it right - and took the second door on the left.

"Holy Crap!"

I found myself standing in a huge, drafty entrance hall, facing a long sweeping staircase, hung with forbidding family portraits. They may have planned the perfect restroom, this family, but they weren't a happy looking bunch! I moved towards the staircase and climbed, gazing at the dark, sombre paintings of ancient people in fine clothes with wholeheartedly miserable expressions. Money doesn't bring happiness then. This place was like something out of *Bridgerton*, even the heavy gilt frames around the paintings must have been worth a bomb! I climbed, mesmerised, and found myself suddenly at the top of the stairs. Countless rooms went off to the right and the left of the galleried landing and naturally – I mean who wouldn't have – I turned down the passageway and opened the first door I came to. I peered in.

"I see! Snooping, are we?!"

I jumped and spun round.

"Holy Crap!" My heart thudded in my chest. "No, I was just...

"Snooping!"

"Looking! And you shouldn't go creeping round and sneaking up on people like that! It's mean and rude and..."

"What?! As rude as snooping?!" He snapped. He was standing close because I'd spun right round into him. He'd changed out of his pyjama shirt and was wearing a tight black tee shirt with a pair of pretty battered combat trousers. He had something tattooed on the inside of his arm, names and dates, but I couldn't decipher what and it was rude to stare. I stepped back and folded my arms across my chest, trying to stand a bit taller.

"I wasn't snooping, I was just looking... there's a difference."

"Oh, really?"

"And I thought you were getting eggs, in the hen house. Instead, you're sneaking round, scaring the living daylights out of a person..."

"Who's snooping round my house."

He raised an eyebrow at me and grinned in a wholly patronising way. God, he was absolutely infuriating!

"I told you, I was NOT snooping, I..."

"Hellooo? Tye? Is anyone home?"

We both turned and he moved swiftly to the top of the stairs. I followed. Just inside the doors stood the most beautiful young person I have ever seen. My gaze moved from her to Tye, whose face lit up at the sight of her. Hmmm, if I'd harboured any thoughts about him – which of course I hadn't – they'd have been wasted. This person was clearly important to him... VERY important.

He bounded down the stairs and there was that peachy arse again. Willa, stop! I averted my eyes and followed him down. I stood a tad awkwardly while he hugged said beautiful person then she stepped back and looked at me.

"Hey," As she moved away from Tye, I did a quick assessment of the look. Yup. She pulled it off! Immaculately clean denim dungarees, baggy, which only emphasised how lithe she was, a white tee-shirt and a huge man's padded plaid shirt over the top, highlighting her femininity.

"Hi" I squeaked, suddenly embarrassed by my creased clothes, wild hair and altogether grubby appearance.

"I'm Cecelia" She had a voice like warm honey, "Cecelia Flood, but everyone calls me Cici as Cecelia is a bit of a mouthful." She laughed, "especially when you're mad or in a hurry." She held out a hand, long, elegant fingers with... wait, was that dirt ingrained into her skin and under her nails? "I work in the farm shop here," she said, following my gaze. "And the garden and I help get some of the produce out of the ground! Hence the nails!"

"You don't just work in the farm shop Cici, you *run* it! Which reminds me, I've done the eggs already and left them by the back door."

"Did you get enough kale for today? And some of the apples from the store would be good too, we're running a bit low."

Tye smiled. Not the sneery grin he'd given me but a full-on Colgate ad for tooth-whitening smile, where the skin crinkled at the side of his face, which by the way was weather beaten and had a light brown stubble on the cheeks, the sort that made you want to run your fingers over it.

"I'll get the kale picked now, always better fresh and I'll bring some apples over with a nice cup of coffee about ten. You OK opening up? It's bloody freezing this morning, have you got gloves with you Cici?"

Cici turned to me. "How rude are we? Rambling on

about the farm shop and I didn't even ask your name. I'm sorry."

"I'm Willa," I said. And as if I wasn't dazzled enough already, Cici smiled at me with such sincerity that I wanted to cry. I almost wailed, "and I've been driving all night and I'm exhausted and..." And now I come to think of it, I never did get that cup of coffee.

"Well, it's lovely to meet you Willa, it's nice to see Tye has finally found someone so..."

"Good God no! No, no, no!" Tye suddenly cried. "No, it's not like that Cici, Jesus No! No, it is definitely not that, no!"

I turned to look at Tye. What the hell? I know we hadn't exactly hit it off but was I that much of an ogre that he had to deny any involvement so vehemently?

"I'm Maud's niece," I said, "Maud Large. She's lent us the house while she's away. We just arrived and... we couldn't get in – long story – and Esme was desperate for the loo, so, well, here we are." I shrugged.

"Esme?" Cici asked. She had a wide-eyed look about her as if everything was a curiosity and a joy.

"Willa's daughter." Tye interjected.

"She's not..."

"You clearly started very young." Tye interrupted as he raised an eyebrow at me. "One of those teenage mums we read about?"

I stared at him, my mouth dropped open and the urge to kick him hard in the shins came back so strongly that I had to step back in case I gave in to it. Well, let him believe what he wanted, I didn't care. Bigot.

"Esme's nine," I said, "and Teddy is seven. They're in the kitchen with Eadie. Would you like to meet them?"

Cici grinned. "I'd love to Willa. Tye? Lead the way."

Tye smiled again and nudged Cici who nudged him back affectionately. I followed on, feeling tired, dreary and like a spare key at a swinger's party.

WHEN WE GOT to the kitchen, my mood instantly got worse. Teddy was banging on a saucepan with a wooden spoon, making one hell of a racket, Basil was barking, and Esme was up to her elbows in a bowl of sudsy water, washing dishes and throwing bubbles all over the place. She was soaked and there was a small lake of water under her feet. Oh. My. God. Why, for once, couldn't they just be sitting colouring or chatting or doing something QUIET?! I caught a glimpse of Tye out of the corner of my eye, and I swear I saw him flinch. Cici, on the other hand, waltzed right on in and started jumping to the beat of the drum and clapping her hands in time. Teddy was delighted and banged even harder. If I hadn't fallen in love with her before, I did now. This girl was BFF material no doubt whatsoever!

"Are you OK?" I shouted to Eadie, "Shall I take them away?"

Eadie was placing the dough into bread tins and seemed completely oblivious. She smiled and hummed as she went about the task and simply didn't answer me. Tye went to the dresser reached into a cup and pulled something out. He handed whatever it was over to Eadie. Eadie fiddled with her right ear, then her left and suddenly started. Ah, hearing aids!

"Oh Lord, what a noise! Teddy, you are a genius making such a wonderful sound. Cici, stop dancing and take the spoon off him please. Tye, put a towel down under Esme and remove the washing up liquid. Willa sit! You, my lovely, are exhausted!"

Both Cici and Tye did exactly what Eadie asked, which was cute, if a trifle puzzling, but then so did I. I sat and Eadie went to the stove to fetch the coffee pot. She poured a mug of rich dark coffee.

"Milk and sugar?"

"Both, erm, please." She placed a steaming cup in front of me and I took a sip. Heaven.

"There," she said, and she brushed the top of my head with her fingers. I held the mug in both hands, suddenly aware of just how exhausted I really was, and I felt the beginnings of tears. Teddy, now minus drum, looked at me and came to sit on my lap. Esme turned at the sink, saw Teddy and came up behind me with wet arms, encircling my neck and placing her warm, damp cheek against mine. I felt the tears roll. Here we were, in a strange house, with people we didn't know, no money and starting all over. I gulped down a mouthful of coffee to stop the wail that was rising in my throat. I hugged Teddy tight and planted a kiss on Esme's little hands. Oh, dear God, what had I done?

FOUR

TYE

Oh shit, tears. Willa Hart, all one hundred and twenty pounds of determined, annoying and quirky gorgeousness was crying, and I felt my insides go to mush. Shit and treble shit.

Eadie and Cici had moved right in, Eadie handing out tissues and Cici patting Willa's arm in that really unique way that she had which was reassuring and kind and not in the least bit irritating. I backed right off and seeing the little guy wriggling on Willa's lap, I winked at him. He winked back. Well, it wasn't actually a wink, it was more of a double blink with both eyes, but I got the message.

"Hey, Ted, do you fancy a ride on my quad bike?"

Willa looked up. "Oh, I don't think that..."

Teddy had already climbed off her lap and was standing by the door. He was wearing fireman pyjamas and bare feet. Eadie looked at me and rolled her eyes.

"He's not going out on that quad bike, Tye, not in his pyjamas he isn't, it's freezing cold, and he's got no shoes on!" Eadie looked at me as if I was some kind of idiot, which I probably was when it came to kids. I hadn't a fricking clue and I didn't know if I even liked them. "You can take Teddy and Esme across to the barn and introduce them to Sandie, Petula and Cilla. Go into the boot room and find some little boots for them and some socks." Eadie glanced across at Willa. "And take them both with you. You can leave Basil." Eadie gave me one of her long hard stares which usually meant, 'I need some privacy.'

"Teddy," I said, "Esme, come with me to get some boots."

Both kids stayed where they were and stared blankly at me.

Eadie threw me another look. Crap. How was I supposed to make trying on boots and looking at cows sound exciting.

"Guys," Willa said, "I bet Tye's got some really big boots that you can stomp around in the mud in and then he'll take you to say hello to the cows. They've all got names – Petula, Cilla and Sandie." Willa smiled to herself. She got the joke; I'd named them all after 1960s pop divas. "I think cows are smelly, what do you think?"

"Of course they're smelly Willa," Esme said, pulling herself up to full height, "But we should go and check to make sure. Teds, I bet they smell of poo."

Willa? That was unusual, not Mum, or Mumma. It was odd, but in a cute way. And she'd done it, she'd made them all excited and intrigued. It didn't make her less annoying, but it was pretty genius.

Teddy had started to snigger. "I bet they've got pooey bums as well," he announced, "and pooey breath."

"Teddy," Willa warned, "Don't get carried away. Now go on, go and get some boots on and tell me whether the cows do really have pooey bums and stinky pooey breath!"

Teddy and Esme laughed at Willa's continuation of the joke and Willa smiled to see their reaction. She had a warm, easy smile; it made her eyes sparkle. Hell, it was plain to see that she loved those kids. And I have no idea why, but it gave me a warm feeling despite the cold.

I whistled, and Eadie snapped, "They're not dogs Tye!" But Esme and Teddy both came to the door pretty pronto, and so did Basil, which did make me a bit uncomfortable. I whispered, "I think I've got some sweets in the boot room..." I put a finger to my lips. They weren't dogs, but they were similar, weren't they? Good behaviour was rewarded with treats. I knew Eadie had picked up on what I was doing, and she didn't approve, but I took Teddy's hand - now that was a surprise, I don't usually take *anyone's* hand, hand holding was not for me - and I opened the door to the passage and the boot room, leaving the girls behind.

FIVE

WILLA

As soon as Tye had stepped out of the room with Esme and Teddy, I knew I was in for it. I'd caught sight of Eadie's face, and she wanted answers; I could see it in her eyes. And who could blame her? A strange woman arrives at the crack of dawn with two kids, allegedly Maud's niece - but there's no proof - she's a mess, she's driven through the night and at the first sign of kindness she dissolves into tears. Things didn't stack up and I knew I had some explaining to do.

"So, you're not just here for the half term holiday, are you?" Eadie began gently. "I'm getting the feeling that you're planning to stay a bit longer than that."

I nodded.

"Do the kids know they're not going back?"

Again, I nodded. "They've been at a new school," I said, "It was Syd's idea, it's a private school, with blazers and hats, and they hated it, well, Esme did, she was so unhappy and well Teddy didn't really care, but he kept getting after school detentions and he's only seven and so..."

"Syd?" Cici asked. "Is that your ex?"

Oh boy, here we go. I'd never been good at sharing things, never. I kept things in, preferred it that way, it meant I could cope. I mean, all the time with Lexi, I never told anyone about it, only Maud knew and then I just dropped out of school to look after her.

I nodded. Syd wasn't *my* ex exactly, but still *an* ex. "And then when Harry told me what Syd was planning, I rang Maud in Costa Rica and the next thing I knew she'd spoken to Miss Kindness...-"

"You know that's not her real name, right?" Cici said, "It's Ella, Ella Blackmore. Miss Blackmore."

"Yes, yes I know, but everyone calls her Miss Kindness, because she's so..."

"Monstrous with kids," Cici said, and we all smiled. It broke the tension.

"Go on," Eadie encouraged.

"Yes, well, Maud said how lovely she was and how good the local school was, and she asked Miss Kind... I mean Miss Blackmore if she had space and she did, so before I knew what was happening, I had a new school for Esme and Teddy and when Harry told me about Syd, well..."

I looked at their faces, still blank confusion.

"Harry?" Eadie asked.

"Harry," I faltered. "Harry's my...Oh, look Harry isn't important," but he was, he was part of the reason I was here. "Syd wanted custody and well, I couldn't part with them, especially knowing that they didn't like Syd and liked Daisy even less."

"Daisy?"

"Syd's new girlfriend, well partner."

They looked at each other. It made sense, well enough sense for now. If it wasn't the whole truth, it was part of the way there and I hadn't lied. Cici got up and came over to give me a hug. She bent down and put her arms around me. She smelled of roses.

"Right, well," Eadie said, standing straight and placing her hands on her hips. "That's the kids sorted then; I feel much better now. I was worrying that you'd done a bunk with them, and they'd be all upset and discombobulated."

"They still might be," I said.

"No, you're all right. The local school and Miss Kindness is right where they belong. They'll be just fine." She turned her formidable gaze on me. "But what about you? How are you going to be?"

I shrugged, but I felt my bottom lip begin to tremble again. In truth, I had no idea how I was going to be. I'd fled, in the middle of the night, with just a thousand pounds in the bank and as many clothes as I could fit around everything I'd brought for the kids, which wasn't much. "Fine," I said, "I think."

Eadie raised an eyebrow.

"Honestly, I think I'll be fine." I stood. I was stiff and cold, and I suddenly remembered how tired I was. "Well, I'll be fine as soon as I get the kids sorted and unpack and get settled."

Eadie went to the door and took a big brown overcoat off the hook on the back of it. "Go and fetch them then," she said "And Tye will settle you in, get the heating on and stuff and you are coming back here for supper..." She looked at me and wagged her finger. "And I won't have any excuses. Cici will be here and her friend Nellie..."

"It's Angelica now Eadie, she's not Nellie anymore."

"Angelica smellica," Eadie harrumphed. "Her mother called her Nellie and that's what she'll always be to me. Right, off you go. We'll eat at six, on account of the kids."

She handed me the coat, opened the back door and

hollered for Tye. I stepped out into the cold, huddled in the huge man's overcoat that Eadie had given me and was led, by the sound of laughter and Teddy shouting, to the cow barn.

The door was half open and I peered in. Teddy was standing on a stack of hay and Tye stood below him with his arms open. Teddy gave a yell and leapt forward. I swallowed a gasp as Tye caught him and threw him up in the air. Teddy shrieked with joy and laughed uncontrollably. As Tye placed him on the ground he turned and saw me in the doorway.

"Snooping again," he said.

I bristled, then I saw him smile.

"No, sorry, I didn't want to spoil the fun." Teddy was shouting, "Again, Again..." as he clambered up the hay bales. Tye grabbed him and lifted him down. He placed him on his feet and put his fingers to his lips. Teddy hushed immediately. Blimey, that was a first!

"Where's..."

"Esme?"

Tye nodded in the direction of cow stalls, and I saw Esme planted on the gate, her face close to a brown cow with huge love-me eyes, and she appeared to be singing to it. I smiled; I couldn't help it.

"That's nice," Tye said, "You know, that's only the second time I've seen you smile."

"Well," I said, "I've not had too much to smile about, being mistaken for a squatter and wrestled to the ground."

"Sorry," he said, holding his hands up, "honest mistake."

I nodded and we stood there in silence for a moment. Teddy had joined Esme at the gate, and I knew within minutes he'd start annoying her, but I didn't want this moment to end. It was nice, warm and... well, to be honest, I was beginning to feel a distinct tingling between my legs, and I had to focus on the hay bales. There were children present. I cleared my throat.

"Do you erm think that we could get a lift back to Maud's?"

"Sure."

He whistled and Esme and Teddy both turned and trotted over to him, accompanied by Basil. I shook my head. What the hell?

"That's rude," I said curtly, "As Eadie said, they're not dogs, they're children, they deserve a bit of respect."

"Says the lady who bundled them into the back of a van in the middle of the night and drove them nearly 500 miles south to a place they don't know, in the middle of nowhere."

I glared at him. Who the hell did he think he was, making judgements about me? He knew nothing. That desire to kick him came on strong again.

"Can we go please?" I snapped. "We need to unpack and, for your information, Esme and Teddy do know this place, they've... they've seen pictures, and they know Maud." I pulled the coat a little tighter round me. "Really well!" I finished. Then I called to the kids and Basil and walked out of the barn.

SIX

TYE

Crap, me, and my big mouth. I knew as soon as I said it that I'd hit the wrong buttons. When she arrived in the barn, she looked so lost and small, wrapped in my dad's old coat that I just wanted to scoop her up the way I had Teddy. Then I made her smile and for a few seconds I had it, right there, the sort of moment that you remember forever; laughing kids, warm barn, the smell of hay, light coming in through the cracks, and a beautiful woman smiling at me. Then I went and ruined it all with my careless, stupid remark. Open mouth and insert foot. The mood changed instantly from warm barn to arctic outhouse, and by the time we got to the Land Rover with the kids and the dog, she was miles away from me again; cross, tense and with that look of utter exhaustion and despair she'd had when she first arrived.

I headed across the fields while Teddy asked me a barrage of questions about cows and Willa sat stony faced and silent. At the copse I parked and jumped out to help her to the house.

"It's fine," she said, "We can manage." Just like that, curt, without looking at me. I helped Teddy and Esme down. I felt peeved. Why the hell was she so difficult? Okay, I said a stupid thing, but she didn't need to be so prickly about it. We all say stupid things from time to time.

"You sure?" I asked, although by now I was hoping that she'd tell me she didn't need my help.

"Yes."

She turned towards the woods and the gate to the lodge.

"If you get stuck..." I said it like I knew she would, and she glared at me.

"I'll find a way round it," she said. Then she turned and looked at me square on. "Because funnily enough, driving through the night to somewhere we don't know and feel completely lost in was my way of finding a way round something, of finding a way out. Not giving up. But then I wouldn't expect you to understand that. You don't look as if you've ever had to find your way out of anything tough. Ever."

And with that she walked away.

Now I was more than peeved, I was fucking mad. She'd assumed that my life had been so sweet that I was a stuck-up prig with no understanding of anything beyond myself. How dare she make judgements about me? She knew nothing about my life! Shit. And shit that she looked so beautiful while she riled me. That was infuriating.

I STOOD and watched her go and wondered what Eadie was going to say when I arrived back at the house within minutes instead of the hour or so it would have taken to get Willa settled. Well damn it, Eadie would just have to say what she would and be done with it. I wasn't going back.

My fury that she had judged me, coupled with a desire to put my arms around her were enough to send me racing back to the jeep. I climbed in and revved the engine, letting the throttle out so quick that I sent a spray of mud up behind me as I screeched off.

BACK AT PEACE SUMMERTON HOUSE I took the lane round the side of the house towards the farm shop and pulled into the small, gravelled car park in front of it. I stopped the engine, took the keys, and threw them into the pocket of my coat as I jumped down. They joined the other set I already had in there. Oh Crap! Maud's new house keys! I should have given them to Willa when she got out. I had a vision of her climbing through the window again, but this time with a fear of her falling. I jumped back into the Land Rover swung it instantly around in a wide arc and headed back in the direction I'd just come.

AT THE COPSE I parked and hurried through the trees towards the Lodge. I came into the clearing and onto the front lawn of the house. I stopped. The lights were on, there was a smell of wood smoke, and the van was neatly parked by the front door, its hatchback open, half emptied. I glanced up. The first-floor window was still open, and I smiled. It seemed I was superfluous, and it also seemed that I'd underestimated Willa Hart.

SEVEN

WILLA

I reached up and suddenly my face was just next to his. He leaned down and his lips were soft and warm and...

Holy Crap! I woke with a start. For one awful moment I had no idea where I was. I sat up quickly and shook my head to clear it. I was on a sofa, I had a blanket over me, I was stiff and cold and one of my legs had gone completely numb. There was a lump of a dog on it, snoring. I sat up, shifted Basil off and looked round.

"Esme?" I dropped my feet onto the ground and stood up. "Esme? Teddy?" I glanced round the room. Empty.

I felt a sudden lurch of fear. "ESME?!" I shouted, hurrying into the hallway. "ESME? TEDDY?"

Nothing. I tried the kitchen; empty. Now I really began to panic. The Lodge was an old cottage, with low ceilings and flagstone floors and it was the biggest house we'd ever stayed in. It had a sitting room, kitchen, a dining room which Maud seemed to use as a general storage area - packed with boxes of God knows what - and a small snug off the kitchen with a wood burning stove and a squishy sofa. I tried every room downstairs then ran outside. All empty. I ran out of the front door, accompanied by Basil, checked the van, then ran round the side of the lodge into the garden.

I carried on shouting, my heart banging in my chest. I ran back inside, all the time wondering if anyone knew where I was, if she could possibly have found me... taken them.

"ESME?!" I hollered, striding the stairs, two at a time. "TEDDY?"

At the top of the stairs, I stopped. There, at the end of the landing, was a small camp. The rugs from the van were draped between the banister and a chair they had dragged from Maud's bedroom, there was a duvet on the floor as a ground sheet for their makeshift tent and the old overcoat that I'd been wearing up at Peace Summerton House covered the entrance. I got onto all fours and crawled up to it, pulling the coat aside. Esme and Teddy were both fast asleep. I was relieved and sorry - as I so often was - that Lexi wasn't here to see this. I manoeuvred myself inside the small space while Basil sat guard outside it, and lay down next to them, my feet sticking out. I closed my eyes. I'd never questioned how it came to this, it just had, and it was hardly the life I'd imagined for myself. But...

I took Teddy's hand and held it. No time for self-pity - it was a phrase I had on repeat - barely time for a wee. What's done is done – another phrase on repeat. But the done is done doesn't stop the pain. Not when you miss someone you love.

"Willa?"

"If we pinch her ear then she might wake up..."

"You pinch her then..."

"No, you do it."

"You're scared..."

"You're a poo-poo head."

"You're a scaredy poo-poo head and you smell...."

"I don't smell. WILLA! WILLA! Mimi said I smell."

I opened one eye. Mimi was a hangover from when Teddy couldn't say Esme.

"You do smell...." Suddenly I lunged and grabbed Teddy, tickling him. "You smell yummy and I'm going to eat you..." He screamed and wriggled free, scrambling out of the tent. I went after him and chased him to the stairs. "Don't run!" I called. He bounced down on his bottom and I threw the overcoat over my head and monster-walked down after him.

"I'm coming to get you! I'M GOING TO EAT YOU!" I tripped slightly on the bottom step because I couldn't see much. "HERE I COME, TO EAT YOU ALL UP!"

"Oooh, I wouldn't, honestly. I should think I'm pretty tough and chewy."

I stopped and pulled the coat off my head. The front door was wide open, where I'd left it in my panic to find the kids, and now a man stood in the porch, letters in hand.

"Percy," he said, "The postman." He smiled. "The tough and chewy postman. Not edible at all, no, no, no."

I smiled back. Lord, what did they put in the water round here? Percy was tall and broad, all pumped muscle, with long blond hair that he wore pulled off his face with a thin black hairband. His face was bearded, tanned (out in all weathers I expect) and he was so Viking that I expected to see a longboat out front. I peered over his shoulder to check. Nope, just a bicycle with a trailer.

"Hi," I said. "I'm Willa."

He looked quizzical.

"Maud's niece," I filled in. Basil, Teddy and Esme appeared, ever curious, and Teddy clasped me round the legs. Not a great look. Basil growled quietly, eyes intent on Percy.

"Teddy and Esme," I added. "Nine and seven. Basil the dog, probably also about seven, but we're not sure. It's OK, he's harmless." I smiled and glanced down at the kids. "They're not!"

"Well nice to meet you all," Percy said. Unlike Tye, he looked completely nonplussed by two kids under ten. "I usually carry dog treats," he said, grinning, "For pesky pooches that go for my ankles." He looked at the kids, "You wouldn't do that would you? Bite me on the ankles?" They both shook their heads solemnly and I laughed. "Good, well then tomorrow I'll bring you some sweets and then I can be sure you won't." He handed over some post.

"For Maud," he said. He dug in his pocket for a treat for Basil and held it out. Basil had no loyalty. He snaffled it instantly and went in for a head pat. "Will she be away for much longer?"

I shrugged. Maud was an intrepid traveller, or at least she had become one since Lexi... I didn't finish the train of thought. I took a breath. She couldn't stay still, it made her too sad, at least that's what I thought. She'd never said, she just upped and left one day and had been coming and going intermittently ever since. "Maud is..." I wasn't sure what to say.

Percy laughed. "A law unto herself," he finished for me.

"Yup. She is."

"I'm glad you're here to take the post in though, I hate leaving it stuffed through the letterbox. Are you staying long?"

Nice. Causal, post related, but the way he grinned at me said otherwise. There was promise in that grin.

"I've moved in," I said.

"Well, that's good news. Peace Summerton could do with some new neighbours, and you guys will certainly brighten the place up a bit." He continued to grin. And stare. And grin some more.

"Thanks."

"You two starting at the local primary?"

Esme nodded. Teddy looked up at me. I nodded at him. "Yes," he said.

"Well, that's good too." A car came up the road in front of the lodge and beeped its horn. Percy looked behind him and waved. "Right then, I'd better be off," he said. "This post won't deliver itself." He turned and headed for his bike. "Nice to meet you Basil, Esme, Teddy and Willa."

Nice. I liked that, addressing the dog and kids first. The sure-fire way to a woman's heart is to be nice to her kids, and her dog.

"Bye," I called. The kids waved as he headed off and glanced back at us. Basil followed him to the end of the drive. Like I said, no loyalty. I watched him go, a biking Viking. A hot one too. I closed the door and looked down at Esme and Teddy.

"Right," I said, "We need to go and get some food. And how about baking a cake for this evening, for dinner with Eadie and Cici?" We headed towards the kitchen. "Esme, organise the coats and Teddy get the shoes." I stopped. "Ah, we'd better get you dressed first, hadn't we? Don't think we can really go shopping in pyjamas."

EIGHT

TYE

I pulled up outside the small shop in the village and saw the camper van. Damn. She was the last person I wanted to bump into. I wondered about driving to the supermarket on the outskirts of Peace Summerton. Come on Tye, get a grip. You're going to have to see her at dinner tonight. But then dinner in the kitchen at Peace Summerton House with Cici and Angelica would be diluted and there'd be little chance to let her get to me, whereas in the mini mart anything could happen. I started the engine again as she came out of the bakery and headed towards the village shop. Teddy saw the car and jumped-up waving at me. Too late. I'd been seen. I switched it off again and climbed out.

She nodded at me. I nodded back.

"Hey guys," I said to the kids. "Ted? How are you doing? Esme, Sandie Shaw misses you already." I walked with them into the shop and took a right, hoping Willa and the kids were taking a left. They were. Escape. "Catch you later," I said. I walked down to the dairy fridge, grabbed the milk, and started back to the counter, passing Alfie

Roycroft, who I saw out of the corner of my eye put a pack of rolls into his ruck sack. I hung back. He added biscuits, and a packet of pasta. Poor kid. I followed him to the cash desk.

"Hey Tye," Ellen, the shop assistant, was waiting for Alfie to choose from the chocolate bars in front of the desk. I could see him eyeing them up, trying to find the smallest and the cheapest. She kept looking at the CCTV camera, as if she was waiting for something. She was. Moments later, Mr Renton, who owned the shop came in from the back. Ellen looked uncomfortable. He approached Alfie.

"Excuse me young man,"

Alfie started and flushed a deep red.

"May I take a look in your bag?"

I stepped forward. "Alfie, can you show Mr Renton what I'm paying for please?" I said, "We agreed you could add a chocolate bar, so why don't I open the bag and you choose what you want?"

I looked at Mr Renton. "Sorry, I told him to just bung it all in the rucksack and I'd pay at the cash-till. We didn't have a basket, forgot to get one on the way in." Mr Renton looked embarrassed.

"I hate doing this," he said, sotto voce to me, "But we've had so much theft from the shop, I don't know what else to do." He emptied the rucksack and Alfie's meagre possessions – a wool beanie with a hole in it, a dog-eared schoolbook and a couple of chewed pens fell onto the counter, along with the bread rolls, the pasta, the biscuits, and a couple of other items I hadn't seen him put in.

"Alfie? Didn't you get the ham and cheese for mum? She did ask you to." I said.

Alfie stared at me. I saw him swallow and the flush on his face receded slightly. "Yeah, thanks Tye." He scuttled off to the fridge and came back moments later with a saver pack of ham and a small slab of cheese. He could have ripped the arse out of that, but he didn't. He was a good kid.

"Right," I said. "Add those to the bill please Ellen and Alfie, grab a handful of Yorkies for everyone will you?" He looked at me agog for a moment, then took three biscuit and raison Yorkie bars and added them to the pile. He stood; head hung down while Ellen rang it all up and I handed over the milk I'd come in for.

Mr Renton said, "The Yorkies are on me."

Ellen smiled at me, relieved. Everyone knew the Roycroft family, but no-one knew how to help. This was small beer. I tapped the machine with my card and put Alfie's items back in his bag.

"Come on mate," I said. I glanced at Mr Renton, then I leant in. "Thanks for that. Next time Alfie is in, and you check his bag, just put it on my tab, will you?"

"I will, thanks Tye."

Alfie and I left the shop.

OUTSIDE ON THE PAVEMENT, Alfie looked at me. He was embarrassed and the flush on his face had angered his rash. He always had a rash, dermatitis, or something. He shuffled from foot to foot. "Thanks," he mumbled.

"No problem, Alfie. How's Mum?"

He shrugged. "Okay."

I doubted that. I hadn't seen her in over a week which was a bad sign. "Come up to the farm shop Alfie, whenever you want. We often have surplus we can't sell." It was a pointless request, but I made it anyway. Megan Roycroft wouldn't let Alfie past the main parade of shops in the village, especially not when the paranoia was bad. "You want a lift home?" I finished.

"Nah, but thanks." I remembered he wasn't allowed in a car either, or on a bike.

"OK but let me know if there's anything you need. You take care now Alfie."

"Thanks Tye, I will." He turned and headed off towards Mallard Avenue where he lived. He was a small, lonely figure and it made me sad to watch him go. I walked to the car as Willa came out of the shop. She stood on the pavement and stared at me.

"What?" I snapped. Suddenly I felt angry. Why the fuck did kids have to suffer the problems of their parents? What in God's name had prompted Willa to uproot two small people and drag them to Peace Summerton where they knew no-one? Like I said, kids suffer the problems of their parents. I climbed into the Land Rover, revved, and drove off without looking back.

NINE

WILLA

Well, that was awkward. And weird. Who rattled his cage? And all I was going to say was how nice that was, with that kid Alfie. Jeepers, the man was exasperating. Hopefully, after tonight's dinner, I wouldn't have to see very much of him. Attractive as he was, he just wasn't worth the stress, way too unpredictable!

I bundled the shopping into the van and took Teddy and Esme's hands. I'd promised them that they could feed the ducks in the pond by the village green. Just for a short while as we'd left Basil back at the Lodge. We'd bought some duck feed in the shop, and a bit of fresh air would do them good. We crossed the road and walked across the grass to the edge of the pond. The ducks saw us coming and immediately began quacking and waddling towards us. This was clearly not an original idea; they had that expectant look in their eyes.

Teddy cowered back and Esme began to wail as the ducks marched on towards us.

"They're only ducks," I said, more confidently than I felt. There was a small army of them rapidly approaching and they threatened to surround us. "It's fine, they won't harm us..." But I caught sight of a large drake with a malignant glint in his eye, and I really wasn't so sure.

Suddenly, from behind me I heard the rush of wind and the flap of a cape. I glanced back and saw a tall thin girl with bright red hair and a long magenta cape swoop past us towards the ducks.

"Timor!" she shouted, flapping her cape as if it were wings, "in omnia te benedicam et custodian!" Blimey, what on earth was going on? She flapped and repeated her Latin chant, running through the crowd of ducks, who probably thought that this was a bird far bigger than them and not to be messed with. They retreated rapidly to the pond and swam off. The girl stopped as suddenly as she'd started and turned to face us, beaming.

"A good spell always works," she said triumphantly. She had a young, pretty face, pearly white skin, dotted with freckles. "I'm Angelica," she went on, "I'm a white witch."

"Hi," I said. I'm..."

"Oh, I know who you are. You're Willa and this is Teddy and Esme, right?"

I blinked rapidly and stared at her. She beamed even wider. "I told you, I'm a witch..." she glanced at Esme and Teddy, "But a good witch, not a wicked one, I only do good things and good spells and stuff." She turned back to me. "And I knew who you were because I can read things and see into the future." She smoothed her cape and tucked her hair behind her ear. "We were destined to meet."

"Wow..." Esme murmured by my side. "Do you know fairies and elves?"

Angelica looked a tiny bit taken aback by this question. She squatted down so she was at Esme's level. "Erm, I know of them," she said, "And some of the elves are really very naughty. Not at all like you I bet."

Esme shook her head earnestly.

"Good."

"We're really pleased to meet you Angelica," I said. "I think we're going to see you later, at Peace Summerton House, for dinner. Eadie said that you were invited."

"Yeah, I know that. I sensed it. And of course, Cici is my best friend." Angelica stood straight. She was about three inches taller than me, and I had to look up at her. She cut a very imposing figure in bright pink with flame red hair that rippled down past her shoulders. "Well, I should get going," she said, "Now that I've saved you from being quacked to death." Teddy sniggered. "Or covered in duck poo," she added, watching Teddy for a bigger laugh, which she duly got. "I'll see you later at..." she held both hands up. "No, don't tell me..." She closed her eyes for a moment and made some waving movements with her hands in the air, to encourage the energy I suppose. "Six p.m. Early, for the children."

I nodded. "Very impressive," I said. She was a Kook, but a lovely one.

"Laters Gaters," she said, "Be on time, not later than 6 on the dot!" And she walked backwards away from us, all the time watching the ducks as if she were controlling them in the water.

Esme turned to me, her face alight with awe. "Isn't she wonderful Willa, the witch?"

"Yes," I said. "Now scatter the seed quickly and let's get out of here, fast, before the ducks come back onto dry land." We chucked great handfuls of seed as far away from us as possible and then headed quickly back to the van. By the time we got there, we looked back at the edge of the pond, and it was a wriggling mass of brown feathers. We'd escaped, just in time. Remind me not to feed the ducks again any time soon.

TEN

WILLA

By late afternoon, we had baked our cake - a light lemon sponge with three layers, lemon curd and cream cheese filling – and we had cleared up. I say we, but mostly it was Basil and me. He licked the floor clean, and I washed everything up. Nine and seven are not really the right ages for good kitchen staff. After that we got ready, but getting out of the house with two small kids is like chopping firewood in a rubber dingy. It might work, but then again, your hand might slip, slice through the rubber and down you'll go, sunk in a second.

I had all three washed and ready by five thirty; Teddy's hair dampened and combed so that it didn't stick out at right angles to his head and Basil contently dribbling, brushed and in his 'going out' diamanté collar and pink lead. Lexi didn't approve of gender stereotypes, especially not for dogs. If only she'd seen Esme's tulle ballerina skirt in lavender and her sequinned jumper in pink, both worn with leopard print wellies and black and white striped tights. Esme was all girl, but with attitude, so maybe that cancelled out the all-girl? Anyway, I left them all watching Paw Patrol, a bit too young for Esme and Ted, but Basil loved it, and I nipped upstairs for a cat's lick and a promise. Fifteen minutes later I was back down in jeans and a tee-shirt, my hair newly washed and drying into an unruly lion's mane. I'd finished my make do outfit with a coating of dark red lipstick, my favourite, to complete the look. Esme looked round; her little face lit by the blue glare from the TV.

"Willa, you can't go to dinner in jeans." She continued to stare at me. "You can't go in jeans and boots Willa; you HAVE to wear a dress."

"No, I don't poppet, I'll be fine. It's a casual meal in the kitchen."

She stood and came across to me. She looked very grave. She shook her head. "No, Willa, you can't go in jeans."

I stared at her. Now normally I'd probably have said, "Oh don't be such a dolt Esme, no-one cares what I wear," but something in her earnest gaze stopped me. It was quite clear that this was important to her; very important. I took a breath and glanced first at Teddy, mesmerised by the TV, closely mimicked by Basil and then at my watch. "I'm not sure that I have time to change," I said, "We have to be there in..."

"Fifteen minutes," she said, already ahead of me. "There's lots of time. You should wear the blue velvet dress." She wasn't budging, she had her hands on her hips and was staring me down, indicating that any argument was futile; the conversation was over. An impressive nine-year-old, this one.

I went back upstairs and rummaged in the drawer. I had thrown everything in a few hours ago under the guise of unpacking. Nothing there. I checked the wardrobe in my room. Nope, I hadn't hung it up; I hadn't hung anything up.

I went into Esme's room, the one she had chosen opposite mine, with a sloping ceiling, a white metal bed frame and small rose buds dotted over the walls. I found the blue velvet dress. It was hanging from a hook behind the door in all its rich, dark beauty. It was hanging where Esme could see it before she went to sleep. I stopped and swallowed down a lump that rose in my throat. It had been my first dress and Lexi had found it in a junk shop for my school prom. It was a 1930's evening gown and it was tired and frayed when she had brought it home. Lexi had mended it for me, taking it up, and in, adding small sleeves, reworking it so that it fell on the bias from my hips, into a swirl of dark blue intensity. She was so clever with clothes; she knew how to bring out the beauty of them. By the time she had finished it was perfect. And here it hung – we called it *Lexi's dress* - for her daughter to see each night as a reminder, as a goodnight kiss.

I took it to my room, undressed, and slithered it over my head. I added a heavy cardigan, my boots, and I piled my hair up into a top knot, securing it with a band. It was transformative and Esme had been right. Now I was ready for dinner in Peace Summerton House. Thank you, Lexi.

We piled into the camper van, I strapped everyone in, and Basil sat in the back giving the house the once over, checking it was all ours in that territorial way that he had. We set off, out of the drive of the Lodge, a hundred yards down the road and right into the drive of Peace Summerton House. We motored slowly, for what seemed like ages, under an arch of interwoven branches from the sycamore trees that lined the drive. Either side, beyond the trees, was open parkland which, in the dark, seemed to stretch for miles. And then we came upon it. The house. I slowed to a stop, and we sat there, just looking at the symmetric loveliness of this eighteenth century manor house, lit by the lights from inside and a line of candle lanterns up the front steps to the grand portico and front door.

"Holy shit," Teddy said.

I turned to him. "That is not at all polite," I said. "Please do not use that word."

"You do,"

"Well, I shouldn't either."

Esme turned to me. "I told you the dress was better."

I smiled at her. "You did, and you were right." I drove forward and parked our shabby van by the steps. "Come on," I said, "I am absolutely starving."

We climbed out and suddenly Cici appeared, flinging the door open – well, as much a heavy double oak door can be flung – and bouncing down the steps.

"You're here!" she exclaimed. "At last!"

"We only came from next door," I said as she scooped Esme and Teddy into a hug. She turned to me and grinned.

"Of course, you did," she said, "But we're still delighted that you're here." Cici was pure gold, through and through. She hooked her arm into mine and led us all into the house.

If the house was impressive during the day, at night it shone. The lamps lit the walls turning them the colour of butterscotch and the chandelier over the staircase sent a hundred shafts of light dancing across the floor. I stopped and looked round.

Cici said; "It always takes your breath away at night, this place." She winked at me. "Even the grumpy old portraits look less forbidding." She glanced up at one on the staircase. "Although not less ugly. You'd think they'd get the artist to touch their images up a bit, wouldn't you?"

"Maybe they did, and this was the best that he, or she, could do."

Cici laughed. "Good Lord, imagine what they really looked like. Thank God Tye isn't related, otherwise he'd be sporting that funny weak chin and pretty big nose."

"Beauty is in the eye of the..."

"Beholder." Esme finished for me. "It means that beauty can get into your eye, and you hold it there and it makes everyone look nice."

"Well... Okay, I'll take that." I glanced at Cici who was still grinning. "Everyone is beautiful to someone, isn't that right Ted?"

Teddy nodded. He was holding Basil's lead and Basil could smell the food. He was having a hard time restraining a dog almost as big as he was. "Some people think Basil is ugly, but we don't, do we Willa?"

"Well..." I shook my head. "Smelly sometimes, and noisy, and naughty, but no, we think he's a very handsome dog."

Teddy was being pulled in the direction of the kitchen and Cici said, "Come on, or Teddy won't have an arm left." We hurried after the impatient Basil, across the hall to the corridor that led to the kitchen, the boot room, the pantry, the laundry and the cloakroom. Once again, I was momentarily lost.

"This way!" Cici directed. "Follow your noses." We did and moments later she opened the door ahead of us, revealing the kitchen transformed into a candle lit dining area.

"They're here!" she called out, a bit pointlessly as Basil had slipped the lead and bounded towards Eadie, all diamond collar and Scooby grin. Angelica turned from the dresser where she was lighting more candles.

"I told you they'd be here on time!" she exclaimed, "I could see into the future, and I just knew it."

She came across and hugged me, then Esme and attempted to ruffle Teddy's head, but he ducked.

"Eadie doesn't believe that I have the powers of a white witch, but your arrival at 6pm exactly is what I predicted."

I smiled. I didn't mention her earlier instruction.

"It's just good manners Nellie," Eadie said, "To arrive on time and I'd say that Willa has excellent manners." Eadie came and hugged each of us in turn. Teddy endured the embrace as politely as he could, and I noticed that Eadie had slipped him a small cocktail sausage as a bribe. Eadie clearly knew a thing or two about seven-year-old boys.

"Where's Tye?" Teddy asked.

Eadie said, "He'll be late, there's something wrong with the Land Rover and he's down at the barn fixing it now.

Teddy was momentarily crest fallen, but Eadie lifted the plate of warm sausages off the table and held it out.

"I thought we girls could have a drink and a few nibbles to keep us going," she said, "Would you be in charge of the sausages Teddy?"

Teddy grinned from ear to ear and took the plate from Eadie. He held it up high, away from Basil, but I'd already seen him slip a sausage into his pocket to give to the dog.

"Oh, the cake!" I said, "We made a cake, and I've left it in the van. I'll just pop out and get it."

"A cake, how lovely! I'll pour the wine while you go and get it. Red or white Willa?"

"White please. But only half a glass please; I'm driving. Teddy, Esme? You OK to stay here for a few minutes?" They both ignored me – a good sign. "I'll only be a few moments." I glanced at the door.

"Second on the right takes you back to the hall," Cici said, smiling.

ELEVEN

TYE

This was clearly going to be a bigger job than I'd thought. I'll admit I'm no mechanic, but I know a bit and I was stumped. I turned the engine off, lifted the bonnet for one last look and billows of steam poured out. Again. Fuck. I left it gushing and headed towards the house. I needed to let Eadie know that I'd be late for dinner, and she wasn't looking at her phone. Nothing new. She never looked at her phone, except to do Wordle.

I hurried across the courtyard from the barn and round to the back of the house. I'd wanted to install security lights around the back, but Eadie said the foxes would set them off and she'd be kept awake all night with flashing lights. Bit of an exaggeration, but Eadie was in charge – always had been. So, it was pitch dark and I only had the torch on my phone. As I came round the corner, at a pretty rapid pace, I banged straight into her. Bam! And almost knocked her off her feet. I grabbed her and held on for a few moments to steady her, and myself, then I righted her and took a massive step back.

"Bloody hell! Are you OK?"

"Yes!" She scowled at me, or from what I could see in the darkness, it looked pretty much like a scowl. "I'm fine," she snapped. "Shocked and lost, but fine. Thank you."

I held my phone up and she blinked in the glare of the light.

"What are you doing out here?"

"Looking for my van. I parked it at the front of the house and took a wrong turn from the kitchen. This place is like a maze. Somehow, I've ended up here. In the dark, knocked down by you!" Her voice was sharp and irritated. My heckles rose.

"I didn't knock you down. I bumped into you. And saved you from falling if you recall correctly."

"Which I wouldn't have done if you hadn't knocked me down."

We stood, glaring at each other. Finally, she said,

"So, what's the problem with the Land Rover?"

"Sorry?" What was wrong with her? She was either snooping or prying.

"What's the problem with the Land Rover? Eadie said you had a problem with it?"

"I'm not sure yet. I've come back to let Eadie know that I won't make it for dinner."

"And?"

I couldn't believe she was so persistent. "And every time I turn the engine on steam pours out from under the bonnet."

She looked at me for a few moments, as if weighing up whether to speak or not and then she said, "It might be one of the hoses. Do you want me to have a look?"

"Sorry?"

"Now that was sexist," she said sharply. "I did a course. I take care of the van myself; it saves money. I had a problem with a hose a few months back, but if you don't want me to have a look because you think I'm a woman and women don't do cars then fine. Struggle on. Alone." She raised an eyebrow and stared at me.

I was an idiot, and she knew it. I hadn't meant it to be sexist, I was just surprised, that's all, by her offer. She'd been so difficult up to this point that I was a bit taken aback by her sudden generosity. But, fair shout, it *had* sounded derogatory. I stared at the ground for a few moments. "Look," I said, meeting her gaze again, "I'm sorry, you're right, I'm being an asshole." I honestly didn't think it was worth arguing my case; I'd only sound lame. "If you don't mind, then yeah, please, come and have a look."

I led the way back round to the courtyard and the jeep. It smouldered ominously.

"Right," she said, moving under the bonnet. It you shine your light here..." she pointed to the right-hand side of the engine, "Just under here there's a hose..." She glanced at me. "It's split, see that?"

I nodded. Now I felt like a real chump.

"I'll fix it, don't worry." She stood straight. "Can I borrow your fleece?"

"Sure." I pulled it over my head and handed it to her "What are you..."

"Sorry, could you turn around please? This is my best dress and I'm not fiddling with your engine wearing it." She looked at me and grinned. "And that wasn't a euphemism."

I suddenly laughed. I turned away while she pulled her dress off and when I turned back, she handed me a sheath of velvet. Wearing my fleece and a pair of DMs, she bent forward under the bonnet and began to wrench the hose free. "Have you got a Leatherman by any chance?"

"What tool?"

"Knife."

I handed it over and she sliced the top of the hose where the split was. "I'll fit it back on for you and it'll do for a day or so. If you get a new hose tomorrow, I can fit that for you too, if you like?"

I stared at her. Her hair had been in some sort of bun thing on the top of her head and now it fell down in strands around her face. She had a smear of engine residue on her cheek, and she had the longest and most beautiful legs - bare to mid-thigh - that I'd ever seen. I gawped. Stupidly. Tongue tied. Fuck. I was never, ever tongue-tied.

"I take that to be a somewhat shocked, yes?" She bent under the bonnet again. "Bloody dinosaur," I heard her mutter under her breath.

"No, it's not that, I..." What was I going to say, that I'd got a hard on looking at her legs? That was hardly chivalrous!

She twisted the hose back into place, straightened and ordered me to turn again while she pulled her dress back over her head.

"Now if you don't mind showing me round to the front of the house, I'll collect the cake I left in the van. Eadie will wonder where I got to."

"God, yes, of course, sorry." She clicked the bonnet shut and we turned to head back to the house. "Thanks so much, for doing that and..." I glanced sidelong at her. "Male or female, that was pretty cool, what you just did. I wasn't being sexist, I was in awe, sorry." That was the closest I was going to get to admitting any kind of feeling; I didn't do feelings. Didn't see the point.

She shrugged, but I sensed she was pleased.

At the van, she bent in and retrieved a large Tupperware.

"She cooks as well," I said.

"Of course, I cook," she snapped, "I've got two kids. We'd starve if I didn't."

Christ, she was off again! I was trying to pay her a compliment and the next thing I know she's at me. I led the way up the steps into the house through the front door. In the hallway I held the door for her and saw in the light that the sheath of velvet was a swirl of intense blue that hung from her hips and draped over her legs showing the full curve of her limbs. I swallowed and looked away. Angry with a full-on boner. That was a first. She walked into the hall and stalled momentarily.

"Second on the right," I said.

"I know," she shot back.

"Really?" I said, stupidly. "Didn't look like it to me."

TWELVE

WILLA

That man is infuriating. Sexist, self-important and... I racked my brains for something beginning with S. Smug. Yes, he was definitely smug. But then I forgot all about him as I walked into the kitchen and saw Eadie with Teddy on her lap and Basil at her knee. Cici was colouring with Angelica and Esme and as we entered, the warmth and kindness in the room was palpable.

"I thought you'd got lost," Cici said.

"I did." I replied.

"Luckily for me," Tye said. "She fixed the Land Rover."

All three women turned and looked at me, but without the least bit of surprise.

"Can't keep a good woman down," Cici said. "Willa, come and sit. Your wine is getting warm."

I took a place at the kitchen table and noticed that Tye put his hand on Eadie's shoulder, where she patted it affectionately. "Can you make the dressing for the salad love?" She asked him. He gave her shoulder a squeeze and headed to the fridge. Now that, I wasn't expecting.

"And get your pudding in the Aga, will you?" she went on, "How long will it take?"

"Twenty minutes. But why don't we save it for tomorrow? Willa's made a cake and mine will keep in the fridge."

"Of course, great idea." Tye beamed. Whatever his relationship was with Eadie, it was strong and loving, that much was evident. At least he had one saving grace.

Eadie continued to read to Teddy, Esme coloured, and I sipped my wine. It had been a long time since I'd felt this, a sense of ease, of being part of something.

"So, where did you learn mechanics?" Eadie asked. "Did you do a course or is it a natural talent?"

"Looked natural to me," Tye said, "She knew right away it was the hose."

Clearly, he was trying to be nice, but the fact that he was so obviously trying made me cross. Was I that much of a pill that he had to make a conscious effort to be nice to me?

"I did a course," I said, "I like to know how stuff works. It's important when you've got kids, on your own, to know what's what. If a pipe bursts, I need to know where the stopcock is."

"The stopcock?" Angelica said. "What on earth is that? I hope it's not what it sounds like." She giggled and I noticed that Cici threw her a look.

"What's a stopcock Willa?" Esme asked.

Teddy sang "Stopcock, stopcock, stopcock," loudly and out of tune, over and over.

"It's an external valve on a water pipe that stops the water coming into the pipe from the main supply," Tye said. I stared at him, and Esme looked baffled.

"It's usually like a little tap sweetheart, on the pipe and

it stops all the water," I said. I almost rolled my eyes. External valve. Really? Esme nodded, her frown clearing.

"It stops all the water coming in from the mains." Tye added, "Just to be clear."

Eadie did roll her eyes at this point, and I saw her exchange a look with Cici. Cici smiled. Eadie handed Teddy down onto the floor and said, "Dinner is ready." She went across to the Aga and Teddy came to stand by me. "So, we'd better eat," she continued, pulling on some oven gloves, "Because my *'Eadie Special'* is ready to be served..." She glanced back over her shoulder and grinned. "Just to be clear." Cici, Eadie and Angelica started to laugh, and Tye held his hands up, grinning. "Busted," he said.

DINNER WAS WONDERFUL. Eadie's special was mac and cheese, which I'm sure she'd made with three different cheeses, and cream, and she served it with a crisp green salad and warm crusty bread - the bread she'd been making that morning. It was heaven and if I'd ever needed a home cooked meal, with a side serving of warmth and laughter, then today was the day. The long, stressful hours of driving, the locked house, the sense of anxiety grinding in the pit of my stomach for the past forty-eight hours all started to fade. The dinner buoyed me up and, as I watched Teddy eat every little scrap and even try to lick his plate, I felt suddenly sure that we'd landed in the right place.

Teddy sat next to Tye and his open adoration was reciprocated with real affection. Tye was a genius with small boys, flipping a coin between his fingers to make it disappear, cajoling Teddy to eat some salad, helping him to sit still and use his knife and fork – all notoriously difficult for my gorgeous, neurodivergent seven-year-old. I even managed to laugh, something I hadn't done for quite some time. I sat on the other side of Tye, the three of us on the high settle that was used as a kitchen bench, and I couldn't help but notice that every time our thighs briefly touched - inevitable as we were squished in so tightly - I got a small, electric jolt of pleasure. There was something innately, but annoyingly sexy about this man and I could feel it right through my body. He'd even managed to smile at me a couple of times and *that* was something I hadn't been prepared for. The intensity of those brown eyes; they seemed to lock onto mine and see right into me. At one point I almost shivered. Blimey, this wasn't going to do, not at all. Get a grip Willa! This is a kitchen supper, with a whole bunch of people and the kids around! And... don't forget he's been a bit of an arrogant prig up until now. Still, the rock-solid muscle of his thigh against mine, even for a nano second went straight between my legs. I thought for one terrible moment he'd sensed it as he glanced away quickly, almost certainly embarrassed by having picked up on my reaction. Oh God, how awkward. I looked at my watch, quite obviously, and said,

"Eadie, I think we should be going. It's getting late and even though we're not at school, I'll have grumpy and grumbly on my hands tomorrow if Esme and Teddy are too late to bed. I hope that's OK?" I was at the end of the bench and shuffled my way out from under the table and stood. "We've had the best time. Thank you all so much."

"Lord, not at all my lovely. We've enjoyed having you, haven't we Tye? Cici?"

Cici beamed. "I LOVE colouring with Esme. She is the best colourer I've ever met." Cici bent and kissed the top of Esme's head.

"And your cake was delicious," Angelica said, "Magical. And I should know!"

"Tye, you should get Willa to cook some cakes for the farm shop," Cici said, "If they're as good as the lemon one tonight then they'll be a sell-out."

"You know that's not..." He stopped as Basil suddenly barked loudly, twice, and moved in front of the table protectively. We all stopped as the back door of the kitchen swung wide open.

"Percy!" Angelica cried, "You're too early!"

Percy the postman stepped into the room, transformed from friendly Viking postman into smouldering Nordic bad-boy. He was in black jeans, a faded tee shirt and a battered old denim jacket. He wore plimsols that had been through the wars and no socks. He looked as if he'd thrown on some clothes effortlessly and somehow created a look of weathered chic. My heart stopped.

"Percy," Tye said. He nodded and glared.

There was a sudden definite ice in the air. What the hell was going on?

"We've finished supper," Eadie said brusquely "And Nellie, you're excused the washing up. Tye and Cici will do it." Eadie stood and seemed to put herself between Percy and Tye. I looked round and Cici had left the kitchen. I didn't even notice her go.

"I walked up," Percy said. "Didn't want Nellie..."

"Angelica," Angelica corrected him.

"Sorry, Angelica, coming home on her own. Took me less time than I thought. I've got a gig tonight and I wanted to see her home before I headed off." He was talking directly to me, as if no-one else in the kitchen existed and his gaze was unswerving. I have no idea why, but I blushed. I put my hand up to my face and felt the heat in my cheeks.

"A gig?" Basil had recognised Percy and stopped barking, but he stood beside Tye, his tail wagging as Tye stroked his ears.

"Hey big boy," Percy said, suddenly turning his attention to Basil. Percy's full attention was difficult to ignore, and Basil trotted over. Percy knelt to give him a proper pat and a hug. "Yeah, I'm in a band and I'm still young enough – just – for it to be cool." He looked up at me and smiled and I smiled back. Bad-boy rock star. Wow. "So, if you're ready Angelica? We'll head off."

"I can give you a lift," I blurted. "We were just leaving anyway."

"It's a hike," Tye said. "They live on the other side of the village."

"It's no problem, honestly," I said. "It's what, ten minutes out of my way?"

"Oh Willa, that would be fab!" Angelica exclaimed. "I'd love it. I knew we'd be friends; I just knew it!" Percy laughed and stood. "If you're sure," he said, "You'd make my witchy sister here very happy!"

"Of course, I'm sure."

"But don't Esme and Teddy have to get to bed?" Tye asked. Oh my God, why was he being so difficult? It was a short drive across the village. "Yes, but it's a hop away. They'll manage." I tried, unsuccessfully, to keep the irritation out of my voice.

"Great, well we'll leave you all to it," Percy said. He beamed at me. "I've always wanted to ride in a camper van. It's a hell of a cool van you've got there. Nells? I mean Angelica?"

Angelica had her cloak on and was gathering up her spider bag. "I'll just find Cici to say goodnight," she said. She disappeared. There was a sudden deafening silence and only the thump of Basil's tail could be heard as it slapped against the table leg.

Angelica reappeared, Esme gave kisses to everyone, and Teddy endured a hug from Eadie and Tye, who was curiously cool and silent. Eadie said,

"Mind how you drive now lovie and pop in if you need anything. Anything at all."

I hugged her and she felt soft, warm and comforting. I felt loved and that made me feel more alone at the same time. "Thanks again," I said, as we made our way to the front door. The hall was cold and echoed with our voices. Tye saw us out, not smiling, quick to close the door as we went down the steps.

"That place gives me the creeps," Percy whispered. "And the Lord of the Manor can be a right pain in the arse."

I laughed and immediately wished I hadn't as Tye had re-opened the door behind us to send us home with Eadie's leftovers. I'm sure he heard the comment and my laugh. He handed the dish to me without a word and went back inside.

"See?" Percy said.

I looked at him, but there was something about Tye's face as he'd handed me the dish that stopped me from agreeing with Percy. Yes, he was difficult, and surly and well, self-important, but... I don't know, he'd looked kind of... disappointed and I have no idea why, but that made me feel bad.

THIRTEEN

TYE

You are so wrong Tye, to trust your instincts. Wrong with a capital R. Bummer. I closed the door and made my way back to the kitchen, that easy, light laugh of hers ringing in my ears. A pain in the arse? Fucking Percy. Takes one to know one.

Before I went back into the kitchen, I took a couple of moments to rearrange my face. I was annoyed and to be honest, I was fucking disappointed. I thought I liked Willa. I mean, liked as in she was beginning to shape up to be quite a decent person, talented, good mum, fun to be around. And she smelled so good. Not that smelling good is a requirement for me to like someone, only, sitting next to her on the bench, every so often I'd catch the floral musky scent of her hair as she moved her head, and it was nice. It was so nice. And I liked the way she speaks to her kids. Her voice changes and she's soft and reasonable, even when she's telling Teddy to stop jumping up and down, she's funny. I loved it when she said, 'Teddy, you'll wear the floorboards out if you keep jumping up and down like that, and you never know, you may end up like Rumpelstiltskin and go right through them." And everyone laughed and Teddy came and sat on her lap while she retold him the story. Result. And she never even raised her voice.

I turned the handle on the door to the back of the house and stopped midway through opening it. Fuck.

I liked her for more than the fact that she was beginning to shape up to be quite a decent person. I liked her. Fuck. I liked Willa Hart. Mad hair, DMs, single mum, part time mechanic and cake maker and not bad at breaking and entering. Willa Hart. Fuck.

"You going in or coming out?" Cici asked.

She stood behind me in the hall. "Going in," I said. 'There's still the washing up to do." I turned to look at her. "You OK?"

She shrugged. "I thought, you know, with Nellie being my best friend and the fact that it's been a few years, well, I thought it would be fine, seeing him."

"But it's not." I tried to keep the venom out of my voice.

Cici shook her head. "No." She placed her hand on my arm. "But I'm a big girl Tye, I have to get over it..."

"No, you don't, not while I'm around you don't!"

She smiled at me. "Thanks, but no thanks. I *do* have to get over it. He's back from his travels, he's delivering letters, he's everywhere and I'm going to run into him."

I felt my jaw clench.

"We can't hate him forever."

"I can."

She batted my hand away and turned the handle, opening the door. "No, you can't," she said, holding the door for me so that I could go ahead. "You're just not made that way Tye." She followed me and walked towards the kitchen. 'Besides, I think you might have other things on your mind."

She opened the door of the kitchen and all the warmth and comfort of that room flooded out. She was smiling as she went in and Eadie, who was sat with her feet up on the settle drinking a whisky, said,

"What's so amusing my loves?"

"Tye's got a thing for Willa," Cici replied and she laughed as my face darkened. "Tye and Willa, sitting in a tree, K.I.S.S.I.N.G!"

I grabbed a tea towel and twisted it, flicking it at her legs.

"Ouch!" She grabbed another and flicked me back. Eadie continued to drink her whisky quite unperturbed by the fight going on around her. I finally got the last flick in and stood behind Eadie so that Cici couldn't get me.

"You may not be siblings, but you blooming-well fight like them," Eadie tutted. "Washing up please, now that you've got tea towels in your hands the pair of you!"

I grinned at Cici, knowing that I'd got the last shot in and waited for her to put the rubber gloves on. She always washed and I always dried.

"And I do not have a thing for Willa," I said loudly, coming out from behind my cover. Eadie glanced over her shoulder. "Of course you don't," she said, "Why would you? She's nothing more than a beautiful, intelligent and accomplished young woman, who's single and who has moved in next door. What on earth could you possibly see in someone like that?"

I stopped mid room and noticed that both Eadie and Cici were staring at me.

"Exactly," I said. Besides, I told myself, taking a sudsy saucepan off the draining board, she's too young, probably no more than early twenties, if that, and she has kids. And I'm too old, nearly into my thirties, too single, too occupied with making this place earn its keep, and as much as I thought I might have liked her, not at all interested in pursuing someone who thinks I'm a pain in the arse. I raised my eyebrow at both of them. Matter closed. Then from somewhere outside we heard a dog barking.

"Basil?"

Cici opened the back door and whistled. Moments later, Basil lolloped up the back steps and into the kitchen. He was mightily pleased to see us.

"Oh, poor old Basil," I said, kneeling down. "Did they leave you behind?" He licked my face and dribbled over the sleeve of my sweater, his tail wagging furiously. "I'd better walk him back," I said. Eadie poured herself another tot of whisky.

"Leave it ten minutes of so," she said, "Then we can have a pet with Basil, and you can be sure that Willa will be home when you take him back." She winked at Cici who turned away grinning. Sometimes, living with two women could be a real pain. But I did what she said and finished the drying up and tidying away before I found my coat to walk Basil back across the fields to the Lodge and home.

FOURTEEN

WILLA

I was in a panic; I couldn't help it. As I stopped the van and glanced behind me to unlock the back door and let Angelica out, I saw Teddy asleep and Esme just about to nod off. In the space between their car seats, where a dog should have sat, there was no Basil. Shit.

"You OK?" Percy asked.

"Oh, yes, erm, it's just that I think we left Basil behind." My heart dropped. He didn't know his way back and... Oh God Willa... Poor Basil.

"Oh bollocks," Percy said. "Oops sorry. I keep forgetting the kids." He checked over his shoulder and saw that Teddy was asleep. "Phew. Asleep." He shrugged. "Look, it's no big deal. He'll be fine," he said, "He's a dog."

"Yes, but he's my dog," I shot back. Correction, he was our dog, our family dog. Lexi had got him, she thought he would stabilise things, once she'd.... I sniffed. And he had, he'd cemented us together in a way that I don't think Lexi could ever have imagined. Big, soft, smart, loyal Basil. I looked behind me again, not believing that I'd been so stupid, so caught up in chatting to Percy. I kept the engine running and said, "I've got to go. Now."

"Ah, right. OK." He lingered and I felt my panic rise. "You sure?" He asked. "You couldn't leave the kids napping in the car for ten minutes and come in for a quick drink?"

I stared at him. In the dim light of the car, he was even more attractive, a darker blonde, and more mysterious. As he reached towards the door handle, his sleeve rose, and I saw the beginning of a tattoo that snaked over his wrist and up towards his bicep. He was super cool and enticingly hot. But he was also way off the mark. Leave the kids napping in the car? Leave Basil wondering where we are? Had he mistaken me for someone else? There were three things that really mattered in my life: Esme, Teddy, and Basil. All the rest was just turkey trimmings.

"No," I said. It came out all snappy, like a little snarl, but that was my panic talking. His face changed and I said, "I mean, thanks, but no. I've really got to go... like now!"

"OK." He opened the door and jumped out. Angelica was already on the pavement. She popped her head back into the car behind me and said, "Cici will look after him, and Tye, don't worry. He's just fine. I know these things." She flicked a long strand of red hair over her shoulder and slammed the door shut.

'Wait," she suddenly cried. I opened the window and she leant into the car, waving her hands theatrically over my head. "Reduc Basilium, reduc Basilium..." she chanted, "Reduc Basilium."

"There." she said, standing back and smiling. She put the hood of her cloak up over her hair. Flame red against magenta silk was quite a combination.

"Erm, thanks, I think," I said.

"You're welcome," she turned towards the house. "He'll come home."

I revved the engine and perplexed, but still waving, I sped away.

BUT TEN MINUTES LATER, Basil wasn't at the house. I called out for him and whistled, waiting several minutes and then I knocked, but no-one answered. My panic escalated. I jumped back into the van again and headed down the long, winding drive a bit too fast, the van bouncing hard over every small pothole and rut. I turned right, along the main road and then pulled into Peace Summerton Lodge, screeching to a halt in front of the house. I jumped out and called, "Basil? Basil? Here boy? Basil?"

A resounding bark came from the back of the house, then three more and moments later, Basil bounded into the front garden and headed straight for me. I bent and put both arms round his neck, suddenly tearful. "Oh Basil," I cried, "I'm so pleased to see you! You are such a clever boy, you..." I began to cry. Stupid really, to be crying over a misplaced dog, but I couldn't stop myself. Great, coughing sobs escaped, and I began to heave and weep, hanging onto Basil's collar. He smelled all doggy and warm and he licked my face with his heavy wet tongue. It made me laugh and I was crying and laughing at the same time, sitting on the frozen ground with Basil trying as hard as he could to sit in my lap. I wiped my face on my sleeve and fumbled in my pocket for a tissue. I didn't have one. My nose was streaming, and my bum was frozen, and the kids were still asleep in the van. I couldn't sit there weeping. I needed to get them inside.

"Come on Willa, enough. Pull yourself together." I

stood up. "No time for self-pity. One foot in front of the other." I sniffed a last time, ran my sleeve over my face and realised I'd have to wipe the snot off my jacket. Bum.

"I am sorry Basil," I said. "You know how much you mean to me. Without you I'd never have survived, not Lexi, not all the things I did wrong with Esme and Teddy, least of all Bloody Syd!" I bent and gave him one last kiss then I opened the front door, let him inside and went back to carry the kids in and up to bed.

FIFTEEN

TYE

Fuck. That was awful. And now I was fucking stuck round the side of the house, lurking in the shadows like some unhinged stalker. There was nothing I could do, I just had to sit it out and wait until she'd got the kids inside and closed the door. Then I could slink away and pretend I'd never been here. The last thing she needed, or I wanted, was for me to suddenly appear. Then she'd know that I'd seen the whole thing, and it would be painful, excruciating. I didn't do emotion!

I leant back against the wall and felt my whole-body slump. I hated to see anyone cry, but Willa's tears had almost cracked me in two. Who was Lexi? And what did she mean about doing all the wrong things with the kids? And the way she'd stood, wiping her face on her sleeve – that made me smile – and then brushing herself down and carrying on, as if she had all this pain inside and that's where it had to stay. I closed my eyes. Boy did I know that feeling.

I waited in the cold and finally heard the front door

slam. I was still holding Basil's lead, so I thought I'd drop it by the front door and head home. But then I thought, what if she pops out again to the van and finds the lead and thinks I was here all the time and saw everything and was too cowardly to face her? Shit, I couldn't risk that. I decided that I'd take the lead and bring it back in the morning. But I didn't move. I couldn't. I didn't want to leave. I just needed to check that she was OK. I waited a bit longer and then a bit longer still. After half an hour or so I decided that the best thing to do was to knock on the door and say that I'd found Basil's lead and wanted to run it over in case she needed it first thing. It was a bit lame, but I really did want to check that she was OK.

I headed from the side of the house into the copse, went through the woods and came out onto the drive of Peace Summerton House. I made my way along the drive and onto the main road, then into the drive of the Lodge. The security lights came on, as I knew they would, and it looked as if I'd come straight from the house. It was an elaborate ruse to save her embarrassment. I knocked on the door and checked my watch. Not too late to call; eight forty-five p.m. I waited a bit longer, knocked again and suddenly the door cracked open a tiny bit.

"Yes?"

God, what an idiot! It *was* too late to call! She was a single woman in a strange house for the first night and here I was, skulking outside in the dark, unannounced, holding a fucking lead.

"Willa?" I said, my voice hesitant. "It's me, Tye. I'm sorry to bother you, I found Basil's lead at the house, and I came right over. Stupidly! I wasn't thinking. This is an intrusion. I'm sorry, I should have left it till morning, I..."

The door swung open, and she stood, illuminated by the

hall light, in a pair of pyjamas with pink flamingos on them, her hair hidden in a white hairnet and a floury, black apron covering the whole of her torso from her neck to mid-calf. She smiled at me.

"Tye! It's fine, not too late. Thank you so much, that was so thoughtful of you."

I held the lead out and she took it. "Would you like to come in? I'm baking."

I glanced behind her, and the kitchen was in full glare. I could smell something delicious.

"Erm, no, it's OK. I should get back..."

"Really? Are you sure you wouldn't like a biscuit? I've just made them. And some tea? It's bloody cold out, you must be freezing, and..." She put her hand up to her hair and suddenly realised that she was wearing the hair net. She whipped it off and her hair fell over her shoulders. She looked away for a moment. "...and to be honest, I could do with a bit of company."

"Well, seeing as you have biscuits..." I bent to take off my boots. "They smell fantastic, is it chocolate?"

"Chocolate and hazelnut shortbread. My own recipe." She glanced over her shoulder and beamed at me. "It's my passion, baking. And cooking. I do it when I'm happy, sad, angry – which can be frequent to be honest – calm, energetic, tired... any excuse really."

I loved her simple honesty. The shaping up into a decent person just notched up a gear. Even if she thought I was a pain in the arse. I followed her into the kitchen.

"Did Teddy and Esme get to bed OK? It's been a long day for them..." I stopped, suddenly embarrassed. I recalled my earlier comment about dragging the kids halfway across the country and by the look of it, so did she. "...And you, for all of you, I mean. You must be tired.

Change is hard. And driving, driving on motorways is hard too."

WTF? What was I wittering on about? Change is hard, driving on motorways? I looked away. When I looked back, she was looking at me, but not in a mean way, just like she was sort of bemused by me.

"Sorry, I said, "I'm not very good at small talk."

"I noticed." She smiled.

"OK!" I smiled back. "But in my defence, I work, a lot. All the time really, keeping Peace Summerton House going, it's quite a..." I wasn't sure how to describe it. It was a burden, but not one I didn't want. It was endless worry about bills and maintenance, and I worried about Eadie and Cici, and yet I'd take it all on again in a heartbeat. "...quite a responsibility." I smiled again. "I don't get out much."

"But you love the house," she said. It was a statement, not a question and I realised that she understood without me having to tell her.

"Yes, I love it. It's... well, it's home. My parents left it to me, they died when I was young, I was eight, and I never thought about anything else except taking it on and making it work. I suppose I could have sold it, people have made offers, but it's the one link I have to my parents." I took a breath. I couldn't remember the last time I'd said so much in one stretch. I'd gone from silent and taciturn to blathering sentimentalist.

Willa offered me a plate of biscuits and I took one.

"I'm sorry," she said, "About your parents. That must have been hard?"

I shrugged and held the biscuit mid-air. Whenever people asked about my life, my auto response was silence. I hated personal questions and I'd already said enough. In fact, I'd already said *way* too much. I looked away and took a bite of the biscuit to stop myself from saying something rude.

"Losing someone you love is always hard." Willa said.

I also hated platitudes, so I just chewed and continued to stare round the kitchen.

"Blimey!" I suddenly exclaimed, "What on earth is in this?"

Willa frowned. "I...erm... sorry?"

"It's amazing! Delicious!" I gobbled the rest of it down in one mouthful. This wasn't a deflection; it was the truth. "Seriously, Willa, what did you put in this biscuit?"

She beamed and I thought, wow, this woman smiles with her whole face.

"Do you really want to know? It's a bit of a cook's answer."

"Yes, I really want to know." I took another biscuit and chewed, more slowly this time. God, these things were so good they were addictive.

"Well, I toast the hazelnuts then I grind half of them so that they add to the flavour but not the texture," Willa said, "And then I add a pinch of salt and some ground coffee, but only half a teaspoon, it makes the chocolate more intense. Then I chop the rest of the nuts, and I tend to crush the chocolate, it gives a better texture than grinding it in the food processor..." She stopped. "Oh God, I'm food waffling..."

"No." I took another biscuit. "Well, yes, a bit... You had me at toasted hazelnuts."

Willa laughed, and I felt the same as I did in the barn half a day ago. Is there a better feeling on earth than making someone laugh, knowing that you made them forget themselves for just a few seconds? I took another biscuit.

"Would you be able to make some of these for the farm

shop? I'd pay you of course. In advance. How long do they keep?"

Willa thought for a few moments. "I think they really need to be eaten fresh. I mean they do keep, but only for about two days. I think they'd have to be a 'buy and eat the same day' product, you know, like Pret a Manger? If you think you could sell them then I could get up early every morning and make them before the kids wake up?"

"That sounds like a plan. We supply some of the cafes in the area with fresh produce, I can ring round tomorrow and see if anyone is interested, and we could send out some samples the following day?"

"OK." Willa crossed to the dresser and took a pencil and a note book out of her bag. She opened it and scribbled a few things down. "Let me do some costings tonight and I'll text you in the morning with a price for each batch." She chewed the end of the pencil. "I'd really love to do this and to be honest, I could do with the money."

"Great. I don't think price will be a sticking point," I said. I knew the cafes well and they were all about quality and individuality, which is why they came to us. "People like the Peace Summerton House brand, it looks smart, different." I stopped suddenly. I caught myself smiling so I looked down at the biscuits. I needed to get a hold of myself. This was a business deal and potentially a good one and it had nothing to do with Willa, or the way she looked at me, or the way her wild hair seemed to fall across her face so that every now and then she had to flick it away with a small movement and a frown. Or the fact that now that she'd taken her apron off, I could see that she didn't have a bra on and the skin on her chest visible where her pyjamas were unbuttoned, was creamy white with a sprinkling of freckles dusting it. I stayed where I was and placed my hands over my lap. I thought about getting a new hose for the Land Rover, about clearing the gutters at the side of the house, about milking first thing, about anything other than Willa, just a few feet away from me, and as sexy as fuck. Without knowing it my erection subsided – it was the gutters – and I said,

"Do you know about the heating and the Aga here? Would you like me to show you how it all works?"

Willa raised an eyebrow, but there was a smile in her eyes. "Does that involve you telling me how to turn it on and off? Or where to put the wood?"

"Well, yes, and a bit more, like the controls and how to vary the radiators. But I'm guessing that you've worked it all out." I raised an eyebrow to match hers. "Obviously."

"Yeah, no need for any mansplaining, it was as easy as fitting a hose on an engine." She looked at me and burst out laughing.

SIXTEEN

WILLA

I honestly think he would have opened the front door of the Aga and shown me how to put a piece of wood in there if I'd let him. But it was a cute offer, and to be fair to him, the controls did take me a while to work out. Maybe I look like the kind of woman who needs looking after? Which I don't. I've been looking after myself for as long as I can remember, and then looking after Lexi and now the kids. Oh, and Basil, only tonight I did a pretty rubbish job at that. Still, it was nice of him, to think of me and to offer and well, if I'm honest, there are some moments when I *do* wish that someone would take charge and let me have a while to myself.

So, I let him off and he took the joke and then we sat opposite each other at the kitchen table and talked about Peace Summerton and life in the village and Peace Summerton House. We swapped numbers, he sent me a wink/kiss emoji and I replied with a heart smiley face. Every now and then our knees bumped each other, and I felt such an urge to put my hand on his thigh that I had to sit on both, which made it difficult to chat because I use my hands all the time to make my points. Plus, my nose was itchy, and I had to keep twitching it which made me look a bit like a demented rabbit.

Tye was hard to fathom, not that I wanted to try, but not knowing where I was with him was confusing, and sexy, which made it even more confusing. I didn't need sexy, and certainly not sexy with complications, which Tye certainly would have been.

"Well," he said, when we finally came to a natural pause in the conversation. "I guess I should go." He made a move to stand up and our knees bumped again as I did the same. I wobbled a bit and he put both hands on my arms to steady me. I caught my breath. Holy smoke, my stomach jumped up to my chest and a sudden warmth spread between my legs. He had literally knocked me off my feet.

"Whoa," he said, "That's better."

I took a quick step back. "Thanks," I said. "And thanks too, for the biscuit offer. It will really help me out."

"It's OK. Works both ways."

"Good. You know, I'd been thinking of asking Percy if anything was going at the post office. I thought that might be something I could do during the day while the kids are at school. You know, maybe a post-person. And Percy has connections, he said he could..." Tye's face suddenly changed.

"Oh, I wouldn't rely on Percy if I was you!" he said sharply.

"I wasn't relying on him, I just thought..."

"Whatever." Tye snapped. He headed towards the door. I stayed where I was and looked at his retreating back. "Tye?"

He turned.

"Is there something up between you and Percy?"

Tye glowered at me for a moment and then brought his face back under control.

"Nope," he shot back. He bent to pull on his boots and opened the front door. "I'd better get going," he said. "It's much later than I thought."

Framed in the doorway he looked tall and strong and yet there was something vulnerable about his sudden emotion, as contained as it was.

"OK. Let me know about the biscuits, will you? About the demand?"

He nodded and without glancing over his shoulder, he left, slamming the door shut behind him. Very confusing. I still had that annoying heat between my legs. And sexy. Confusingly sexy. I went back to the kitchen, cleared up and made my way upstairs.

I cleaned my teeth, checked on Esme and Teddy, and tiptoed back downstairs to see if Basil was all right. He'd been in his bed since his return from Peace Summerton House. I knelt and gave him a quick, guilty hug and finally made my way up to bed. I'd made up beds for the kids earlier that afternoon in the two spare rooms that Maud had, but I'd left mine, or rather Maud's room because she had a huge bed, and I simply hadn't the energy to tackle it. I now wished I had as I suddenly felt so tired that I could have laid down on the bare mattress and fallen straight to sleep. Not a good idea, it was freezing, and I'd be awake in an hour, shivering and looking for blankets.

So, I found sheets and a duvet cover and lugged a couple of blankets off the top shelf of the wardrobe and set about making my bed. I heaved the monster mattress, panting as I fitted the sheet and stuffed what felt like half a mile of duck down duvet into a cover, smoothing it out over the bed and spreading the blankets on top. Maud had a ridiculous number of pillows; big square ones at the back, soft ones in front for sleeping and harder ones in front of those to make the bed look nice. Then there were the cushions... But I abandoned all of it except one soft down pillow, found a pillowcase and finally, feeling like I'd done half a triathlon, I climbed into bed and wondered if I should go back downstairs for a hot water bottle. The bed was icy cold. But, as I lay under a feather duvet and two blankets, I began to feel the sensation of my toes again and I started to relax. I closed my eyes and felt myself begin to drift off.

Crap! What was that?

I sat up and listened. There was a car in the drive.

I got out of bed and crept to the window, parting the curtains a tiny bit so I could peer out. I saw the Land Rover and what looked like a trailer on the back, reversing into the drive.

What the hell?

Pulling a blanket off the bed, I wrapped it round me like a cloak and opened the window. A blast of freezing air slapped me in the face. I was annoyed, almost angry when I saw Tye jump down from the truck.

"Oi?!" I half shouted, through clenched teeth. I didn't want to wake the kids. "Tye? What on earth are you doing?"

He stood looking all around him for a few moments, not knowing where the voice was coming from.

"Up here! Tye!" He glanced up and me. "Oh, never mind!" I growled. I shut the window and made my way downstairs. I yanked open the front door and there he was, unloading logs and stacking them into the porch.

"For the Aga," he said, puffing with the effort. "Solid fuel and environmentally friendly. We use fallen trees, so..."

He looked and me and shrugged. "There's enough here to keep you going for a few months."

He was making a neat stack, he was clearly skilled in wood piles.

"Erm, thanks?" I offered.

"I thought I'd do it now..." He looked at me and shrugged, leaving the sentence unfinished.

"Do you want help?"

"No. I'm fine."

"Sure?" If I'd been confused earlier, now I was completely baffled. After a dramatic exit, he turns up half an hour later with a truck full of logs and barely speaks to me, unloading them with the precision of a brick layer.

"Sure."

He was now out of breath, but he'd emptied half of the trailer. He worked fast.

"We could have waited until the morning; we have enough logs for the next few days."

He stopped for a moment and looked at me. "Yes, I suppose you could have," he said, then he carried on until the trailer was empty and I had a perfect wood stack in the porch to the lodge. He stood straight and wiped his forehead on the hem of his tee shirt. I caught a glimpse of his muscled torso and quickly looked away. An image of a rippling 6 pack was the last thing I needed right now.

"Thanks," I said.

He nodded and made for the truck. I pulled the blanket closer round me. It was bitterly cold, and my breath made small white clouds in the light of the porch. Was that it? I honestly couldn't fathom him one iota. He climbed into the truck and started the engine. I stood there, not sure whether I should wave him off or go inside. He accelerated forward then suddenly the Land Rover stopped and the brake lights came on. He jumped out and came back.

"You did the right thing, asking Percy. Even though he's a right pr..." He stopped himself. "Of course, you've got to think of the kids first, find something to fit round them." He cleared his throat and stared at a place just above my right shoulder. "You're always thinking about the kids. You're a good mum Willa."

He nodded as if he was pleased with what he'd just said and then he turned on his heel.

"Tye?" He glanced back.

"I'm not a..."

He held up his hands as he interrupted me. "Yes you are Willa. And I won't hear otherwise." Happy that he'd had the last word, he carried on to the Land Rover, climbed back in and drove off.

I went inside and shut out the cold. "I'm not a mum," I said to the empty hall. "I do the best I can Lexi, but I'm not a mum, not their mum."

I went upstairs, almost tripping over my blanket-cloak and climbed into bed, still wrapped in the thick wool. I reached for my iPad and touched the photos icon. I pressed play on the video I wanted; it was one I played often. Lexi's face came onto the screen.

"So, little sis, you are now the one in charge and it's not easy. There'll be lots of times when you'll feel lonely and upset and freaking furious that I landed this on you. There'll be times when you'll even want to walk away... but you won't. And that's why I landed it on you because I know that you'll never leave them. I know you're not their mum, I am, but you're the closest they'll ever get to knowing me and remembering me..."

I stopped the video and reached for the box of tissues on

the bedside table. I blew my nose hard and wiped my face. I pressed play again.

"And I'm here for you Willa. I'm right beside you, not in person, but here on the screen and in your heart and in your thoughts and in the decisions that you make. Hell, I practically brought you up girl! So, keep this playing and talk to me. Tell me what's up and even though I can't answer you, you'll know, that despite the FC, somewhere I'm listening, and I've got your back."

I wiped my face again and propped the screen up on my knees. The FC was her 'Fucking Cancer,' the video was one of twenty or so she had recorded for me before she died. Lexi was my sister and my best friend. I swallowed down the rest of my tears.

"There's this man, Tye," I said out loud, my voice wobbly. "God Lexi, you should see him, he's really hot, like smoking..." I smiled, knowing that she'd loved that expression. "But I can't work him out, not at all! He's not like Harry - who, you'll be glad to know, is no longer my boyfriend – it's OK, it was mutual. Not that Tye is boyfriend material - I don't think he's the slightest bit interested in me and two kids - but he's also not like any other man I've ever met, he's... well, he's kind, but he hates showing it and he's infuriating, and he just delivered logs, which I think was kind of an apology for storming off earlier, which was baffling as I had no idea what I said to make *that* happen...then and on top of all that, he's incredibly sexy, it's like this chemistry thing, you know? He just sets my body off and there's nothing I can do about it..." I had a momentary mental image of a muscled abdomen and quashed it immediately. "So... as you can see, the whole thing is impossible." I sighed heavily.

"But we're here, in the middle of nowhere, like I told

you we would be. I just hope I've done the right thing Lexi." My voice wobbled again, and I swallowed down the lump of tearful doubt that rose in my throat. "I've blocked Syd for the time being, just until I get settled and I'm down to the last of my savings. But we're OK, I think, if it wasn't for some stupid half-crush on the man next door, who also happens to be my landlord and may become my boss if the biscuit thing lands."

Lexi was serious and nodding and it made me suddenly laugh. She was never like that; she rarely took anything seriously and men problems she always put down to loving the wrong sex. I blew my nose again. The last thing I needed, any of us needed, were the complications that love brought. I stopped the video and dropped my iPad onto the bed, Lexi's face on the screen close to mine.

"Night Lexi," I said. "This will all look better in the morning, won't it?"

I could hear her agreeing and I closed my eyes. "Love you," I said.

"Love you," a little voice echoed from the door. I pulled back the covers and Esme, holding Teddy's hand, came forward. Half asleep, they both climbed in next to me and I switched off the light.

"Night Muma," she said.

I glanced down at the iPad, but the screen was dark. She was talking to me. "Night Esme," I answered, "Night Ted."

SEVENTEEN

TYE

Well, I'd made amends; made up for being a bit of a dick when she mentioned Percy and storming off like a teenager, and I think it worked. Although why it bothered me that she might think I was a dick was another thing altogether. I generally couldn't give a flying fuck what people thought of me – there were only two people whose opinion mattered; Eadie and Cici. The rest could go hang for all I cared.

I parked the Land Rover and went round the back of the house, in through the kitchen. It was dark, with only a small lamp on. Everyone was in bed and that's exactly where I needed to be. I opened the door, stepped into the warmth, and bent to take my boots off.

"You're late?" Eadie said.

I jumped in fright, practically an inch off the ground. She was sitting in the big wing chair, unseen. "Jeeze Eadie, you scared the life out of me!"

I walked around the chair and stood opposite her.

"I dropped some logs off at the Lodge."

"Did you now?"

"It needed doing, the log store was full, so I thought I'd get rid of them."

"And you had to do it now, tonight, at..." she glanced at her watch, "Ten p.m."

I averted her eye. "No time like the present."

"Well, I'll be off up to bed then. Now that you're in."

She was already in her dressing gown, and she stood, crossing the kitchen.

"You don't have to wait up for me Eadie," I said, smiling. "I'm old enough and ugly enough..."

"You certainly are." She interrupted. She placed her mug in the sink. 'Old habits die hard Tye. And..." She turned. "And I wanted to let you know that it's OK to be happy."

I frowned at her. "Yeah, I know."

"Well, maybe you do... and maybe you don't. You spend your life worrying about the estate, looking after the house, me and Cici and keeping up with all your responsibilities..." She looked at me and I noticed that her face was finely lined.

"Trying to prove yourself," she went on, "to make two people who died a long time ago proud of you." She smiled. "Well, they would be. And it's time you had a bit of joy, Tyler Malloy. You deserve to have your share of happiness when it suddenly appears on the horizon."

"Eadie, I..."

"No. No Eadie I this, or Eadie I that. Just listen to what I'm saying. And then get yourself to bed. You're never up this late."

I nodded.

She headed for the door, stopping for a kiss on the way. "Night love." And she was gone before I had the chance to say another word.

EIGHTEEN

WILLA

"No, Teddy, it's not going to taste very nice raw, I... See? It's not nice, is it? I did say... No! No, don't spit it on the floor! Get a cloth! No, don't walk in it, it's impossible to get cookie dough out of the... GET A CLOTH!... Oh, thank you Esme. No Teddy, you do it, it's your mess! It's not Esme's spit and half chewed biscuit dough on the floor now, is it?"

I wiped my face on my apron. I was sweating. The best laid plans of mice and men and all that. So much for getting up early (before the children got up) to bake my batches of trial shortbread. Teddy was up at five a.m., and he thoughtfully took Esme in a cup of milk to wake her up, some of which I had to scrub off the stairs. Thank goodness he missed the runner and spilt it on the wooden steps. Spilt milk smells like rancid feet after a few days, not that I know what rancid feet smell like, but I imagine that they're disgusting.

"Good, thank you Ted. Yes, put it in the sink. Now, off

you go and play." I glanced across to him. "Why don't you do some colouring?"

"Where's the pens Willa?" He had flour all over his face, so I tore off a piece of kitchen roll, dampened it, wiped his mouth and cheeks, took his floury apron off, all whilst checking my oven timer. I was adept at multi, multi-tasking.

"In my room, in a box somewhere. Have a good scout around and see what you can find...."

Crossing to the table, I picked up my list as Teddy slipped out of the room and I closed the door with my foot keeping Basil out. I crossed off batch number nine. One more to go, plus the one that Esme was making. That one couldn't go out to customers though as I think I saw her pick her nose midway through rolling out the dough, but I'd got enough ingredients to cover myself for a couple of mis-batches, so we could have her lot for tea.

Tye had secured ten trial orders, which was amazing and last night he'd sent over some images of the labels for the packaging. They were gorgeous, all smart and sophisticated. I'd printed the image out on Maud's circa 2013 printer and stuck it on the fridge as a sort of incentive and to boost my confidence. The label said, *'Choc-hazelnut shortbread by Willa Hart for Peace Summerton House.'* There was an illustration of the house, white on blue underneath and my name was in italics. Nice. Classy. I'd been looking at it on and off since I'd printed it. That was me, my name, and the biscuits in the pack would be my biscuits! I hugged my arms to my chest. Then I sniffed the air.

"Oooh, time for batch nine to come out Esme. They smell..." I sniffed again and smiled at her. "Perfectly baked." Just as I said that the timer went off and we both looked at the Aga. "Have you got the cooling rack ready?"

Esme nodded and jumped down from the chair she was kneeling on. "Can I do it Willa, can I take them out?"

I began to sweat. Again. "Sure," I said. She needed to learn, to be involved, but the whole procedure was a health and safety nightmare. She held her arms out and I put the extra-long oven gloves on her small hands to protect her whole arm, then we crossed to the Aga, and I knelt and opened the main oven door.

"Right," I said, leaning forward. "I'll slide the baking tray out towards you, and you be ready to lift it carefully up from underneath and take it to the table. OK?" We'd lost one batch earlier to a wobble and a small trip on the uneven flagstone.

Esme nodded solemnly. I knelt, opened the oven door, slid the tray out and held it up while she placed her little hands underneath it. I took a big breath and said, "OK... Off you go! Hold it firmly and take it over to the table. And please hold it away from you too because it's really, really hot and it'll burn if it touches you." I almost couldn't look. I'd got enough flour, chocolate and hazelnuts for a couple of mistakes, but we'd already had two. I held my breath as she took tiny baby steps towards the table, the baking tray tilted at an angle, the biscuits slipping, very gently towards the edge. Learning independence is hard... on me, not on Esme. She was loving it, I was terrified.

She placed the tray on the table and stood back beaming. So, this is what it's always going to be like, I thought, relief washing over me. You let them fly and prepare yourself for a fall. No wonder some people found it so hard to let go.

"You are a super star Esme! Fantastic. Now you can roll your dough and cut some biscuits out. I thought we might keep your lot for ourselves as I think they're going to be the best." Esme grinned. 'Do you want to choose the shape cutters? They're all in the box that I haven't unpacked yet. Over there, by the door."

Esme scuttled over and opened the box. I could hear Basil scratching at the door and I suddenly remembered Teddy. Uh oh, a silent, missing Teddy was not a good sign.

"Esme, keep the door closed, will you? Basil isn't allowed chocolate, it's not good for him and even though he's whining, do NOT let him in. OK?"

Esme nodded, engrossed in her selection and I headed for the door. I squeezed out, kept the door closed behind me and looked at Basil.

"Don't give me that face. I'd let you have a biscuit if it didn't have chocolate in it, Bas. You know it's not good for you, now, don't you?" I could hear Lexi's voice as I said that. *He's not going to answer you, you do know that don't you Willa?* I smiled to myself and checked in the sitting room for Teddy before I made my way up the stairs.

I loved the Lodge, even though we'd only been there for two days. I loved the higgledy-piggledy nature of it, Maud's eclectic paintings, the warm, mismatched kitchen where no cupboard was the same and I loved the comforting smell of home. Not that I could identify what that was exactly, it just smelt, well... cosy.

I called for Teddy, Basil at my heels, but he wasn't answering. Also, not a good sign. Climbing the stairs, I checked the room he was sleeping in first. His toys were scattered all over the floor, the bed had clearly been bounced on, but he wasn't there. I tried the room Esme had bagsied next. Hers was neat and tidy, with everything lined up in its place, a place she had clearly thought about. He wasn't there either, which I have to say I was quite relived about. Teddy running amok in Esme's room was a frequent problem. Finally, I went into Maud's room, or mine now, and there I found him, quietly colouring in his art pad, using the small array of lipsticks that I kept lined up in colour order in a box, as pens. At his side were the three he'd discarded, two broken in half, one, the dark red one, my favourite, worn right down to the case. In front of him was an oily, wild mess of red and pink and bronze squiggles, splotches, and smears of thick lipstick. There was also quite a bit on his face.

"Well," I said, fury rising in my chest. "Don't you think you should have asked if you could use those to colour with?" I spoke through clenched lips, afraid that I was going to explode.

He looked up at me innocently. "You said to look for the pens and I found them."

I put my hands up to my face. Oh, dear God! *Have a good scout around and see what you can find,* I'd said. Oh Willa, you absolute twit. I stared down at my former collection of lipsticks and swallowed down the urge to weep, rant and stamp around, flaying my arms and wailing about the demise of the only bits of decent makeup I possessed. I took several very deep breaths. I counted to ten. I took another deep breath.

"Yes, I did and well done for doing such a lovely picture." I said at last. My chest was heaving at the effort. Teddy beamed up at me.

"Can we put it on the fridge? Please Willa, please?"

"Yes." I said, "Of course we can."

NINETEEN

TYE

"Hey you two? You look as if you're up to no good!"

Cici and Angelica had their heads together, bent over something on the counter as I came into the shop.

Cici looked up at me. "Angelica is casting a spell," she said, grinning. "I've got a lock of your hair and we've put it on Willa's name. It's a love spell."

"You are both full of nonsense!" I moved past them to the store at the back. "How old are you? Fifteen?"

"He's smiling!" Angelica exclaimed triumphantly, "See, I told you it would work. He's already in love."

"Oh please," I moaned.

Cici laughed. "But she's right Tye, you never smile at stuff like this. Something's going on!"

"I'll tell you what's going on," I said. "I am smiling because I've cleared my afternoon, and I have some free time! So, I am off to deliver biscuits to all the local cafes. Talking of which, could you make a note that I've taken twelve little brown carrier bags please Cici?"

"But who are you going with?" Angelica asked.

"Willa and the kids," I said.

"Ah ha!" Angelica cried. "I knew it!"

I stood and looked at them both.

"And he's still smiling," Cici said, raising an eyebrow.

I shook my head. But Cici was right, I was smiling, and I had no idea why.

"It's just work," I said. "Nothing more, so don't get your hopes up. Right, I'm off. Message me if you need me..." I glanced around the shop, hoping to find a job I could remind Cici to do, but as always, the place was in perfect order. The wooden shelves were stocked with all the jar and bottle labels facing the right way, the produce was artistically displayed in the wooden crates and the cheese counter was stacked with our local cheeses in alphabetical order, all with small, beautifully handwritten descriptions.

"See you..." I called and I headed out and down the drive towards the Lodge.

Willa was driving, as she had the car seats, and together we'd planned to go into each café, introduce her and the biscuits. I'd done the route and had left the best café until last. I was planning on buying everyone tea and cakes, but that was something I certainly wasn't going to mention to Cici and Angelica. I glanced down at my phone to message Willa that I was on my way. Perhaps it was a little bit more than just work, but a love spell?! As if...

"Whoa! Shit!" The impact was less than the shock, and I staggered backwards for a few paces, momentarily dazed, then righted myself.

"Alfie? What the hell?" I stopped. Alfie had managed to spin the back wheel of his bike to a stop to miss me, but he dropped the bike to the ground now and stood looking at me, his face deathly pale and tear stained.

"Alfie? What's happened?"

"It's Mum," he said, "She's locked herself in the bathroom and the water's running and it's coming through the ceiling. We can't get in. I've tried to climb in the window, but I can't. I've left Libby at home with the others. I didn't know where else to go and you said..." He started to cry. "Can you come Tye? Please?" He wiped his face on his sleeve.

"Of course," I said. "I'll come now. Follow me." I ran back down the drive to where I'd left the Land Rover.

"Chuck your bike in the back!" I called. "I'll be two minutes."

I put my head in the door of the shop. "Cici, can you call Willa and let her know that there's an emergency with Alfie and his mum?"

Cici hurried across to me. "Can I do anything?"

"No, I'm heading over there now. Don't know when I'll be back..."

I turned and headed to the car. "Tell her I'm really sorry, will you?"

Cici nodded. I climbed in, unlocked the door for Alfie and we drove off.

ALFIE'S little sister Libby opened the front door as we arrived at the house. I ran in carrying the toolbox I'd grabbed from the back of the truck. There was water running down the walls of the small, front room.

"Water first," I said. "The stopcock's probably in there." I tried the handle of the cupboard under the stairs, it was locked. "Alfie? Can we get in there?"

He shrugged.

Shit, I muttered. I took a pace back and gave the door an almighty kick. The lock was flimsy. It broke almost immediately, and the door splintered. I pushed it open, put the torch on my phone and found the stopcock. I turned it off.

"Right. Stay here, keep an eye on Libby and the kids," I said. Whatever had happened to Megan, Alfie wasn't going to see it. I ran upstairs, found the bathroom, and took the same action. Taking a pace back I smashed the door with a kick. Inside the bathroom the floor was two inches deep in water. Megan was in the bath. The water was up over her neck, and she seemed to be unconscious. By some miracle, her head had fallen backwards, away from the water and not forwards into it. I slammed the door behind me, checked her pulse. It was still beating, but faint. I turned the taps off and reached down under her for the plug, pulling it out to drain the bath. I took out my phone and dialled 999.

"Ambulance."

"Yes, I need an ambulance... 0782544359, location... erm, it's Mallard Avenue, number, erm... I think it's number twenty... Yes, emergency. I've just found the householder, Megan Roycroft unconscious. Yes, she's still breathing. She's in a bath, she's got a pulse but it's very faint. I think... I think this might be a suicide attempt." There were several empty medication bottles floating in the water. "No, I don't know medical history, but I know there's mental health issues...Thank you. Do you know how long? Yes, yes, I will..." I pressed end and went into the bedroom to find a pillow and some blankets. Alfie appeared at the top of the stairs.

"Alfie, can you do me a favour? Can you go outside onto the street and wait for the ambulance? They'll be here in about 15 minutes. It'll be much easier if you're outside and you can wave them down. OK?"

He stared at me; his face was tight with anxiety.

"I think Mum's unconscious, OK? So, we need the paramedics to get up here quickly." I reached out and touched his shoulder, holding it for a moment. "It's OK Alfie, she's still alive." I looked at him. "But I need your help, OK? Keep Libby and the kids downstairs and go outside to wait for the paramedics." He seemed frozen with shock and fear. "Go on, go. It'll be OK." He turned and headed down the stairs. I dropped my head into my hands for a moment. Why the fuck did I keep saying OK. This was not fucking OK.

TWENTY

WILLA

I glanced at my phone again. Nothing. It was after three and we'd agreed two p.m. That wasn't late, that was *not coming*. I looked at the neat stack of packaged biscuits in the basket on the table and wondered what to do. I'd tried to send Tye a message, and call, but the message was undelivered, and the call went straight to voicemail. I could hear the whine of the iPad as Teddy and Esme watched endless Paw Patrol and wondered how long the quiet would last before one or both got bored.

"Right," I shouted into the snug, "we're going out! Come on, iPad off, shoes on!"

I headed for the hall. There was only one thing for it, I'd drive up to the house and see what was going on.

"Come on!" I shouted, "We haven't got all day!" I grabbed my keys and opened the front door.

"Exactly!" Percy stood with his hand outstretched. "I was just about to knock and say the same thing! Nels, I mean Angelica, mentioned that you were going to deliver biscuits and I've just finished work, so I wondered if you'd like any help?"

"She did?"

"Yup. It occurred to me that I might be useful as I know the area and if you drive, I can direct. How does that sound?"

I grinned. "That sounds amazing. Thank you. I was supposed to be going with Tye, but he's not showed up... So..." I hesitated, but only for a nano-second. I was ready, this had to be done and well, if Tye wasn't going to show up or message me then I might as well get on with it. "So, that sounds great. Thanks. I have the list of cafes somewhere that he sent me..." I found the sheet of paper in my bag. "Here." I held it out. "I don't see why we can't make a start. He's probably been held up with something."

"Or forgotten."

"Oh no, I don't think..."

Percy raised an eyebrow. "This *is* Tye we're talking about," he said, "He's not known for putting other people first." He shrugged and put his head inside the door. "Never mind, don't let that stop us. Teddy? Esme? Basil?" he called, "COME ON! If we get done early, we can go for afternoon tea!"

"Right," I said, marching back to the kitchen and picking up the basket. Bloody Tye. It's incredible how easy it is to be taken in by someone. "Kids, shoes on in the car. Let's just get going! Come on Basil!"

We all headed outside, Teddy still holding the iPad.

"No, that goes back," I said. "It's a house only thing."

"Ohhh," Teddy moaned.

"Yes, Ohhhh." I grinned at Percy; my spirits suddenly lifted. I handed him the list of cafés. "You've come at exactly the right moment," I said, "Because these biscuits aren't going to eat themselves."

TWO HOURS LATER, as we left the last café, with Percy waving and smiling out of the window at the owner as we drove off, I finally let my shoulders relax.

"You were amazing," I said. I started to laugh as I did an impersonation of Percy. "And here's Willa, the extraordinary chef. Beautiful and talented!! Now you cannot ignore the biscuit, not with her standing right here... She'd be terribly offended!" I nudged him in the ribs with my elbow. "That was genius! It worked every time. How many orders did we get?" I was truly amazed by his bravado and charm; I know I could never have done that on my own. Super-hot and charming was a pretty impressive combination.

"We scored eight out of the ten cafés, all of them saying they'd buy, but..." he shrugged. "I don't know the specifics! I didn't make a note of how many, exactly, I just shook hands and encouraged them to buy. Tye can call them tomorrow and sort all that boring stuff out. He's good at that. We did it though!! Yay!"

Percy glanced over his shoulder. "A hip, hip hooray for your mum please kids?"

Teddy screwed up his face in thought. "She's not..."

In the rear-view mirror, I saw Esme reach over and cup her hand over his mouth to shut him up. He bit her hand and she screamed.

"Oh dear," Percy said behind him. "I think someone needs something nice to eat because hands must be very chewy!"

"Teddy, you mustn't bite!" I snapped. I was tired and

although I felt for Teddy - Esme was very much in control all the time – I had no truck with violence. "Teddy..." I warned sternly, the joy of the afternoon threatening to disappear.

"But Esme gargled me."

"I think you mean 'gagged' and yes, I saw that." In the rear-view mirror I saw that Teddy poked his tongue out at Esme when I said this. "Esme, apologise to Teddy for gagging him and Teddy keep your tongue in your mouth. You're not Basil." Basil's ear pricked up at the sound of his name.

"Sorry," Esme said.

"Now Teddy, sorry for biting you Esme."

Teddy repeated what I'd said but without enthusiasm.

"No Teddy," I said, looking at him in the rear-view mirror and catching his eye. "Say it properly."

"NO!" Teddy shouted. I gripped the steering wheel, my patience wearing thin.

Percy glanced at me. "Right," he said. He turned and looked at Esme and Teddy in the back. "Who's for afternoon tea?" he asked. "Hot chocolate, biscuits and cake?"

"Me, me, me, me, me..."

"Me, me, me, me..."

"Great! Then both say sorry. Nicely!"

He waited. "No sorry, no cake."

"Sorry," they both said together.

"Right, then let's go!" He turned back. "That's one way to stop an argument." He grinned. "If only cake could stop wars as well! Take a right at the lights, there's a lovely farm shop café a couple of miles away. It's a bit out of the way but I think you'd like it." He touched my arm. "My treat."

"Thank you," I said, "and thanks for today." I smiled back at him. "It was good fun." I pulled up at the lights, "and productive. I couldn't have done it without you." Tye's no show still rankled. "Thanks for everything, Percy."

"Well, if Tye doesn't recognise how brilliant you are then I do. It was a pleasure Ms Hart. Anytime!"

ESME AND TEDDY were high on sugar when we finally pulled into the drive at the Lodge, bouncing in their booster car seats and singing loudly to the soundtrack from Frozen. I was tired and if I was honest with myself, quite discombobulated. I'd spent the afternoon in the company of a charming, funny, intelligent man, who resembled a cross between Thor and Harry Styles, a striking mix of highly masculine, arty, and sensitive and yet I was feeling cross and disappointed. As I yanked on the handbrake, I turned to thank Percy again and to say goodbye, but he'd jumped down and was round the side of the van, opening the doors and helping Esme and Teddy down. Basil bounded out and stood by the front door, tail thumping.

"Keys?" He called to me.

I took them out of the ignition and threw them to him. He opened the front door, let Basil and the kids in and came back to the van.

"You gonna sit there all evening?" He opened the door for me.

"Sorry, have a bit of a cake slump." I jumped down and we stood facing each other.

"So," he said, smiling.

"So," I repeated. "I'd better start thinking about supper for the kids."

"Good idea," Percy said. He followed me inside. "Wow, something smells wonderful!"

I took my coat off and hung it up. It wasn't that I didn't

want him there, it was more that I just wanted to be alone. I needed to be alone, get the kids organised, get my head straight.

Percy went to the Aga and opened the bottom oven. "Someone's been busy," he said.

I'd done a vegetable tagine and I'd done it with some of the veg I'd bought in the farm shop up at the house yesterday. I thought I was being clever as I'd planned to ask Tye to stay for supper and impress him with the tagine so that he'd want me to make batches of it to sell in the shop. I'd left it in the slow oven, the oven that Percy was still peering into.

"Looks pretty big for three?" he said.

Suddenly I smiled; God loves a trier. "You are a subtle as a brick through the window. Would you like to have some supper with us Percy?"

"I thought you'd never ask," he answered grinning, "I'd love to." He stood. "Hang on a minute...". He left the kitchen and went outside to his bike. A few minutes later he came back with a bottle of wine. "I came prepared," he said, holding it up. "Shall I open it?"

"Great." I got some glasses from the cupboard, left them on the table and went in search of the kids. Miraculously they were colouring in the snug, both on the floor bent over a shared piece of paper, eating the last of the cake they'd brought back in a box from the café. Basil had his nose to the ground, snaffling crumbs the moment they fell.

"I hope you'll have enough room for supper," I said.

Teddy looked up at me. His face was smeared with icing. "I've always got room for supper," he said. He wasn't far wrong; he had the appetite of a small horse.

"I'm in the kitchen if you need me," I said. "I'll call you in half an hour or so."

I headed back to the kitchen and Percy. He was on the phone.

"Yeah, of course I told her and no, she wasn't too bothered. We did it together actually, Willa drove, and I directed her."

He glanced up as I came in and mouthed '*Angelica.*'

"Ha-ha, very funny. Who's the post person round here? And who managed to find his way round the world? Yes, thank you, I do have a good sense of direction. So no, we didn't get lost, and we got to all the cafés on the list. It was a great success; we made a great team! OK, no problem. Thanks, Angelica."

Percy had poured me a glass of wine and I took a sip, moving to the other side of the kitchen to avoid looking as if I was eavesdropping, which I was. A minute or so later, he finished his call. "She wanted to make sure you got the message."

"Really? Was Tye asking?"

Percy shrugged. "No, I don't think so. He'd just asked her to pass the message on that he was busy, and she wanted to make sure I'd delivered it. In case Tye asks."

"Right. Which I'm guessing he won't."

"Probably not."

"I see."

"You'll get used to it," Percy said, "If you have more to do with Tye." He pulled out a chair at the kitchen table and sat down. He swept his hair back with his hand and looked at me.

"Which I'm guessing you'll try not to do," he said. Then he grinned. 'Why have a cart horse when there's a stallion in the field?"

TWENTY-ONE

TYE

"Right kids, we're here." I pulled to a stop at the back of the house and yanked the handbrake on. I thought the back was less intimidating than the front of the house, with the steps and the huge double doors. I glanced sidelong at Alfie, whose face was still ashen and tear stained, then I looked behind me at the other three. I felt momentarily overwhelmed by their confusion and sadness.

"Hey," I said, in my jolliest voice – which Eadie had told me had a touch of 'threatening pirate' about it. "This is going to be fun! A sleepover, and Eadie will have made something AMAZING for tea. Who likes cake?"

Libby put her hand up and smiled wanly, Tommo sucked his thumb and Carlton just stared at me. Of course he did, what did I expect? There was no-one else at the hospital to take them and they sure as hell weren't going to social services for the night, not on my watch. But they hadn't got a clue who I was, and Alfie was the only one of the four who'd met me before. Plus, they'd just spent the past five hours sitting in a waiting room playing with a sad selection of battered toys, wondering what the hell had just happened. I smiled at them all and then at Alfie.

"Come on," I said, "I'll help you all out of the truck." I opened the door and to my utter relief, Eadie and Cici came out of the house and headed towards us, arms open and faces wreathed in loving smiles.

The doors were opened, seat belts unclicked, and small people lifted up and out of the Land Rover. Cici carried Carlton who was four and Eadie reached for Tommo who was a small five-year-old. Alfie helped Libby down. She was ten, but she seemed older. She was used to caring for Megan and for her siblings and I guessed she'd had to grow up pretty quickly.

"Libby, what's your favourite colour?" I asked as we headed to the kitchen. "I thought it might be pink, well, I'm hoping it might be pink?"

Libby nodded.

"Phew! That's great because Cici has put a pink duvet cover on your bed. And..." I smiled. "There're pink pyjamas too? If you'd like?" She nodded again and reached for Alfie's hand. Alfie glanced at me and almost smiled, and we went into the house together.

An hour later, Eadie had fed and bathed everyone and changed the younger ones into clean pyjamas. Eadie never, ever threw anything away and in the interval between my phone call from the hospital and arriving back at Peace Summerton, she had found clothes and bed linen for small children - things that Cici and I had used ourselves - washed it, dried it and had it all waiting for them. She took them up to get them settled while I washed up with Alfie.

"It's big," Alfie said, "your house."

"Yes," I handed him a plate to dry. "It's nice to have it

full." I meant it too. I'd always imagined the house full of kids and family.

"You don't mind?" he said, "Having us here? I mean, you didn't just do it cos you had to?"

I was glad that my hands were in the washing up bowl otherwise I think I would have hugged him, which I'm not sure he would have wanted. He looked so lost and so sad. I kept my voice casual, but I was flooded with memories.

"No, it's cool." I glanced at him. "I'm glad you're all here."

'Thanks."

Cici appeared in the doorway. "Alfie, you're wanted upstairs," she said. "I think they're all a bit nervous. Are you happy to go up and sit with them? You can borrow my iPad and watch something if you like?"

He shrugged. "I often go to bed with them. Sometimes it's the only way I can get them to sleep."

Cici caught my eye. Alfie reached for another plate off the rack to dry and I said, "Don't worry about that Alfie, you get yourself upstairs. If you want a shower, my bedroom, sitting room and bathroom are on the top floor, at the end of the long corridor. You can use them if you want?"

"And there's a pair of Tye's old trackie bottoms on his bed and a clean tee-shirt I left out for you," Cici added, "I mean, if you don't mind looking pretty uncool, just for tonight!"

Alfie smiled. 'Thanks..." he said again. He crossed to the door. "For everything Tye." He disappeared with Cici, and I finished the washing up.

Cici appeared in the doorway a few minutes later.

"Megan's OK isn't she Tye?"

"Yeah, she'll be in for a while though. They need to check for liver damage and then there'll be a psychological assessment, not that they'll find anything new or do anything about what's already wrong." I shook my head. "Alfie did well, coming up here so quickly."

"You both did well." She came across to me. "Hug?"

Cici gave me one of her hugs. She was small and petite and I pretty much enveloped her when we hugged. "Are you OK?" she asked, her voice muffled by my chest.

"Yeah, I think so." We broke apart.

"Sure?"

"Yeah, sure." But to be honest I wasn't sure. I turned away and went back to the washing up.

"Tye, it's OK if you're not fine you know. Seeing Megan like that, well, it must have... well, reminded you..."

"It was completely different," I said. "I just did what anyone would have done and honestly, I'm fine." We didn't go there; I didn't go there. The best thing about the past was that it was a long time ago and that's where it should stay.

"Good," Cici said, and she reached up and kissed me on the cheek. Although the way she looked at me told me that she didn't quite believe me.

"Talking of fine, was Willa OK when you rang her? I thought I might pop down there and see if we can rearrange our café trip."

"Ah, about that...". Cici shook her head. "You didn't leave us her number you numpty, and we couldn't get hold of you at the hospital."

"Oh shit, of course!" Fuck. Numpty was the least of it!

"It's OK, crisis averted. Angelica rang Percy who dropped by with the message after work. Angelica rang him a bit earlier actually, just before you came home, and he said it was all fine."

My heckles rose. Percy was involved. Who the fuck thought that was a good idea?

"Great." I lied as I pulled the plug in the sink and the sudsy water drained away. I dried my hands. "I think I will go and see if we can rearrange though and apologise. It makes good business sense what we're aiming for, I'm keen to move it forward." Cici was staring at me, one eyebrow arched. "What?"

"I'm sure it does make good business sense." She laughed. "God Tye, you're so transparent!"

Eadie popped her head round the door. "Tye, could you pop up and say goodnight to the kids? I think it'd be nice for them, you know, seeing as you brought them here."

"Sure. Then I thought I'd walk down to the Lodge."

"Did you now?" Eadie said, but she smiled.

"I won't be long," I said.

"Won't you now?"

Eadie winked at Cici and once again I was the butt of their private joke. I went past her and out towards the hall. It was polite, to make sure there was no misunderstanding, and if the trial orders for the biscuits were anything to go by, this really did make good business sense. I made my way up the stairs. And the fact that I thought Willa was absolutely gorgeous had absolutely nothing to do with it.

TWENTY-TWO

WILLA

Finally, finally, finally I got Esme and Teddy into bed. The bathroom looked like a war zone, my hair was a mass of frizz from all the steam and splashing and Teddy had to be bribed with two stories in bed to clean his teeth. I was tired, sweaty, and right at the end of a long, frayed tether. I read the shortest stories I could find, tucked them both up and went downstairs.

Percy was outside the back door of the kitchen smoking. I started on the clearing up.

"Here, let me help," he said, coming in. "I don't suppose that Maud has any spare bottles of wine lying around that we could drink and replace later?" He grinned at me.

"No, I don't think so." I wasn't a party girl, I'd never had the chance to be. Two kids with a hangover were a living hell, so one glass was my limit.

Percy sat down and emptied the last of the red wine into his glass. "I'll just finish this and then I'll get up and help," he said.

"Sure." I cleared up round him. I was quick, force of

habit from running Syd's café back home, and I'd loaded the dishwasher, wiped the table, and put the leftovers in the fridge by the time he'd drunk up.

"Oh," he said, looking up, "You've done it."

"I have, and now I need to get to bed. It's been a long day. Sorry."

"Ah right, of course." He stood and took his wine glass over to the sink, where he left it. I was going to let him know that the dishwasher was right by his legs, but honestly, I couldn't be bothered. He'd been kind, helping and then the tea out with Teddy and Esme, and I *was* glad of his company. Single parenthood could be very lonely.

Percy headed for the front door, and I followed him. He pulled his jacket on, checking he had his cigarettes in his jeans pocket, then opened the front door and we stood for a few moments, facing each other.

"Willa, today was good fun..."

"Yes, it was," I said.

"And you are lovely..." he said, "really lovely..." Then he leaned towards me and kissed me.

Shit! I should have immediately pulled back, but it took me a few moments to realise what was happening and then his tongue flickered over my parted mouth, and I was so surprised that I sprang away.

"Oh... I... erm... I..." My face was hot, and I couldn't find the words. "I'm sorry, I..."

"You weren't expecting that?" he asked.

"No! I..."

"I'm sorry." He grinned. "Should I have asked?"

I stared down at the ground. "Well, erm, yes."

He tilted my chin up to look him. "And what would you have said?"

My heart was thumping. Percy was gorgeous, smoking hot, funny, intelligent...

"I'd have said... not now, not tonight."

He stared at me. "But not never?"

I shrugged.

He stepped back. "You're tired, it's late, and I must go. Thank you for a wonderful supper." He headed towards his bike and stopped when he got to it to light a cigarette. He was also super-cool. "Night Willa," he said.

I held my hand up. "Night Percy."

I watched as he cycled down the drive, stopping to put his helmet on before he headed into the main road. Not now, not tonight and probably not ever, I thought, as I went inside and closed the door. What the hell was wrong with me?

TWENTY-THREE

TYE

Fuck. Talk about wrong place, wrong fucking time. Percy. Percy fucking Dunstan. Percy and Willa. My blood boiled. I'd seen it all, from a distance, the kiss, the moment of tenderness, the fucking waves goodbye. Fuck. I took a deep breath, lifted my shoulders back and down and stood tall. This was a business deal and I'd come to rearrange the meetings. Nothing more, nothing less. I carried on to the house and knocked lightly on the door so as not to wake the kids. Willa opened it almost immediately, her face a mixture of annoyance and concern.

"Oh Tye! It's you. I thought it might be..." she broke off. 'What are you doing here?"

She looked tired, and even though I was only here on business, I had the ridiculous urge to scoop her into a hug.

"I came to see if we could rearrange the meetings, with the cafés? I'm sorry I missed it today, I..."

"I know," she interrupted, "something came up."

I bristled. "It did, actually. Didn't Percy tell you?"

"Yes, he did. He explained everything. I get it, you were busy."

"I was busy?"

"Yes. And it's fine. We've already done the cafés; I went with Percy. We got a whole bunch of orders, which I think you could follow up on tomorrow."

"You've already done it? You've got a whole bunch of orders which you think I could follow up on?" I was suddenly exasperated. I did the air quotes as I repeated her words, despite knowing how infuriating that was. "How kind of you, to let me be involved. Those were my contacts, and I should have been there."

"You didn't message me." She said, as if that was explanation enough.

"No, I didn't! As I explained, I was busy." Fuck, what was her problem?

"So, you keep saying. Good for you."

"Is that all you can say? Good for you?" Was she missing a sympathy gene? Did everything have to evolve around Willa?

"What else do you want me to say?"

"Erm, sorry? Sorry for going ahead without you and not thinking..."

"Not thinking what? That I should wait until Tye, the Lord of the Manor was ready to spare me a little time?"

I took a pace back and a deep breath. "Not thinking that this is my business, and you would be operating under my name." Outwardly, I kept my voice low and calm; inwardly, I was seething. "Not thinking that the right thing to do was to wait for me so that I could take you to *my* customers and introduce you!" I took another pace back. *Lord of the Manor?* The jibe rang in my ears.

"Well, I'm sorry that I didn't think about putting you first. I'm sure that isn't something that you're used to."

I shook my head. "You are unbelievable..."

"Oh yeah, well it takes one to know one!"

"And you are a fucking child. Is that all you can come back with? It takes one to know one?" I shook my head again, stared at her for a few moments longer then turned on my heel and walked away. Un-fucking-believable.

TWENTY-FOUR

WILLA

Shit. That went well. I slammed the door, then remembered the kids, went halfway up the stairs to see if I'd woken them, which I hadn't, and finally sat down on the bottom step and put my head in my hands. How could what had promised to be a lovely day with Tye, meeting new customers, serving him a delicious meal that he'd want me to cook for the farm shop, spending a whole afternoon and probably some of the evening with him, turn out so wretched? So completely wretched. God, what was that all about? He didn't even have the courtesy to properly apologise. He just turned up with a brief '*sorry*' and expected me to be waiting and simpering. Well, tough luck! I'd gone ahead and got the job done without him. And done it well, got loads of orders. Perhaps that's what really irked him, the fact that I'd done it just as well on my own as I could have done with him.

I closed my eyes, his words swirled round my head, and I knew that wasn't the real reason he was upset. What he said was right. I should have waited for him. But then why couldn't he just have called me, or even said sorry for not calling, for leaving me hanging? I rubbed my hands over my face and opened my eyes. What had Percy said? That Tye did his own thing and everyone else had to work around that? But then why did he make me feel important, because he did, when I was with him. Well, he did, up until just now.

I wandered through to the kitchen and stood by the Aga, my back to it, the warmth of it seeping through me. I felt cold and stupid, I felt cross and confused, but mostly, I just felt sad.

TWENTY-FIVE

WILLA

I was pleased with myself. It was Friday morning, the last day of Esme and Teddy's first week at their new school and I'd got them both out of the house on time with lunch, PE kit, show and tell for Esme that wasn't my vibrator (which she'd been insistent on taking, thinking it was a massage tool, and which had taken some delicate negotiation and subtle explanation on my part to deter her).

"I think a large fir cone from the garden is far better," I said, as we walked from the village green where I'd parked, to school. "I just don't think a massager is very interesting for children."

"But it's the same shape as the fir cone," Esme said earnestly. "And it wobbles. The fir cone doesn't wobble."

"No." I coughed. "Still, a fir cone is part of the natural world, and you can talk about the wonder of nature." I gave her hand a little squeeze. "Also, think how lovely it will look on the winter table in the classroom. You can add it to the display, can't you?"

"What am I going to take Willa?"

"I think you're down for the last week of term Teddy, so why don't we try and think of something Christmassy."

"Snot fair!" Esme whined, "He gets to take one of our precious things and I have to take a smelly old fir cone."

"It won't be one of our precious things Esme, not for show and tell, not with Teddy. I was thinking that we could make something, like a Christmas cracker or some Christmas biscuits and then you could eat them after show and tell Ted? What do you think of that?"

"Yay! Biscuits, biscuits!"

"And you can take some in for the class Esme, as a Christmas treat."

Esme nodded seriously. "But I don't want to give biscuits to everyone."

"No?"

"No."

"Well, if you take biscuits into school then you really have to have enough for everyone in the class Esme, otherwise some people might feel left out."

"Well some people should share their jumbo colouring pens then and not be mean about them."

"Perhaps the jumbo colouring pens are precious?"

"So are biscuits."

Esme had an answer for everything, and I was about to enter into what would undoubtedly be a challenging exchange when Teddy shouted, "Tye? TYE! Look Willa, it's Tye!"

I glanced up and across the playground to see Tye talking to Miss Blackmore and holding hands with two small children.

Oh shit. That was the last thing I needed. For nearly two weeks he'd been avoiding me. He'd received over fifty orders for the choc hazelnut cookies, which came via email to me – he couldn't even call – and I'd fulfilled all of them as soon as they came in with not so much as a thank you or a well done. God, it made my blood boil! It was all so childish. He dropped the packaging off outside my door, I made the biscuits, put them in the packaging, and delivered them back to the shop - a place he'd suddenly developed an aversion to. I'd tried to catch him out a couple of times as he came by with the packaging late at night so I'd waited up for him. But getting up at 5am to cook always got the better of me and both times I'd nodded off on the sofa and woken face to face with Basil who was gently snoring in my ear.

"TYE!" Teddy shouted again, waving his arms and Tye looked across. He waved back at Teddy and grinned.

"Who's that with him?" I asked Esme. It was a small school, and if anyone was going to have their ear to the ground it would be Esme. She didn't miss a trick.

"Tommo." Teddy said. "He's in my class and he's awesome."

I looked at Teddy. "Awesome?" I had a small American on my hands.

"And Libby is in the class above me," Esme said. "Their Mum is in hospital and they're staying with Cici and Tye and Eadie. Libby said Tye reads them a story every night and he does all the voices."

"Really? How nice." I kept my voice neutral when all the time I'm thinking, of course he does, he's Mr Perfect to everyone else except me. But Esme's explanation was cutting through my angst. He had kids staying while their mum was in hospital. Hmmm.

"Hey?"

I glanced up. There he was, in faded grey cords, the sort that had seen hundreds of washes and still looked good - in a macho, scruffy sort of way - and a baggy, thick wool sweater.

How did he manage to dress in a way that looked so deliberately unselfconscious but must have taken tons of effort and thought. No-one was that good at throwing things on, surely?

"Hey." I nodded and he smiled.

"Your biscuits are a best seller! We've had loads of repeat orders the last few days."

"Oh?" And you couldn't pick up the phone and tell me? But I didn't say that, I said,

"Nice one."

He looked at his watch. "I've gotta go. I must be somewhere. Hey Teddy, how are you doing? Esme? Still as stylish and lovely as ever I see."

Esme smiled, Teddy held up his hand for a high five and the fact that Tye was so nice annoyed the hell out of me.

"See you," he said. He looked sidelong at me, and I wasn't going to give him the satisfaction of returning his gaze. He hurried away across the playground, and I bent to kiss Teddy and Esme.

"Why are you so cross?" Esme said. Yeah, nothing gets past her.

"I'm not cross," I said.

"Your mouth is all pinchy," Esme continued. "and your eyes are a bit squinty."

"And I think you're beautiful too," I countered. "Now skedaddle and I'll be here at half past three." She looked at me, her head on one side, as if working it all out and then she turned, saw a friend, waved, and ran off. Teddy had already gone. I could see him jumping in the sandpit near the classroom with Tommo. I turned and made my way to the van.

"Willa? Hey, WILLA?" I glanced behind me and saw Angelica, bright red hair billowing, long green velvet skirt bunched up in her hands, and her trademark magenta cloak flying out behind her as she ran towards me. "Willa Stop! STOP!"

I'd already stopped, and Angelica caught me up, panting heavily.

"I had your biscuits..." she said, between mouthfuls of air, "...and ...they are amazing! I'm... going to a... witchcraft fair... in Glastonbury...and I wanted to ask if... if you could make me some Halloween Biscuits to sell there. I mean, I'd split the profits..." She took a few big gulps of air and started to ferret in her giant bag - in the shape of a spider – for her inhaler. She'd gone very pale.

"Pass it!" I said sharply. She had bent double and handed me the bag, struggling for air. I delved, found the inhaler, and whipped it out. "Here." I handed it over and she started puffing.

I waited and gently rubbed her back. Finally, she straightened.

"You OK?"

She nodded.

"Good. Sure?"

She nodded again and some of her colour came back. "Sorry. I shouldn't run in the icy air."

"Well, at least not in those boots."

We both looked down at her high heeled lace up boots.

She started laughing and suddenly reached forward and gave me a hug. "It's so good to see you, Willa. You haven't been up to the house for ages! Cici and I miss you! Obviously, you know that I live there, well practically live there, and so I'm quite all right to invite you. You have to come up, it's been such fun with the kids there! You'd love it and so would Esme and Teddy..." She was talking so fast that she began to pant a little again.

"Angelica, slow down! Kids? What kids? Why are there kids up at the house?"

"Oh, Tye rescued them. You know what he's like, he's just the nicest person ever, and their mum was rushed to hospital..." Angelica leant in very close to my ear.

"It's been awful. Especially for Alfie. He didn't know where else to go, so he cycled up to the house. Tye drove him home and..." She stopped, suddenly embarrassed. "Tye will tell you all about it."

"Can't you?"

She looked uncomfortable. "Oh, I don't think so, Willa, it sounds like gossip if I... you know..." She pulled a face to show how bad she felt. "You know what I mean?"

"Yes, I do." Suddenly, I loved this young woman.

"When did all this kick off?" I asked. "I mean if its ok to tell me that much?" I was beginning to have a slight sense of unease, like a tiny fluttering, right in the pit of my stomach.

"About two weeks ago, I think." She narrowed her eyes. "No, ten days ago. It was the day I asked Percy to deliver the message that Tye had been called away on an emergency and couldn't do the biscuit run with you."

"Wait, what?"

"He told you all this, didn't he?"

I blinked.

"Tye dashed off and asked us to call you and we didn't have your number, on account of you having just moved in and us, me and Cici, only just having met you, cos it'd be like, kind of weird to meet you and go, hey, nice to meet you, can I have your..."

"Angelica?"

She stopped. "Sorry," she chirruped. "got carried away." She took another puff on the inhaler. "Anyway, I rang Percy and asked him to stop by and let you know all that. Tye ended up in A&E all day and then he brought the kids home because there wasn't anyone else to..." She stopped.

"Willa? Are you..."

"No!" I wailed. I was NOT OK! I had both my hands over my head, I was pacing the pavement and I wanted to scream! How could I have been so stupid! Percy had delivered half a message and instead of finding out what had really happened to Tye, I'd jumped in and assumed that whatever Percy said was right. I'd been so concerned with myself that I hadn't bothered to look further than my own feelings of indignation.

"What's the matter?" Angelica asked.

"Oh God..." I moaned, "Everything! Everything's the matter!"

Angelica put both her hands on my shoulders. "Look at me Willa," she said sternly. I stopped pacing and faced her.

"You've fallen out with Tye, that much is obvious. He's walking round with a face like thunder and you're conspicuous by your absence. Was this anything to do with Percy?!"

I nodded.

"I'll kill him!" she announced. "I'll bloody kill that brother of mine! He is always causing trouble for Tye, he does it like it's sport! Jesus! I could swing for him! He is definitely getting one of the horrible spells I'm working on." She took a big breath. "He didn't pass the message on, did he?"

I shook my head. It was as if I'd been struck dumb.

"That explains an awful lot." She released me and ferreted in her bag again. She brought out a bottle, glanced at the label and chucked it back in. She dived back into the velvet spider and this time found what she was looking for.

"My magical protection potion," she said. She held it out to me. "Here. Take a swig."

"Really?" I took the stopper off the small bottle and sniffed. It smelled like apple juice.

"It's apple magic," Angelica said. "It protects you against harm and it also gives you a leg up with getting your dreams."

"A double whammy then," I said. I took a swig. It was delicious. Her potions were covering all eventualities.

"We've got to fix this," she said, "because you and Tye... you're... " She stared off into the distance. She was thinking. I could tell because she had put her finger to her lip in style of the Rodin sculpture. "Aha! I think I've got it." She hooked her arm though mine. "Walk with me round the green, will you?" She grinned. "Because I think I have a plan."

TWENTY-SIX

TYE

I put the kettle on in the kitchen and came back into the small front room to have a good look at my handy work. I could paint a wall; I mean who couldn't with a roller and a tin of cream emulsion paint? But the truth was staring at me; I was rubbish at cutting in. The edge between the ceiling and the wall looked like a dog's dinner. It was going to be even worse when I tackled the upstairs. The kids and Megan had all chosen the colours for their rooms, Eadie reckoned a nice fresh house to come home to would do them all the world of good, but the colours they'd picked were going to challenge my decorating skills to the hilt. There was a light blue for the boys –okay, could probably just about get away with that one, sunny yellow for Libby – a bit better but still tricky and... a deep mauve for Megan – might have to get a professional in for that one!

The kettle boiled, I made tea and turned the radio on. I took the mug back to the front room and opened the tin of paint. I'd done two walls, had two to go and even though it was a shit load of work at the end of my day, honestly, I was glad to be doing it. Alfie had helped a bit, but Cici and Angelica had insisted he do his homework tonight, which was fair and... well, I was glad of the solitude. I was still as mad as fuck with Willa and seeing her this morning hadn't made any of those feelings go away. She looked defiant. And so fucking gorgeous. Shit, I had no idea whether I wanted to ignore her or kiss her. And Eadie was no help, dropping hints with all the subtlety of a fucking sledge-hammer. You're so good with kids, you'd make a great dad Tye, wouldn't it be lovely to see you settled, blah, blah, blah. I was heartily sick of everyone thinking that my perfect woman was down in the Lodge. They were so wrong. She may have looked perfect, but she was far, far from it.

I drank my tea, poured the paint into the roller tray, and turned the radio up. There was a banging on the front door. Fuck. I hoped to God it wasn't social services. That was all any of us needed.

"Coming!" I yelled. There was another loud, insistent thumping. The panes of glass in the door shook. For fuck's sake. I stomped to the door and looked through the glass. There was nobody there. This was pissing me off. I waited in the hall to catch them out the next time they knocked. Fucking kids. There it was... I flung open the door.

"What the hell do you think..."

Willa fell forward, lost her balance, and dropped a fucking enormous toolbox, just missing my foot. I jumped back, she fell in the door, stumbled forward several paces and grabbed the banister to right herself.

"Oh... Jesus... I..." She stabilised, turned, and looked at me. "Phew. That was a close one." She smiled awkwardly. "I've erm... I've come to ... help. If you'll have me."

I eyed her suspiciously.

"And to say I'm sorry. I misjudged you, I shouldn't have said, or done..."

She looked on the verge of tears; I jumped in. "Me neither," I said, "I was an idiot, and..." I broke off and smiled. Just being in the same room with her made me feel good. "Can I assume your decorating is on a par with your mechanics?"

She grinned back. "Slightly better actually. I painted our house twice, once when Lexi was pregnant and then... well, a few years ago, to cheer us all up."

Lexi? Who was Lexi? I was going to ask, but she took her coat off and hung it over the banister and she was wearing a vest with shoestring straps and dungarees over the top. Her arms and neck were a pale creamy colour dusted with the same freckles that she had on her face.

"So," she said. "Where are you at?"

I led the way into the front room. I'd covered all the furniture with dust sheets, the paint was ready, and my handiwork was in full view. Willa looked at the wall.

"Hmmm," she said. She stepped in closer and stared up at the ceiling. "Hmmm." She turned to me. "Not bad. Cutting in needs a bit of repair work, but the wall is even and well, not bad at all!" She grinned.

"Is that a gold star for me?"

"More bronze I think..."

"Bronze? Come on, there's two coats of emulsion on that wall! And no splashes on the floor."

"A few on you though." She laughed. "Shall we get started? I've got blue masking tape and a special brush for the edges."

"Of course you have." I looked at her and raised an eyebrow.

"I'll ignore that and get on and redo the cutting in," she

said. "I'll make sure the line is straight then I'll come and roller the other wall. You happy with that? Have you got the white ceiling paint?"

I found the other tin of paint and opened it with a screwdriver. "Do you need a tray?"

"Please," she called as she went into the hall for the cumbersome toolbox. She lugged it back in and opened it up.

"Right," she said, armed with paintbrush and tape.

I fetched the ladder for her, put it up and watched as she scaled it effortlessly, with the tools and paint in her left hand.

"Is there any limit to your talents?" I asked.

She glanced back over her shoulder and her look gave me an instant erection.

"That's for me to know and you to find out," she said. And she smiled.

TWO HOURS into it we had finished the room. It looked clean and bright and the edge between the wall and the ceiling was perfect. We had worked quickly and companionably, singing along to Magic FM - she took the higher notes, I did the baritone - and honestly, it was the best fucking time I'd had in ages. I had no idea what the time was, but I knew that I didn't want it to stop. As we stood back side by side, paintbrushes in hand and looked at the walls, I said,

"Shall we do the hall next?"

Willa glanced sidelong at me. "Well..."

"I mean, if you have time, that is. If the kids are OK, with the babysitter? Who is...?"

"Angelica." Willa said.

"Ah. And did Angelica by any chance tell you I'd be here tonight?"

"She might have done..."

"I see."

"Which is why Alfie had to stay at the house and do his homework."

"I guess."

"Oh."

"Are you implying that you'd rather have had Alfie here instead of me?" She was staring at me, a smile playing on her lips.

"No..."

"Good. Cos you'd better not be..."

"Or what?" I stared right back at her. We were standing so close that I could feel the heat from her body.

"Or this!" She suddenly swiped a paintbrush over my arm. I looked down at a stripe of wet emulsion. "Hey!" When I looked up again, she had darted to the other side of the room. "HEY!" I darted across the room after her and flicked my brush in her direction. A splattering of paint shot off it and hit her across the chest. She gasped, a look of shock and outrage crossed her face. I thought, oh fuck, I've blown it now.

"Right!" she cried, "That's it." She laughed and flicked back. It got me in the face. I lunged forward and grabbed her hand with the brush in it. She lifted the hand and swiped me across the face with the tip of the brush. I tasted paint.

"Yeow!!" I still had her hand and was holding her fast to my side. "That tastes..."

Suddenly her mouth was on mine. I felt her warm lips, her tongue and then the sweet, explosive taste of her mouth. She pulled back for a tiny moment.

"Disgusting?" she whispered, smiling.

"Fucking amazing," I whispered back. "You are fucking amazing."

I brought my hands up to her face, her hair and felt the soft tangle of it. I wrapped my fingers in the long curls and eased her face gently towards mine. I opened my eyes to look at her.

"Oh God, Tye, I don't..." And as suddenly as she kissed me, she pulled away.

TWENTY-SEVEN

WILLA

I stopped and took a breath. Tye stared at me.

"You don't what?" He'd moved away, but his eyes never left my face, and he still held my wrist.

"I don't know what I'm doing..."

He smiled. "Me neither."

"This is the... last thing... either of us..." He rubbed his thumb gently over the skin on the inside of my wrist and I shivered. I couldn't think straight, let alone talk any sense. "...Need."

"No."

"And there are so many reasons not to... erm you know..."

"Yes." He bent and put his mouth lightly where his thumb had been. He licked the skin and the muscles in my stomach contracted.

"So..." I took a step closer to him and I could smell the scent of his skin.

"So?"

I had no sense or reason left. I kissed him again and this

time he took the lead. His tongue was forceful, insistent, he knew what he wanted. I lost myself, barely breathing. His hands were in my hair, over my back and then as he bent his head and kissed my neck, he moved his fingers up under my vest and rubbed my nipple through the lace of my bra. Bizarrely I thought, thank God I'd put on decent underwear and then, wait, did I know this was going to happen? But those were the last semi-intelligent thoughts that I had. I moaned as my body connected my nipples and the sweet spot between my legs and I was consumed by the warm, pulsing ache that flooded through me. Tye pulled back.

"How the fuck do you...?" He was twisting the fastening of my dungarees, unable to undo them. That was a good sign, he obviously wasn't an expert at removing clothing.

"Here." I unclipped the straps and the front fell down. Two more buttons at the side and the whole lot slipped to my ankles. I lifted my arms, pulled the vest top over my head, and stood in front of him in my bra and pants. But only for a moment.

"Fuck." Tye pulled me back into his body and began running his mouth down over my chest until his lips found my nipples. He sucked through the lace, his hands moving behind me to find the bra clasp and I gasped as I felt the warm wetness of his tongue, sucking, gently biting, making my nipples hard. I reached down and hooked my thumb under the waistband of his jeans and found the fly button. I wriggled it free, unzipped and slipped my hand down inside the front of his pants, wrapping my fingers around his erection. He moaned loudly.

"Willa, that's, oh god, that's so fucking good..."

His hands moved down my body, I was out of breath, and as his fingers slipped inside the edge of my knickers, spreading my thighs, I was dizzy, my head blank and swimming. I moved involuntarily, shifting the lace down to my ankles and kicked them off. I brought my hand up to my mouth and covered it in saliva, slipping it down inside his jeans to run the wetness of it over the top of his cock. He moaned again and worked his fingers deep inside me, making my legs buckle.

"Oh God, Willa, stop..." He inched back and stood straight. "Shit, this is so fucking hot and... where the fuck can we....?" He was looking around the room, his eyes darting over the furniture covered in dust sheets. I kissed his cheek briefly and walked naked into the hall. I found my coat, brought it back and laid it on the floor. He pulled me back to him and kissed me.

"Lie down," he ordered. I was always in charge, always giving instructions and the surrender was blissful. I knelt, then sat back and watched him slide his jeans down over his hips. What I'd felt in his jeans was even better on sight. He got to his knees in front of me and parted my thighs.

"Lay back," he said hoarsely. He put his hands under my buttocks and lifted my hips up, putting his face between my legs. I felt his tongue, the same determination and hot slippery wetness that had been in my mouth was now... probing, licking, pushing inside me. I started to moan and move my hips; I was moving on a wave that was pulling me deeper into a flood of pleasure...

"Tye, oh God, Tye..." He kept on, flicking his tongue, small movements, then thrusting it deep into me. I was being washed away, drowning...

"Oh yes...Yes...YES!" My body began to tremble as the best and biggest orgasm OF MY LIFE pulsed and shook through me. I pushed my hands back against the wall behind me, my moans became cries, became shouts...

"Oh fuck...YES......! I'm coming...YES, YES!"

It crashed into me, a whole-body convulsion, from my clitoris up to the tip of my head. It crashed and shuddered and rolled until finally my body went limp, Tye moved his mouth, and I closed my eyes in blissful calm. Tye gently kissed the inside of my thigh and sat back. I opened my eyes, and he had a look on his face that could almost be described as smug. I nudged him with my leg and reached towards him, taking his erection in my hands.

"Be careful," he said, 'That's about to go off."

"Really?" I slipped my hand up and down him, smoothly working him.

"Yeah. You coming like that is..." He stopped and looked down at my fingers. "Jeeze, that is so fucking good..."

"Me coming like that is...?"

"Electric Willa. You are... Oh yeah, don't stop..."

He moved up over me. I licked my hand again and slid it, wet and slippery over his balls and the base of his cock. I continued to pump, slowly, long strokes.

He moved his face over mine and started to kiss me. I could feel myself wanting him all over again. "Can we... I mean do you want to..."

"Be inside you?" His voice was not more than a whisper. "Fuck, yes! I haven't..." he started to lose his breath. "I haven't... got... anything."

I worked him harder, faster, moving my fingers to the tip of him. He started to moan. "Yes, do that, don't stop Willa, Oh god, yes... I'm..." He tensed and opened his eyes, locking them onto mine. I felt an intensity that shook me; exhilarating and terrifying. He exploded in my hand.

"Wow."

I smiled as he sat back and dug in the pocket of his jeans on the floor next to him.

"Here," He handed me a handkerchief. "For your hands."

I looked at it, a clean, neatly ironed square of soft, white cotton.

"This is very... erm... very gentlemanly."

He grinned back. "Oh yeah? Well, a gentleman always has a clean handkerchief about his person."

"To wipe the semen off a young lady's hands?

"Exactly. When the occasion arises, of course."

"Of course."

We both started to laugh, and Tye lay down next to me, propped up on his elbow. He ran his finger along my collar bone and down to my nipple.

"You are exactly as I imagined," he said.

"Ah, you imagined this?"

"I did. And it was way better in real life. Did you?"

"Never crossed my mind," I said, grinning. And to some extent that was true. I mean, I hadn't exactly spent hours and hours fantasising about lying on my coat on the floor in a half-decorated house with Tyler Malloy's face between my legs. But it hadn't come as a complete surprise that his mouth was luscious and hot and... I glanced down as I felt his erection pressing against my thigh.

"Do you, I mean are you...erm..."

Tye followed my gaze. "Yup. And yes, my god, I'd love to...erm..." He leant in and kissed me. "As you so beautifully put it." He sat up. "You are irresistible Willa."

I ran my fingers down his back, and he shivered. "So...?"

"So..." He caught my hand and brought it up to his mouth. "I am going to have to exert extreme willpower to have any chance." He kissed my fingers. "But we've got some more painting to do."

I sat up as well. He was right. We were in the middle of

decoration chaos, and I was also about to catch a chill. Tye stood and pulled me to my feet and then in close to his body. He held me and it was warm and calm and complete. But to feel like that was also the very last thing I needed.

"We should erm..."

"Get dressed?"

"Yes, and get on, with the hallway." We broke apart and Tye began gathering up his clothes. He pulled on his tee-shirt, jeans, his boots. Had they come off in the fray? I didn't remember seeing him take his boots off... God, had the sex been that good? I'd practically lost all sense of time and place. Tye was looking at me as I fastened my dungarees.

"Those are definitely easier to get on than get off," he said, grinning. He kissed me one last time and I forgot myself again for those few moments.

Yup, it *had* been that good. This man was dangerously gorgeous.

TWENTY-EIGHT

TYE

I didn't want to be a dick about it, but when I kissed Willa goodbye and closed the door of her van at a bit past ten, I watched her go, then I turned towards the house and punched the air. I was grinning from ear to ear. Jesus! That was fucking incredible! We'd decorated three rooms, I'd had some of the best sex of my life (even if it was only a hand job, it was still sex and the best), and she'd even cleaned the brushes and cleared away with me. She was far more capable than a bloke, more fun, and at the same time she was soft and vulnerable and hot and wet. I stopped myself right there and thought of the guttering on Peace Summerton House. My erection subsided. If I didn't get a grip on my thoughts about Willa, I was going to be walking around for the next few months with my hands in front of my crotch to cover the massive boner I got just picturing her.

I switched off the sockets, made sure that the heating was off and left my brushes and tools neatly stacked. I turned off the lights, locked the front door after me and made my way out to the Land Rover. I wanted to follow Willa home, have a box of condoms and be in bed with her, making her come in every way possible so that she looked like she did tonight; wild and soft and sexy. But I got into the jeep, started the engine, and drove carefully through the icy, foggy darkness towards home.

I slowed down as I drove past the entrance to the Lodge and saw Willa's van. She was home safe and out of this icy fog, so that was good. But in the drive to Peace Summerton House, opposite the copse that separated the estate grounds from the Lodge, I stopped and looked for the lights on in Willa's room. I couldn't stop myself. Ridiculous, but I wanted to imagine her tucked up in bed, hopefully thinking of me. Damn shit. There it was again. Hard as a rock. I put the Land Rover into gear and drove off, focusing on seeing through the mist and not on thoughts of a naked Willa in bed.

"HEY TYE." Cici was at the sink when I came into the kitchen.

"Hey Ci."

She was washing a saucepan and had four mugs of hot chocolate made on the kitchen table. I glanced at the clock. It was ten thirty. She followed my gaze.

"Are the kids still up?"

"Yup. Waiting for you to read them a story."

"No?!"

She smiled. "No. They're all a bit hyped actually, except Tommo, he's sleepy but won't give in."

"Megan? You told them she's coming out?"

"Yup, Eadie and I did." Cici put a tray down and began

to place the cups on it. "What time are you collecting her on Monday?"

"The hospital said to come about 10.30 a.m. There's paperwork and stuff, so I guess we'll be back around lunch time." Megan was coming home to Peace Summerton House after the weekend, to join the kids for a couple of weeks. The hospital had asked that she be supervised, and this was the best option. I thought it was a lot for Eadie, but Eadie had been insistent.

"It'll be OK Cici," I said, although I wasn't at all sure of that statement.

"I hope so," she replied. "Alfie's worried I think, and embarrassed, in case she does something, you know, odd, or difficult."

"Yeah." I knew. Megan could be erratic, sometimes unreasonable, but it was different when we were watching from the side-lines; now we were involved. "I'll go up. I'll take the drinks."

Cici glanced at me and raised an eyebrow. "You might want to put your tee-shirt on the right way round first," she said. "And it's inside out." She giggled. "Well, Nellie said she'd cast a spell, and she did. It worked."

I pulled my tee-shirt over my head and switched it round. "It's not what you think," I snapped.

"No, of course it isn't, Tye." She giggled again and I flicked the top of her head the way I used to when she annoyed me as a child.

"Oi!" she yelped, although I knew the action was all hair and no impact.

"Oi yourself," I said taking the tray.

"Oi yourself, what?" Eadie asked, coming in from the laundry room with an armful of clean washing.

"Nothing," we both said at the same time.

"You were late tonight," Eadie commented as I went past her. "Did you get much done?"

Cici started to giggle again, and I shot her a look.

"Is there something I'm missing here?" Eadie said. "Hey, wait up a minute young man."

I stopped and turned. Eadie was the only person in the world who could call me young man and make me feel twelve again.

"The hot chocolate's getting cold" I protested. "I've gotta go."

Eadie took a long hard look at me. Then she smiled. "Go on then. And when you speak to Willa later, tell her I said hi."

I left the kitchen as fast as I could. What was with the women I lived with? Did they have sixth sense or something? I passed the huge, long gilt mirror in the hall and caught sight of myself. No, no sixth sense. I was smiling. Just a small smile, that played around the corners of my mouth, but it was a smile nevertheless and I had absolutely no idea I was doing it. So that's what happiness looks like, is it?

"Who's for hot chocolate?" I called up the stairs. "Pyjama huddle, on the landing, now." I heard footsteps and whispering. When did my life suddenly get so full?

TWENTY-NINE

WILLA

"OK, so that wasn't the best idea in the world. It was hardly a well thought out plan of action now, was it Willa?" I sat on the toilet in the bathroom upstairs looking down at the bristle rash I had between my thighs and feeling hot and aching down there all over again. "Having sex with your biscuit boss, and your landlord wasn't sensible. He might be the sexiest man on the planet, with the most dextrous tongue, but that's no excuse." I wiped, stood, and pulled my still damp pants up. I moved to the sink and looked at myself in the mirror. "And the talking to yourself has got worse." I glanced heavenward. "I blame you Lexi. You can't up and die on people and then expect them to be normal." I washed my hands, dried them, and went downstairs. Angelica was flicking through a cake book in the kitchen. She glanced up.

"The spell worked then," she said.

"Hmmmm?" I filled the kettle and put it on a hot plate on the Aga. I had my back to her, which was just as well because I was suddenly hot and pink, and a prickle of sweat had started under my armpits.

"Willa?" I could hear her get up and move across the kitchen. She stood opposite me. "Willa?"

I turned away and took a couple of teacups down from the shelf.

"It worked, didn't it?! I knew it! You and Tye, you..." She spun me round to face her and my cheeks were flaming. "You had jiggery pokery, didn't you! You and Tye?!"

"Jiggery pokery?" I burst out laughing.

"Yes! Willa stop! Stop laughing, Willa?!"

I couldn't. I was bent double. I could hardly breathe.

"Willa?!" Then Angelica began to laugh, mostly at me laughing, I think. And we stood in the kitchen in hysterics until I could get it under control and wipe the tears off my cheeks. Jiggery pokery indeed!

LATER, when Angelica had gone and I was in bed, I did something that I knew I had to do. Perhaps it was the confidence that being close to Tye had given me, or maybe it was Angelica's spell which made me feel looked after and loved, or perhaps it was just that I felt more settled, and it was about time. But whatever the reason I had the strength to find out what had been happening since I'd left. I found Syd's contact details, unblocked her number, and waited for the messages to download.

Holy Crap! My phone went mad. I waited, shocked as the iMessages flipped up, one after another, every second another one. I started to scroll, words jumping out at me; disappeared; Harry; missing; money; theft! Theft! Oh my God, what the hell had happened? I couldn't look. I dialled Harry and waited for him to pick up.

"Harry? What the hell is going on?"

"Hey Willa, I'm fine thanks and how are you?" He said sarcastically.

"Harry stop! I've just unblocked Syd's number and all these messages have come in! She's furious and she's ranting about theft? Theft? I thought you said you were going to smooth it all over, I thought..."

"Willa, it's fine." Harry interrupted, his voice calm and soothing. "Honestly, it's fine. You're panicking, calm down."

"Calm down? You can't be serious, I..."

"I am serious, and you need to calm down and listen." Harry had this authoritative tone when he spoke, not sharp or hard, just the sort of tone that lets people know who's in charge.

I took a big breath and tried to exhale it slowly. Harry and I had been a thing once, a long time ago and ever since he'd come to work with me at the café, he had my back; he was always looking out for me. I trusted him. In fact, if it hadn't been for Harry, I'd have loads more problems than I did now. He was the one that told me that Syd was going for legal custody of the kids and that I might lose them; he'd overheard her talking to Daisy her new partner. It had been his idea to bolt – he thought that was the safest option and he was right. I know that Lexi had agreed with Syd before she died that I would look after them and stay in the house, but things change – people change.

"Look Willa, Syd is pissed because I left the café a few days after you, that's all."

"You left the café? Why?"

"Well, it was Syd's café and even though you and I ran it, she was invested in you, you know, because of the kids and you being her ex-wife's sister and all that. She didn't feel the same about me, I was just another manager, so I reckoned with you gone, I probably wouldn't last that long. Anyway, I've always wanted to travel, so I thought now is as good a time as any."

"You've always wanted to travel?" That was news to me. Harry got FOMO if we drove out of Newcastle to the countryside for a walk. "So, what's all this stuff about theft then?"

"Oh God, it's Syd being heavy handed, that's all. She's throwing empty threats around, trying to scare you."

"But theft Harry?"

"Yeah, it's bollocks, isn't it? Have you even read all the messages Willa?"

"No, I skimmed them, and they looked so menacing that I rang you right away."

"Well don't bother then. Block her number again and stay low until she calms down. I'd give it a month or so, probably until Christmas, and then message her. She'll have worked out by then that you mean business and that she's not having the kids."

"But what's been stolen?"

"Doh, the kids silly!"

"Oh." Relief washed over me. "No money?" I don't know why I was so worried about the allegations; I'd never stolen anything in my life, and I certainly didn't want Syd's money. She'd paid me well for running the café and she paid the mortgage on Lexi's house, so why would I steal from her? We had enough to be comfortable, the kids and I; I'd never asked for anything. It made no sense for me to steal anything, and I'd have hoped she'd be able to see that for herself. "You're sure?"

"Yes. I told you, it's idle threats. She'll have to pay a hefty legal bill to get custody Willa and all this nastiness works in your favour."

"OK." I went back to my contacts and re-blocked Syd's number, then deleted the messages. I felt immediately better, calmer, more confident.

"So, apart from getting yourself in a tizzy about Syd..."

"It was not a tizzy! Don't gaslight me Hal, it was a genuine concern."

"OK, so apart from your genuine concern about Syd, how is it all going and where are you?"

"I'm in Peace Summerton."

"Peace what? Where the hell is that?"

"Oh, it's a lovely village in the South. I'm staying in Maud's house."

"Maud?"

"Our Aunt."

"I didn't know you had an Aunt?"

"You do now." I wasn't a sharer; hadn't been since Lexi died. I kept myself to myself, even in close relationships and Harry and I were close, or at least we had been once.

"And how is she, old Aunt Maud?"

"She's away actually, which is why we're here. She's loaned us the house."

"Nice." Harry was silent for a few moments. He sounded distracted. "Look Willa, I've got to go, I've got another call coming in, probably about flights."

"Oh right, of course."

"Stay calm Willa, and keep Syd at arm's length, OK?"

There was that authority again; it was hard to resist, and it made me feel safe.

"I will. Thanks Harry."

"You're welcome Willa. Bye."

He ended the call and I looked at my phone. Typical Harry, sensible and in control.

"Which is more than can be said for you Willa," I

commented to the empty room. I plugged my phone in to charge, switched off the lamp and settled down to sleep.

THIRTY

TYE

I hated hospitals. I don't think anyone likes them, but I *hated* them. Every time I entered one, I was eight years old again, and all the same feelings I'd felt back then returned with a vengeance and punched me right in the guts. Fucking hospitals.

It was Monday morning, and here I was at the Kimberton General Hospital. Not a great way to start the week. I parked in the visitor's carpark and tucked the ticket into my coat pocket. The parking was fee was exorbitant. They didn't make it easy to visit sick people, but I'm guessing that was the point. Made you want to get out of there and get home quicker if no-one was coming to see you.

I followed the signs to the psychiatric ward down a maze of grey painted corridors, through a barrage of double swing doors and wondered if I was just going round and round in one giant loop. I wasn't, it all just looked the same. I found Megan's ward and Megan, sitting on her bed, dressed, and clutching a Tesco carrier bag full of the dregs of whatever we'd brought in over the past few days. She was staring blankly at the wall.

"Hey," I said brightly. I hadn't got the right tone; it was way too chirpy; I was trying too hard, and it was more children's entertainer than sympathetic friend.

She glanced at me briefly then went back to staring at the wall. I looked round for someone to help and felt momentarily at a loss to know what to do.

"Megan, I'm here to take you home," I said, "You're coming to stay with us at Peace Summerton House, just for a bit. We're looking after the kids. I bet you're looking forward to seeing them all, aren't you? They can't wait to see you." My words sounded stilted, forced and I realised that I was completely out of my depth.

Megan said nothing, nor did she look up. I made my way back to the reception desk.

"Hi, erm I've come to collect Megan Roycroft. Is she ready to go?"

A nurse had just stepped behind the station and was reaching for a pen. My question registered, she glanced momentarily at me and then she carried on with what she was doing. "Just wating for meds to come back from the pharmacy. She'll be ready to go as soon as they're back." She stepped back round the other side of the station and was gone.

"Right, thanks..."

I went back into the ward and across to Megan's bay. I sat in the chair and smiled at her. She didn't meet my eye or smile back. I took out my phone and went to my pictures.

"I've got some pictures of the kids here Megan," I said. I got up and went to stand near her so that she could see my phone. I started with one of them lined up in their borrowed pyjamas on the first night they'd stayed. They all looked small and weary and uncertain. But as I scrolled right to show Megan the selfies we'd taken and all the pictures of landing acrobatics and milking cows, riding the trailer on the back of the Land Rover, baking with Eadie, dressing up with Cici, I realised that those same pinched white faces were relaxed and smiling and well, I hadn't even noticed the transition, but mostly they looked happy. I watched Megan's face for a few moments then she looked up at me.

"Thank you," she said, "for taking care of them."

I nodded. She held the bag and gave it a little shake. "The sweets were lovely," she said, glancing down at the carrier. "And the biscuits. I shared the sweets, but not the biscuits." She gave a little guffaw.

"I'm not surprised. I wouldn't share those biscuits. Willa makes them for us. I'm glad you liked them."

The nurse from the station arrived at the bed with a carrier bag.

"Meds," she said. She handed them to me. I glanced down; there was an awful lot in there.

"Three months' supply," the nurse said, seeing my face. "And Megan, you know what you have to take and when, don't you?"

Megan nodded.

"It's all on the boxes," the nurse said to me. "But I'd supervise it if I were you, just for the first week or so until she gets into a routine. She's staying with you, is that right? That's what we've got on the discharge form."

"Yes. The kids are staying with us already."

"Are you a relative?"

"No, just a friend."

The nurse looked at me then and her manner changed. Her face softened and she smiled. "That's nice. It's good to have friends you can rely on. You'd be surprised how many people in Megan's situation leave here on their own." She went to the bed and offered Megan her hand. Megan took it and stood. "Let me see you off the premises my lovely," she said, and she winked at me. The corners of Megan's mouth turned up and I think it was the first time I'd ever seen her smile.

EADIE AND CICI came out to the Land Rover to see Megan as I pulled up. I wasn't sure if it was a bit much, but Megan's face relaxed when she saw Eadie. They didn't know each other but Eadie had a look about her that comforted people. She was a good-looking woman in her early sixties, but naturally so, always in jeans and a jumper, and a pair of clogs inside the house, riding boots outside. She was tactile and warm, she smiled at everything, but she wasn't fluffy or flaky. Eadie was in charge. Simple as that. There was no mistaking the feeling that with Eadie you knew you had someone to rely on. Oh, and Eadie told it like it was. You always knew where you were with Eadie which could be hard, but which meant that if she loved you, you never, ever had to doubt that.

I pulled on the handbrake and looked at the both of them, standing in the cold, waiting with open hearts and open minds and even though the feeling of loss never went away, I knew I'd been lucky to have them both.

"Megan," Eadie said, opening the door. "Come on in love. You must be tired. That old thing rattles the bones something chronic."

Megan stepped down and Eadie put her hand gently under Megan's elbow. It wasn't touching, just gently guiding. "I've just put the kettle on," she went on. "I expect you're gasping for a cuppa. Hospital tea is always so stewed."

I stood and watched Eadie take Megan inside while Cici stood beside me.

"She's a wonder your mum."

"A miracle of modern science."

"Ha. Did Willa drop the biscuits up yet?"

"Funnily enough, she didn't." Cici put her finger on her chin mockingly pensive. "I wonder why they're late this morning. I don't suppose you might pop down and collect them, might you?" She was grinning.

"I think I might," I said. "I'll just check on Megan first and then I'll take a stroll over there."

"Not before you've changed your underwear!" Cici called as she made her way towards the shop.

I rolled the finger out at her and went inside to see if I was needed.

THIS WAS CRAZY. I didn't really know what I was doing. All I'd thought about for the past twelve hours was Willa. I had a farm shop to run, an estate, livestock, a family of five living with us and all I wanted to do was find Willa and bury myself deep inside her. I wanted her to move and roll her hips like she did last night, under me, on top of me... Fuck, there I go again. I needed to get a grip. I did not have time for this. I needed to collect the biscuits and get on with things. I picked up my pace and strode across the fields, glad of the effect the cold was having on my erection.

I arrived at the Lodge ten minutes or so later and knocked on the door. The smell from the house was warm and chocolatey; that fresh baking smell that sells properties. I peered through the glass. I could hear the radio and through the frosted pane I could just about see into the kitchen. It was blurry, but there was a figure that flitted past the door every few moments. Wait, was that Willa? Was she dancing? I grinned and knocked again. This woman never ceased to amaze me; her dancing, from what I could see of it, was wild, completely unselfconscious. The music stopped and after a short pause, Willa came to the door. She peered out through the glass as I peered in, then she yanked the door wide open.

"Were you dancing?" I asked.

She smiled. "Maybe."

Basil appeared by her side, and I bent to stroke his head. He wagged his tail, dribbled on my hand a little bit, and suitably acknowledged, lost interest in me, wandering back inside. I straightened.

"Do you often dance in the kitchen?"

"When I'm happy I do." She looked at me in the way she'd done last night. Her lids were lowered, and she stared up at me. It was so fricking hot.

"Willa..." She cut me off with her mouth and pulled me inside. I slammed the door shut with my foot and lifted her inside the hall, pressing her against the wall. She wrapped her legs round me and I held onto her thighs, moving my hands up to her... what, wait?

"Aren't you, I mean don't you have any...?"

"Nope. Completely naked under here."

"Wow..."

I held on to the smooth rounded flesh, finding that place... that naked place between her thighs. I stroked; she was already wet. I heard her moan, a small breathless sound that sent a shiver up my spine and a rush of blood to my cock. I bent and kissed her neck, her chest, my tongue darting over the skin. She moved her hands from my back and reached down, unbuckling my belt. She took me in her long cool fingers, wrapping them round the hot, hard flesh.

"I love the feel of you," she whispered, tightening her grip.

"I love that you love the feel of me..."

A small giggle escaped her. "I love that you love that I love the feel of you..."

I stopped as a snort of laughter rose in my throat. "Has no-one told you that sex is a serious business?" I was grinning and she shook her head, her giggles barely suppressed.

'Well, it is..."

"Completely serious," she said, smiling as she kissed me. I luxuriated in her warmth and laughter while my stomach somersaulted, and my cock ached with a pulsing hardness that threatened to blow us both away.

"Completely," I echoed, kissing her deeper.

My phone rang.

Correction. My phone rang with the ring tone I reserved for Eadie. That meant something serious. Eadie never rang me. It buzzed in my pocket.

"Oh shit, sorry... that's my..."

"Phone?"

Willa smiled and pulled back.

"It's Eadie," I said. "It must be important. Sorry..."

I released Willa's legs, and she stood while I dug in my pockets for my phone. I found it and answered. I zipped my jeans up with one hand as I talked.

"OK, how long? Really? No, she can't do that, yes, I'll come now. I'll be ten minutes."

I pressed end and looked at Willa. She had bed hair, and her mouth was pink, the edges blurred from kissing. I leant in and kissed her again.

"I have to go, I'm sorry. It's Megan. I just collected her from the hospital and things aren't right. Eadie's worried."

"Go." She stepped back and straightened her skirt and sweater. "Not a problem. Honestly, go." I looked at her face and knew she meant it. There was no pretence with Willa; I felt that I saw the whole of her, nothing secret, nothing hidden.

"Right, I'll..." I opened the door and turned back to her again. "See you later?"

She smiled. "I'll bring the biscuits up. Let me know if I can do anything."

I slammed the door shut behind me and headed for the copse. When I was out of sight of the house, I ran.

THIRTY-ONE

TYE

"She's called a taxi," Eadie said. "I tried talking to her, I just couldn't get through."

I added milk to the teas I'd made, chucked my coat over the back of a chair and headed towards the entrance hall of Peace Summerton House. As I went in, I stood for a moment, unsure of what to do. Megan sat on one of the gilt chairs under a painting of the Earl of Penchester - ugly bastard, scowling down at her - two large bin bags by her feet, the Tesco carrier bag on her lap. She sat rigid and looked straight ahead.

"Megan?"

She didn't turn.

"I've made some tea. You could do with a hot drink. It's bloody freezing in here."

She turned her head at the words "bloody freezing," and stared at me. That had made sense to her. She looked chilled to the core.

"Here. I've put a couple of sugars in." I handed one of the mugs across, and she took it. "Are you leaving?"

Megan held her mug in both hands, but she made no attempt to drink the tea. She didn't answer me, but glanced at the two bin bags to indicate that I was stating the obvious.

"Do you think that you could wait until the kids get back before you go? They're expecting Cici to pick them up from school."

She shrugged. A shrug was better than nothing. I pulled up a chair from the other side of the console table and sat down next to her. "I've been painting," I said. "Remember we chose some colours in the hospital? I've done downstairs and was going to start on upstairs tonight." I took a sip of my tea. "It looks good. The paint smells though." I didn't look at her. "I don't suppose you'd stay a couple more nights until I can get it finished, would you?"

I watched her out of the corner of my eye, and she took a sip of the tea. Was that a good sign? I hoped to God it was. "I get a bit OCD about these things," I went on. "I'd like to finish it. I mean if you didn't mind. I really hate leaving stuff half done." I had no experience of mental illness; I was working on gut instinct. I was hoping that if Megan felt she was helping me, and not the other way round, it might feel, well, less difficult, as if she was less of a problem. It was simplistic, and probably a stupid idea. I glanced at her. "You'd be doing me a favour if you stayed and then at least I could get it done. It'll annoy the hell out of me if I don't."

"I called a taxi," Megan said. "It'll be here in a minute."

"Right. Understood. Maybe Eadie can use it? She has to go into town for some shopping." Was that too quick? Was I too pushy? I didn't want Megan to leave; the kids would be upset, the house was in chaos, there was no one to monitor her medication ... I stopped and stood up. I couldn't force her to stay, and I didn't want to insist. She didn't need that. I tried one last time. "It'd be great if you stayed. Plus, we did tell the hospital that you were coming here, but..." I shrugged and let a silence hang for a few minutes. "Anyway, your choice. I'll give you a hand with the bags when the taxi arrives." We both looked at the bags. Had she just thrown everything the kids had into bin liners? I had no idea what was in them. I looked at her one last time and headed back to the kitchen.

"Any luck?

Eadie was standing by the sink, looking out for the taxi. It was usually Sam who drove, and he always parked round the back of the house to say hi to Eadie.

"I don't know." I crossed to the sink and poured my tea away. Eadie touched my arm.

"You've done the best you could Tye," she said.

I nodded, but she wasn't right. What I'd done wasn't good enough.

Eadie turned on the taps and began filling the sink. She always had a bowl of soapy water on the go. "You know, you can't save everyone," she said quietly, not looking at me. She focussed on washing up a few baking things. "You couldn't save your parents Tye, and you can't spend your life trying to make up for that."

"Don't Eadie," I warned. I moved away from her. Whenever anyone mentioned my parents a feeling of confused panic rose in my chest. I never spoke about them.

"Don't what? Tell you what you need to hear?" Eadie dried her hands on a tea towel and faced me. "When I arrived at the hospital that night Tye, you kept asking me what you could do, how you could save them, over and over you asked me. You might not remember but you really thought, at eight years old, that you could make it better. You couldn't, of course you couldn't. Your parents were so badly injured in the crash Tye that there was nothing anyone could do to save them." She came across to me, but I couldn't look at her. The memory of that night brought back an overwhelming sense of pain and failure.

"I think you've spent your life trying to make up for that, for not saving them. You avoid love, if anyone gets close you push them away - I'm assuming in case you can't save them from danger - and you've tried to do everything right. Everything. For me, for Cici, for the house, the estate, for people you employ, helping them with their problems and now the Roycroft kids, and Megan." Eadie placed her hands on my arms. I knew what she was doing. She was holding me in place because I always walked away when conversations got heavy. I hated anything like this.

"Tye? Do what you can, but this isn't your problem to solve. Sometimes you have to let people work it out on their own. Even if you know that they might mess it up."

I was itching to move away, to stride the room, anything to avoid Eadie's scrutiny. She held onto me.

"But what about the kids?" I asked. "And the house, the house is only half decorated..."

"You can pop round later and straighten the house and we'll find a way to help the kids if it comes to that."

She released me as we heard a car pull up outside.

"Right, that's Sam. Let's help Megan out with her bags. Lord only knows what she's got in there. Probably all our stuff." She smiled and shrugged. "Hey ho, it's only stuff!"

Eadie went to the back door to let Sam know we were coming and I headed to the entrance hall.

"Megan?" The bags were there but Megan had gone.

"Eadie?!" I shouted. "EADIE?!"

Eadie appeared in the doorway.

"Megan's gone. I'll check outside, can you check upstairs?"

She hurried towards the staircase as I flung open the doors and hurried down the steps towards the back of the house.

"The car is for Megan Roycroft," I said to Sam, "but she's disappeared. I'm just going to..."

"Tye?" Eadie appeared in the doorway. "She's in Libby's room. She's resting."

I stopped as relief flooded through me. "She's..."

"Staying," Eadie said. "For now, at least." I headed up the steps towards her and Eadie put her hand on my shoulder. "I'll take her up a hot water bottle and sit with her for a while. "Are you OK?"

I nodded.

"Good. Can you pay Sam for the wasted journey? My purse is on the dresser in the kitchen."

"It's fine, I've got it," I said. I headed back towards the car to pay Sam and on my way back to the house I saw her coming up the drive. Willa. My heart did a double back flip. Willa.

THIRTY-TWO

WILLA

He was standing in front of Peace Summerton House as I came up the drive. A taxi went past me, and the driver waved. I waved back even though I didn't know him because that's what everyone did in Peace Summerton; they acted kindly. But all my attention was on Tye. There was something so self-assured about him, as if he knew who he was and what his place was in the world. It was deeply sexy. And yet, when he kissed me, when he was close to me, he had a vulnerability that was almost palpable. That was even more sexy. Actually, it was more than sexy. If I was honest with myself, it was completely irresistible. This man was completely irresistible. I waved at him, and he smiled.

"Hey."

"I have biscuits." I handed the shopping bag with the boxes of biscuits in over to him. "And I've been thinking about something else."

He grinned. "So have I. All the time."

He had lowered his voice and even though it was cheesy, I loved it. It made my skin tingle. "No, not that, I said, "Although I have thought about that too. A LOT." We both smiled like goons. I took hold of myself. "I was wondering if I could make some meals for the farm shop?"

"Like ready meals?"

"Yes. Home cooked ready meals that you could either sell fresh or freeze. Really lovely things, like beef in red wine or something simpler but equally as good, like a luxury mac and cheese?"

He was staring at me.

"What? Have I got a bogey or something on my face?"

"No! No, it's just that, well, it's a really good idea!"

I smiled, mostly with relief. I'd been expecting him to say he'd think about it. Tye was a good businessman; the farm shop was a real success, and he knew how to sell the biscuits. They'd been an overnight sensation. His enthusiasm meant a lot.

"I think it sounds great and it's just what we need. We could trial it over a weekend and see what the demand was like. Also, we have a big mailing list, so we could do an email to promote it and..." His face broke into a wide grin. God, I loved that man's grin, even his eyes sparkled with amusement. "I think it's got legs Willa; I really do!"

"Me too and I wondered, I mean, if you have time, whether I could get started right away? I thought maybe I could look in the farm shop, see what you've got and make something today for you to try? What do you think?"

"I think..." He leant forward and brushed my lips with his own. It was chaste and sexy at the same time. Weird. "I think that's exactly what you should do. Why don't you cook it here? I can commis chef for you?"

"Would Eadie mind me taking over her kitchen?"

"I shouldn't think so. She loves to see other people working!"

We both laughed.

"And you're not too busy?" I guessed that he probably had heaps of stuff to do, but he shrugged.

"OK, let's do it."

"Good. You go to the farm shop and see what's there and I'll pop in and just check that Eadie isn't planning a great feast or anything today."

"Right."

"Right."

We both stood where we were, smiling at each other.

"We should..."

"Yes."

We didn't move. I just didn't want to. I mean, I knew I *had* to move - this was getting a tad awkward - but my legs were keeping me glued to the spot.

"I'll..." Tye pointed in the direction of the house.

"And I'll..." I pointed to the shop.

"Right."

We stood for a few moments longer, staring and smiling and finally, we both moved off. It was like we had to tear ourselves apart.

"See you in five," he called.

"Yup. Can't wait." I headed to the shop, not daring to glance over my shoulder. Can't wait? What the hell was that? I cringed. What are you, Willa, five years old? I opened the door of the farm shop and stepped inside.

"Can't wait, eh?" Cici said and she burst out laughing.

THIRTY-THREE

TYE

Well, I wasn't expecting that. Willa cooked in a precise and neat way, everything ordered and efficient. Hell, she was like a professional chef. Wild hair pulled back into a ponytail and a napkin wrapped over it, clean apron, which she'd brought with her. Hands washed between each prep, ingredients weighed in advance, chopped, lined up. Used bowls, utensils, pots all put straight into soak or stacked neatly away from the food prep area. Knives sharpened. And she moved around the kitchen with balletic ease, speedily, effortlessly, tossing sautéed vegetables for the sauce, throwing them up into the air and catching them back in the pan like a juggler on coke. I was mesmerised by her.

I'd done my bit, chopped all the veg and then Willa had finely diced it, without a word, just discreetly making it look uniform in size and shape. She had three frying pans on the go at once and swiftly moved from one to the other without pause. It was like watching MasterChef, but with a contestant you just knew was going to win because they were so fucking brilliant. And the smells! Seared beef, bacon, onions and garlic, wine. If I hadn't been so rapt, watching her gorgeous, rounded bum encased in leggings I'd have been salivating. As it was, I was trying to keep a raging erection at bay so that if Eadie walked into the kitchen I could at least stand up without my crotch greeting her first. There was something so fucking hot about watching the person you really liked doing something they were really good at. It was like seeing that person for the first time all over again. Wait. I stopped myself. The person I really liked. Fuck, I'd known Willa all of five minutes flat and already I was describing her as the person I really liked. Even if it was just to myself. The thought made me suddenly uncomfortable, and I felt like I needed some air. I stood. Well, at least that had got rid of the boner.

"I'm going to pop out for some air," I said. "It's hot in here."

"Sure." Willa was bent over, checking the temperature on the Aga. The sight of her beautiful ass gave me another immediate hard-on and I made a quick exit. Outside in the cold air I felt instantly better. I took a few deep breaths.

Yeah, I did like Willa. Man-up Tye. I liked her a lot. She was full of surprises: kind, strong but soft. Fuck. I made her sound like an ad for toilet roll. She was, if I was honest with myself, completely irresistible and watching her move around the kitchen in those tight leggings with style and efficiency was driving me crazy. It was at times like this that I wished I smoked. I could do with an excuse to stay out here in the cold.

"Tye?" Cici came round the back of the farm shop and caught me loitering.

"Hey."

"What are you up to?"

"Not much." At least that much was true.

"I was on my way in to ask for the Land Rover keys. I'm going to pick up the kids."

"God, is it that late?"

I opened the back door to the house for Cici and she went into the boot room. She stopped at the door to the kitchen. Willa was holding a spoon out for Megan to taste the stew.

"It's not cooked yet," she offered, "the flavours will all blend in the oven, but you can taste the wine and the redcurrant jelly with the meat juices, can't you?"

Megan tasted and handed the spoon back.

"It's nice," she said to Willa.

"Thanks. It's not so hard to make. When you get home would you like me to make you some? I can drop it round."

Megan nodded and I saw Willa gently touch her arm and smile. "You can try it tonight and then put your order in. You're staying until the weekend though, aren't you?"

Megan shrugged.

"Good," Willa said. "I can make you more biscuits." And suddenly, just for a nano second, I thought I was going to burst with love. Love? Whoa, fuck. Slow down. Love? What the fuck was I thinking?

"Hi," Cici said, moving into the kitchen. "That smells lovely."

They both turned. I saw Willa catch sight of me and her face softened. She smiled. God, she was beautiful.

"I'm going to collect the kids from school." Cici said. She took the keys for the Land Rover off the dresser. "Megan, would you like to come?"

Megan looked away and I saw Cici exchange glances with Willa.

"I hate standing at the school gates," Willa said, "especially on a day like today. It's so cold. Best to stay in the warm I'd say." She spoke softly, with kindness. There was that feeling again; it washed over me. Shit, this was freaking me out.

Willa lifted the casserole and took it over to the Aga. "I'll get this in the oven, and I'll head off to school too," she said. "I'll be two ticks."

The door opened and Eadie came in with a basket of washing. "Haven't you left yet?" She placed the basket on the table and began untangling a bundle of wet clothes. Cici rolled her eyes at me; Eadie was always at least twenty minutes early for everything.

"I'm gone." Cici said. "Willa, shall I drop you at the Lodge?"

"Yup, coming now," she called out.

I grabbed Willa's coat off the back of the chair and held it for her. She took it, shrugged it on and I walked out to the Land Rover with her. Just walking alongside her made me want to reach for her hand. I brushed her thigh with my fingers, and she glanced sidelong at me and smiled. Outside, Cici was waiting by the jeep.

"What was that all about?" she said in a hushed voice. "Why won't she come with me?"

"She's nervous," Willa said. "She doesn't know how they'll react, the kids. They might be angry with her, distant. And she doesn't want to face the other mums. They can be... well, you know, a bit..."

"Shitty?" Cici always told it like it was, she was her mother's daughter. "Yeah, I get it."

She climbed into the Land Rover and started the engine. Willa looked at me and I turned the collar of her coat up, pulling it in close around her. I wanted any excuse to touch her. She glanced at my fingers, and I felt her desire to kiss them. She didn't.

"But they're staying until the weekend," I said. "I don't know how you managed that. But at least it gives me a few nights to finish painting the house. There's a huge amount to do, but I might just manage it."

"We." Willa said. "*We* might manage it. I'll help." She raised an eyebrow at me and smiled.

"Help what?" Cici called through the open car door window.

"Paint Megan's house."

"If you help then I'll babysit," Cici said.

Willa caught my eye and winked. "You're on Cici," she announced. Then she climbed into the jeep, waved and they drove off. I went back to the house to get on with something constructive as I'd practically wasted a whole day watching Willa cook. It was good to get back to work, but I couldn't help feeling disappointed that she'd gone.

THIRTY-FOUR

WILLA

It's funny how sometimes you see people who are the same age, or around about the same age, and they seem either older or a whole lot younger. I reckoned that Cici was a year or so younger than me, but she had all the enthusiasm and verve of a teenager. She made me feel a hundred, like an old mother hen. When we arrived at school, Cici threw the Land Rover recklessly up on the curb outside the main entrance, jumped down and skipped into the playground, waving at the other mums, her face wreathed in smiles. I parked in the designated car park by the Green, and hurried to the school gates, late and anxious, arriving just in time to see the kids streaming out after the home-time bell.

School pick-up was a novelty for Cici, and a temporary one at that. I'd been doing this since I was twenty and Esme started in reception class. It had all been a bit of a shock to be honest. I'd arrive exhausted after the café closed, Teddy on my hip, or - a few months later - Teddy running round with me trying to catch him and stop him from running out of the school gates. I'd seriously wondered if putting him on a lead would look bad. I'd tried to look enthusiastic, to join in, but mostly I was about fifteen years younger than any of the other mums, and, well, I'd just lost the only person I'd ever loved, and I didn't have the brain space to make friends.

Here, at Peace Summerton, it was my second week and I had zero expectations. A school gate was a school gate, wherever you were in the country, and I guessed that all of them had the same level of infighting and gossip. I took my place just inside the gate and waited for the kids. I pulled my woolly hat on and clapped my hands against the cold.

"Here."

I turned. A young woman in a green parker with the hood up, jeans and workman's boots held out a small tin. "Try this. It's a hand warmer and it's brilliant."

I took it and looked at it.

"Pop it in your pocket. It'll stop you freezing your tits off."

I smiled. "Thanks." The tin was warm, I slipped it into my pocket and put my hand in after it.

"See? Nice, eh?"

"Lovely." I looked at her and smiled. She grinned back.

"I'm Amy," she said, "Love a glass of wine, preferably more than one, and hate people who have that sign 'Live, laugh, love' in their house. Who the fuck needs reminding to do those things?"

"True. I'm Willa. My sister had a sign that said, 'don't be a turd today' I liked that one."

Amy smiled. "Yeah, cute. Could do with that in my house, only I'd add Joe on the end. You're new, aren't you?"

"Yes."

"Living up at Maud's Lodge?"

"Yup." Here we go, small village, big gossip.

Amy smiled again. "Don't worry, you're not the hot topic. I know Cici, we went to school together."

"Ah, right."

"Settling in?"

"Yeah, I think so."

"Met the gorgeous and unattainable Tyler Malloy yet?"

"Hmmm, not sure I know who you mean."

Amy laughed. "Yeah, right." She looked across the playground. "Ah there's my lumps." She waved her arms. "MOLLY? PETE?" She hollered.

Twins with shining red hair raced towards us, grinning, holding paintings aloft. Amy scooped them both into a hug, mindful of paintings and produced large apples from each of her pockets.

"You should join the mum's WhatsApp group," she said. "It's more review the latest love egg than recipe swapping. It's a laugh."

"Thanks." I saw Cici chatting with Miss Kindness as Esme made her way across to me. 'Where's Teddy?" As if I didn't know.

"Ah, the 'Incredible Ted'," Amy said. "Pete told me he's got at least ten words for poo."

Oh God, I could feel my stomach lurch. How many words for poo, excluding the swear words, were there? Amy touched my arm and winked.

"Pete is extremely impressed. He must come for tea."

"Really?" Ted had never been home with a friend for tea. Well, not for a full tea anyway. He'd made it back to a friend's house at the beginning of the term in his old new school, but they'd been playing hairdressers and he'd cut his little friend Lucy's plaits off. I was called to collect him. Lucy was hysterical. He'd cut them off above her ears.

"Of course," Amy said. "I think bum-dump is genius by

the way." She snorted with laughter. "Come on you two. Ted's going to come for tea Pete. How about that?" She headed off and waved as she went. "Keep the hand warmer, it'll give us an excuse to meet up!"

I waved back. Esme looked up at me and rolled her eyes.

"Bum-dump," she said. "Honestly."

WITH TEDDY securely in the van after staying behind to help clear up the classroom – he volunteered (miracles do happen) - we made our way up to Peace Summerton House for a cup of tea and a play. Cici had insisted, she wanted to divert attention away from Megan, make it all a bit more natural. Besides, Teddy and Esme loved it up there and with Libby, Carlton and Tommo, they had the run of the place, hiding in linen cupboards and attic rooms, hunting down ghosts and generally using the huge old house as an historical playground.

We parked round the back and went in via the boot room. They took their shoes off and pulled on a pair of the slipper socks that Eadie kept in a basket there. Rarely did they ever find two that matched, but they didn't care. Coats hung on pegs, shoes lined up, slipper socks on and they were off.

"See ya" I said to the empty space.

In the kitchen Eadie was ironing. Alfie sat with Megan at the table. He was doing his homework, Megan sat silently beside him.

"Hello love," Eadie nodded towards the Aga. "There's tea in the pot. Help yourself."

I took a mug off the side and poured myself a cup.

"That beef smells delicious. Megan and I were just saying, weren't we love?"

Megan didn't answer and I saw Alfie glance at his mum.

"Alfie love, will you take these upstairs for me? The linen cupboard is the fourth door on the landing."

I could see Eadie's diversion tactics. She was one smart lady.

Alfie stood and took up a bundle of sheets and pillowcases that Eadie had ironed. Eadie was old school - who on earth ironed their bed linen nowadays? As he passed through, the smell of freshly washed linen, freshly ironed, almost convinced me to go home and get the iron out. Almost.

"Mind a small child doesn't jump out at you when you open the cupboard," Eadie said as Alfie made his way to the door. "Lord only knows what they get up to."

"Who and gets up to what?" Tye asked, coming in and bringing a gust of cold air with him. Eadie looked across the kitchen at him and I saw something in her face change. Love, pride, joy, all rolled into one. It was a look she had only for Tye and Cici. She smiled and I felt myself smiling with her. I think I must have had a daft look on my face because I just caught Eadie throw a quizzical glance first in my direction, then in Tye's before I got it under control and looked away.

"Never you mind," she said to him. "We'll need potatoes for the beef. Can you get peeling love? Willa, are you staying."

"No, thank you though Eadie. I'll get my two home and settled. It's a school night." There it was again, I sounded ancient. "And I said I'd help Tye this evening, so Cici is going to babysit."

"Ah." One word, one syllable. She nodded to herself. I blushed, actually blushed and Tye grinned. I could have thrown something at him. Why was he grinning like that?

"In fact, I should probably get going," I said quickly. I stood. "I'll call the kids. Goodness knows where they are."

"Here," Alfie said, pushing open the door of the kitchen with Tommo on his hip and Teddy gripped by the wrist at his side. "They were looking for something to sit on so they could ride the stairs. I caught them just in time."

"Oh." I crossed to Teddy and took his hands. A catastrophic image flashed into my head. The stairs were long and steep, and God only knows how that would have ended. I knelt to his level.

"That sounds like fun," I said, "But maybe not a very good idea? I should think the bumps on the stairs would hurt your bum and..." I knew from bitter experience that telling Teddy not to do something, and he'd do it right away. Danger was not a word he recognised.

"And how about we actually build you a proper slide?" Tye finished for me. "Outside, in the woods? We could do that at the weekend. What do you think?"

I turned and looked at him. The gorgeous and unattainable Tyler Malloy had just become a super-hero.

"Can we do that Willa?" Teddy asked. His face was a mix of amazement and sheer longing. "I think so, I..." I had no idea.

"Yes, we can," Tye said. "We'll all help. Alfie, how are you with a hammer and saw?"

Alfie shrugged. "Don't know."

"Then we need to find out. You're gonna love bashing up pieces of wood and nailing them together." He grinned.

This slide was beginning to sound more dangerous than a tray down the stairs, but Teddy's face had lit up.

"Thanks Tye," I said. "The kids will love that."

"He'll love it more," Eadie piped up. "Tye will be out on

that slide when you're all at school. There's motive in his kindness."

Everyone laughed and I had a warm feeling that started in my toes and spread right up into my heart. For the first time in years, I felt that this is where I belonged.

THIRTY-FIVE

WILLA

When I arrived at Megan's house, Tye was in the middle of setting things up. He'd left the door on the latch for me and was on all fours, laying the dust sheets in the hall as I walked in. He stopped what he was doing and looked up at me and for one small moment the world tilted on its axis. I caught my breath and then I thought, oh shit, this isn't happening, it can't be. But it was, I was powerless to control it and actually, I didn't want to.

"Hey,"

"Hey."

Tye stood and came across to me. He kissed me and the scent of his skin and hair made my head swim.

"I've wanted to do that all day," he said. "And more." He pulled back. "But there's a fuck of a lot to do. I'm not sure how I'm going to manage it to be honest."

We both looked at the hallway with its peeling wall-paper and dirty scuffed paintwork. I followed Tye's gaze up the stairs.

"The rooms upstairs all need clearing and that's before

we even start painting." He shrugged. "Still, it's not going to get done with me moaning, is it?"

I smiled as I took my coat off and threw it over a chair in the front room. "Have you always been like this?" I asked, coming back, and rolling my sleeves up.

"Like what?"

"Oh, I don't know, positive, active. There's nothing passive about you Tye."

"I watched this interview once, with Michael Caine, you know, the actor?"

I grinned. "I'm young Tye, not living in a bubble. Yes, I've heard of him."

"Ha. Anyway, he said, *'Use the difficulty.'* I was watching it with Eadie and Cici, God it was years ago, and he said that whenever you have a difficulty, use it, make it work for you, and if you manage it, even in a tiny way, then you've won. I never forgot it."

"That's cool," I said.

"Yeah, it is, isn't it?"

"So how are we going to use this difficulty?" I asked, nudging him gently and moving a bit closer.

"To hone our painting skills," he said, kissing me again. "What else?" He went to kiss me one more time but pulled back as we heard a banging on the front door and bit of a rumpus outside.

"What the fuck? Who's that?"

We both looked towards the door, and I popped my head into the front room to look through the bay window. There was a small crowd gathered outside the house and I spotted Angelica in... wait, was that a boiler suit? She was holding a paintbrush.

"The whole of the village by the looks of it," I said. "You

are never going to believe this, but..." He opened the door, and I didn't finish.

"SURPRISE!!" Angelica cried as she led a band of people into the hall.

Tye looked bewildered. It really *was* a surprise. Following Angelica, I saw Ellen and Mr Renton from the village shop, Ellie Blackmore, aka Miss Kindness, the man who drove the taxi, Sam, who introduced himself on the way in and Amy who I'd just met at school, still in her green parker but wearing an old paint splattered tracksuit underneath. At the back of the crowd, closing the door behind them all, was Percy. Yay for the village and oh dear for Percy. Percy and Tye in the same house didn't seem like a very good idea at all.

I moved into the front room.

"Bloody hell, this is amazing!" Tye called over the din.

"It's Peace Summerton," Ellie Blackmore said, "it's what we do. We help each other out."

"And it looks like you need help." Percy said. I saw Tye's jaw twitch very slightly and I reckoned he was gritting his teeth. Uh oh.

"We do need help," he said. "There is tons to do. Thank you all for turning up, it's incredible, it really is. Now, let's get going."

There was quiet as Tye began organising the troupe. He sent Mr Renton and Sam the taxi driver upstairs to start on clearing and lifting furniture into the centre of each bedroom, set Ellie, Ellen and Amy on peeling wallpaper. I was on sanding the woodwork with Angelica, and Percy was painting with Tye. Not sure how that was going to work, but I got the feeling that Tye wanted Percy where he could see him.

Within minutes we'd all started on our jobs and half an

hour later the house was a hive of worker bees. The radio was blaring, there was chat and laughter and I was part of something; something good.

"How did you make this all happen?" I asked Angelica.

"Cici and Eadie," she answered, her head bent over her sanding. "Cici told Ellie Blackmore at school and well, Peace Summerton is a small place. Besides, everyone loves Tye." She raised an eyebrow. "Well, almost everyone." She sat straight and stretched the curve in her back from bending over. "There are people organised to help every night this week. Cici set up a WhatsApp group." She smirked. "So, you're off duty, which I'm sure you're relieved about. Can't think how you'd have got through all those boring hours here on your own with Tye."

I elbowed her.

"Ouch!" she laughed. "You have to give the other single ladies in Peace Summerton a bit of alone time with Tyler Malloy, you know. They are literally queuing up to get a paintbrush in their hands."

I laughed and Tye glanced over at me. He smiled, but stared a bit too long and lost his balance. He wobbled dangerously for a few moments at the top of the step ladder.

"Concentrate Tye," Percy called out. There was a silence and I saw that twitch in his jaw again. He went back to painting the ceiling, but his face was set in a grim frown of concentration.

"Percy and Tye," Angelica said quietly under her breath. "They're always at it. They fell out years ago and there's no amount of magic that will help. I should know, I've tried."

"Why did they fall out?" I whispered.

She shrugged. "I have no idea," she said. 'But Cici sides with Tye, she's always edgy when Percy's around."

"Oh."

"Honestly, I think Tye's a bit jealous. Percy went travelling round the world, plays in a band, has no responsibilities, whereas Tye has been stuck here with the house and the farm shop and everything..." Her voice trailed off.

I glanced at Percy, singing to the radio as he worked, wondering if maybe Angelica had a point. Percy *was* carefree and looked like a man back from travelling the world; tanned, confident, exciting. He caught my eye and winked. I blushed and looked away. Oh hell, that was awkward. When I looked up again, Tye was scowling as he climbed down from the ladder.

"Break everyone," he shouted. "I'll put the kettle on."

Tye disappeared into the kitchen and Percy put his roller down and came across to Angelica and me. "Willa, is there anything that you're not good at? Look at that handy work?! You're smart, funny, gorgeous and you even sand woodwork to a silky-smooth finish."

I laughed and Angelica groaned.

"Is complementing your decorating skills Percy's way of flirting?" Tye said. He was standing in the doorway scowling. "Or is it just more of his bullshit?"

Whoa, that was unnecessary! I felt the sharp edge of unease cut through the atmosphere. Percy turned.

"I'm sorry, did I miss something? Did you say something of value?" He paused for a moment and then smiled. "Oh, no, my mistake, it was just the usual Tyler Malloy self-important drivel. Ignore him Willa, he's full of it."

The punch was quick and hard. Percy was thrown against the wall with the force of it.

"You fucker!" He yelled.

He came back and landed a right hook just under Tye's jaw. Tye reeled, staggered a few paces and grabbed Percy by the neck. I leapt out of the way, pulling Angelica to the safety of the front room while Sam the taxi driver took the stairs two at a time and dodged past them to open the front door. They fell out of it, and he followed them. He ducked as Tye threw another punch at Percy which Percy took on the chin, coming back even harder to grab Tye's shoulders and wrestle him down. There was a smash as the two of them crashed through the small wooden fence in the front garden onto the pavement.

"Enough!" I suddenly shouted, darting out of the front door. "Stop it! That's enough!" I grabbed Tye and yanked him round to face me. Percy stumbled backwards and Angelica joined me in the front garden, her arms around Percy to restrain him.

"What the hell are you doing?" I shouted at them. "You're worse than kids!" I rarely shouted, hated it, but now I'd started I couldn't stop.

"Go home both of you! Go home and cool off! Go on! Get out of here!" I was spitting in my fury and making shooing motions with my arms. I'm sure I looked ridiculous, but I was so angry I didn't care.

"Go on! Both of you! Get lost! NOW!"

Tye hung his head while Percy wiped his face. His nose was dripping large blobs of red blood onto the ground.

I turned and faced the small crowd in the hall.

"Let's get on," I said. "Mr Renton and Sam, can you take over in the hall, painting the ceiling and walls?"

"Will do," Sam said. "As long as these two bozos can be trusted to bugger off."

Tye nodded. "I'll get my things," he said.

But Amy had his jacket and keys already. She handed them over at the front door and without another word, Tye walked away. Percy attempted to play the crowd for a couple of moments, shrugging innocently, as if it was all nothing to do with him, but Sam said,

"You too Percy. Bugger off mate."

Amy had Percy's jacket in her other hand. She gave it to him, and he too walked away, in the opposite direction to Tye. There was a tense, collective silence for a minute or so and then Amy said in a New York accent, "Show's over folks, back to work." And everyone laughed.

THIRTY-SIX

TYE

The words total and dick spring to mind. What the fuck was I thinking? I had just made a monumental arsehole of myself, which to be honest I couldn't give a monkey about, except that it was in front of Willa. Fuck. It should never have happened. Never. It's just that Percy is so fucking smug and annoying. If it was my story to tell then I'd plaster his weaselly, nasty behaviour all over the village on giant posters, with his smirking surfer-dude mug on them. But it wasn't. So, I kept quiet, and it bugged the crap out of me. HE bugged the crap out of me. I know he did it just to wind me up but the worse he behaved, the more I reacted and the worse *I* looked. Fuck.

I parked the Land Rover in front of the house and sat for a while, not wanting to go inside and tell Eadie why I was back so early. Not that she would need much of an explanation. I glanced at my face in the rear-view mirror and realised that the bruises and my swollen eye would tell the story for me.

Of course, I'm sure there were lots of psychoanalytical

reasons for doing what I just did and I'm sure that if I paid someone enough money, they'd be able to work them all out for me. Maybe that's what I needed, a good therapy session. It certainly felt like that now, especially when I thought about Willa. I felt the overwhelming compulsion to be with her and then a desire to run as far away as fast as I could. She made me laugh, impressed me, excited me and could be so damn annoying and not necessarily in that order. I wanted to spend all my time with her and that scared the hell out of me. And for some bizarre reason – and this I couldn't fathom because I genuinely didn't rate him - I wanted to knock Percy right out of the picture. Literally.

I took my phone out and did what I usually do when I'm unsure of myself. I rang Cici.

"I'm an arse," I said, when she answered. "Yes, I know you know that already, but I thought I'd confirm it for you. Cici, I got into a fight with Percy tonight. Yes! Yes he did deserve it – he always deserves it - but well, it was pretty fucking embarrassing. No, he didn't get the better of me, but it was in front of all the people who came to help decorate and in front of Willa." I waited for Cici to vent. "Yeah, I know. I did say I was an arse."

But after she told me what I already knew, she told me that I should apologise to Willa and do it quickly. Willa, she said, and I also knew this already, was not the sort of woman who was impressed by a fist fight.

"Should I say why Percy fucks me off?" I was testing the water, but I pretty much knew what her answer would be. "No, of course not and you know I understand. Look Ci, you never have to say anything, to anyone, never, not as far as I'm concerned. OK?" I could hear the distress in her voice, and I wished I hadn't asked. "Look, text me when Willa gets back will you?" I could hear Basil barking in the background. "Everything OK there?" I asked. Then I laughed. Basil was apparently singing. I pressed end, and still smiling, I went inside to face Eadie.

ON A NORMAL NIGHT I'd have fallen asleep waiting for Cici to call me. If I had the Land Rover and she couldn't drive herself, I usually picked her up from wherever she was, and I'd doze until I got the call. Not tonight. Tonight I was wired. When Eadie went to bed, after telling me off and ordering me to put something on my bruises and the cut over my eye, I paced the kitchen in my socks wondering how Willa would react when I saw her.

When I got Cici's message to say that Willa was home, I left immediately, knowing that this would be better out of the way, for better or for worse. I drove straight to the lodge, parked, and knocked on the door.

"Hey," I said when Willa opened it. Basil pushed past her and gave me his habitually enthusiastic welcome. At least he was pleased to see me.

"I've come for Cici," I said.

Willa looked at me for a few moments, then Cici appeared in the hallway behind her.

"I'm sorry about the fight," I said. "Can I explain?"

Cici stared at me, but she knew I'd only tell the story we'd agreed on.

Willa glanced over her shoulder at Cici.

"I can drive myself home," she said. "You can stay Tyc."

I looked at Willa. "Please?"

She nodded and opened the door to let me in. Cici and I passed each other, and I handed her the keys to the Land Rover. She hugged Willa briefly; they exchanged words that

I couldn't hear and Cici left. I stood lamely in the hall, feeling like the dick that I was.

"Percy and I have history," I said. "It goes back a long way and we've never really got over it."

"So, you punch him whenever he gets on your nerves."

"No. No, I've never punched him before. I don't hit people. I've never hit anyone before."

"So why tonight?"

Fuck, that was a hard one. Well, not hard to work out, but impossible to say out loud. I ran my hands through my hair. Why tonight? Because I knew that Percy had a thing for Willa, and I felt threatened because I like her so fucking much. And I'm not sure how she feels about me, if she likes me in the same way, so when he took the piss out of me, it really got my goat. He humiliated me and I saw red. I took a breath.

"I was jealous," I said. "Because I... I really like you and I thought he was making me look small to impress you..." I stared at the ground. There. Fuck. It was out. I'd said it.

There was a long pause, and I didn't dare look up. Then I felt Willa's touch. She put her index finger up to my face and said, "Ouch," in her best ET voice.

I nodded. "Yeah, ouch."

She stepped aside. "Come into the kitchen. Have you put anything on those shiners?"

"No."

"I've got some arnica and I'll disinfect that cut. You've no idea where Percy's been."

Suddenly I smiled, and relief washed over me as I followed her into the warmth of the kitchen.

Willa pulled out a chair for me.

"Sit. Cici said you've got beef with Percy. It doesn't excuse you though."

"I know. I'm sorry. Fighting is never the right way to deal with things. Is that all she said?"

"Yes. Oh, and that you haven't been in a fight, ever, so she thought it was probably quite funny to watch. She asked me if you'd resorted to slapping and pulling his hair?"

"I was tempted."

Willa came over to the table with a bowl of salted water and some cotton wool. "Right, this might hurt." She dipped the cotton wool and gently bathed the cut. It did hurt and I was trying hard not to wince. Suddenly she smiled.

"You can say ouch, you know. I know how manly you are already."

"Fucking ouch!" I said loudly. "That really stings!"

She continued to bathe my eye, then she pressed a warm flannel on my bruises and dried my face gently with a towel. She stood over me, while I breathed in the warm scent of her skin and her hair brushed the side of my neck. It was the most erotic thing I had ever experienced. No wonder people fell in love with their nurses.

"Do you think we could do the arnica later?"

She glanced down at me. "Sure. Why?"

I reached up and pulled her face down to mine. "Because I really want to fuck you now."

I put my mouth over hers and I could feel instant desire spark in her, like lighting a match. I ran my hands over her thighs, her bum and reached down to unfasten her jeans. She slipped them down and took her knickers with them. Her mouth locked on mine, she unzipped me, and I shrugged my jeans down to my knees. She straddled me, then suddenly pulled away. As she lifted her tee-shirt up over her head and threw it down on the floor, I fumbled in my pocket and found the packet I'd put there a few days ago. I unclipped her bra and freed her breasts, taking her rosy, pink nipple in my mouth. She moaned and took the packet out of my hand, ripping the top off it with her teeth. She handed it back to me and moments later I slipped inside her, hot and tight and wet. She cried out.

"Tye, that is sooo...good..." I began to move her hips, kissing her more deeply, feeling her slide up and down my cock, putting myself inside her as deep as I could go, lifting her the length of me. We found a rhythm, I licked and sucked her nipples as she rode me, her head tilted back, the moans mounting and lengthening as she got nearer to coming.

"God, Tye, don't stop, I'm..."

I wanted her to come, I wanted to feel her shudder and spasm around my dick and so I pushed her harder and faster until she was breathless with endless heat and desire. I felt her body tense, I felt the waves wash over her and I felt her muscles contract and release in glorious pulsing tremors as she climaxed. Moments later I let go. She dug her fingers into my shoulders and hung on as I came. I closed my eyes and the world disappeared and finally, her body went limp as she released me.

"Bingo," she whispered.

"Full house," I said. And we both started laughing.

BACK IN HER jeans and tee shirt, Willa crept up to check on the kids. We'd been pretty noisy, but the kitchen door had been shut to Basil and I didn't reckon Teddy or Esme had heard anything. When she came back down, she gave me the thumbs up.

"Fast asleep. Sofa?" she asked.

"With Basil?"

We both looked at Basil who had been banished for the

last half an hour or so and who looked decidedly put out. I'm sure he was pulling a sad face.

"Yes, with Basil. We can just snuggle?"

I smiled. "Snuggle?" It was so gloriously cute and a million miles away from the Willa astride me, moaning and riding my cock. "Snuggle it is," I said. I followed her into Maud's scruffy, comfy sitting room and put another log on the fire. Not that it needed it, this was a well-made fire by someone who knew what they were doing. I sat down and Willa came in with a couple of glasses of wine.

"Here," she said, handing me one. She put hers on the floor and I made room for her so that she could sit in the crook of my arm, with her legs tucked up under her. Basil climbed up after her. He had lap-dog delusions, but I guess it was too late to correct him.

Willa leant against me and sighed.

"You're amazing, you know that don't you?" I said.

"Yes," she replied. "Of course."

I could hear the smile in her voice. "No, I mean it Willa." I stroked her hair. "I know that things have been hard for you. I don't know the circumstances, but I'm guessing there was a very good reason for you to come here because you're a good mum and you put the kids first." I ran a long strand of her kinked hair through my fingers. "And you tell it like it is. You're strong and honest and I love that about you. You are who you are." I kissed the back of her head. I was usually a man of few words, and I don't think I'd said as much to a woman for a long time. If ever. Probably helped that I was talking to the back of her head.

"There's so much I love about you," I went on softly, "your tits, your hair, your bum... no, seriously. I love that you can paint a room and build a fire and I love that you're smart and funny. I love..." I paused to phrase my next sentence and heard the faintest of snores. I looked over at Basil. He was wide away and stared right back at me.

"Most I love the fact that you didn't hear any of that," I said. Willa had fallen fast asleep.

"I want to tell you everything, about my parents and Eadie and how much she gave up coming to look after me. She was my Mum's best friend, she owed us nothing; it was sheer kindness. And I want so much to explain about Cici and Percy and how he treated her, and what a complete and utter dick he is, but I can't. I promised Cici I wouldn't say anything until she was ready..." I sighed, already feeling better that some of the unspoken things between us had been said. Albeit to a sleeping Willa.

Gently and slowly, I manoeuvred myself off the sofa, placing a cushion under Willa's head and a blanket over her legs. I patted Basil, called him to the kitchen let him out of the back door for a pee, waited for him to come in, then I locked up, turned the kitchen lights out and went back to stack the fire with more logs in case Willa got cold. I bent, planted a small kiss on Willa's cheek, then I left.

I let myself out of the Lodge, closing the door firmly behind me and checking that it was locked. I made my way back to Peace Summerton House, missing her the moment I'd left her.

THIRTY-SEVEN

WILLA

I woke with a pain and numbness in my legs and for a moment I didn't know where I was. I was toasty warm, I knew that much, and my body felt luxuriously relaxed, and content. There was a heaviness in the lower part of me though. I opened my eyes. Basil. I was on the sofa with a blanket over me and Basil lying on my shins, under the blanket. How did that happen? There was a roaring fire in the grate and the house was dark and silent. It was two a.m.. No Tye.

I eased myself up and wondered if I should make it upstairs to bed, but there was only three hours until I was due to get up to make my biscuit batch, so I decided against it and shuffled down the sofa again, closing my eyes. I thought of Tye. I thought of the camaraderie at Megan's house and the laughter and painting. I thought about Teddy's invitation to tea, and I thought about Cici's kindness and how much Esme loved colouring with her. And then I thought about Tye again and I realised that for the first time since Lexi had died, I was happy. I sighed and felt myself drift off to sleep again and I'm sure that I dreamed all night with a smile on my face.

THIRTY-EIGHT

WILLA

"Hey opp. Mind yaself lass."

Amy squeezed past me with a huge pan of cheese sauce. She plonked it on the trestle table that Tye had set up along the back wall of Maud's kitchen and went back for the second pot.

"I know I'm from the North Aims" I said, smiling, "But that doesn't mean I've got a flat cap and a ferret down my trousers."

"Ha!" Amy brought the second pot over to the table. "Ready to mix?"

"Yup." I stirred the tray of macaroni with pancetta as Amy lifted the pot and poured the cheese sauce over it. Once it was covered and glossy, we moved on to the next tray. There were five in total, and we were up to a hundred portions in one session.

"Right." Amy scraped the last of the sauce out of both pots and took them over to the sink. "Let's wash while they cool."

"Are we OK for labels?"

"Yup, Cici printed a hundred and fifty this morning. I picked them up from the farm shop on my way here." Amy began running hot water into the sink. Her face was pink, and her long red hair tucked up into a white hairnet. I was constantly amazed by her efficiency. For someone who'd never worked in a professional kitchen before, she was a marvel. She turned and looked at me.

"Yes, I know, this is most flattering. Joe is always begging me to put it on when I come to bed. He says the dinner lady look is very sexy."

"You can pull anything off Amy," I said.

"That's what the boys at school used to say."

I burst out laughing.

"I know, I'm wasted in a kitchen. I should be in stand up!"

I joined her at the sink and began drying the things she'd already washed. We were a cottage industry and it never felt more 'cottage' than washing and drying all the pots and pans we used in cooking. I longed for the dishwasher we had in the café, but we were still a way away from that.

We finished the washing up, stacked the pans and utensils in the plastic boxes under the trestle table and I checked the temperature of the Mac and Cheese.

"It's cool enough to package," I said. "What's the order for today?"

"I've got it here," Amy replied. She took a spreadsheet out of the folder and went into the hall for the packaging.

"I miss Basil," she said, coming back with an armful of metal containers. "Having to slip in and out of the kitchen without him getting anywhere near the door was quite an art. I enjoyed the challenge."

"He's better off where he is." He was up at Peace

Summerton House with Tye. He went every morning while Amy and I cooked. Dogs and commercial kitchens didn't mix.

She placed the containers down on the kitchen table and began counting. We usually split the Mac and Cheese into containers for eight, six, four and two, often with about ten individual portions for one person as well. Half were for the farm shop and half went out to the local cafés in the area. They sold out every day. Tye was a smart businessman, that much was clear.

"Right, I've got it all here," Amy said. 'And there's a few extra because I think we'll have some left over." She recounted the containers to make sure. "Do you want to check them?"

"No. I trust you completely."

"Fool!"

I grated parmesan and cheddar cheeses for the topping and added them to the breadcrumbs we'd made earlier. Amy and I worked in companionable silence. Once she'd laid out the containers, we filled, topped with cheesy breadcrumbs, and put the labelled lids on. We were done in half an hour and an impressive stack of ready meals lay on the table.

"Is Angelica collecting today?" Amy asked, "and will she put a spell on these, do you think?"

"She puts a spell on everything. She says it's her magic that's made the food so popular."

Amy snorted with laughter. "Nothing to do with your genius as a cook then Willa,"

"Or your skill as a sous chef!"

"Aw, you're too nice," Amy said. She went over to the sink, filled the kettle, and placed it on the hot plate of the Aga. "Coffee?"

"Please. Angelica will be here in about half an hour." Angelica collected all the food and took it back to the farm shop where Tye had installed some big fridges and a freezer for the meals.

'You know, it makes me feel good, looking at what we've done this morning, and every morning," Amy remarked.

"Me too."

"Thanks Willa, you know, for asking me to do this with you. I really love it and..." The kettle whistled, but she left it singing while she spooned coffee into mugs and added milk. She made the drinks and handed me one. "Well, it's made all the difference to me. I know we haven't known each other very long, or been doing this for very long..."

"Just over a month,"

"Yeah, just over a month, but it's been good, Willa. Really good. It's got me out of the house, I earn a bit of cash and I've got a new BFF."

"Whoa, steady on." I smiled and sipped my coffee, but Amy was right. It had been good. From the biscuits and the beef in red wine that I'd first made, to Angelica's Halloween biscuits that I made for the Paranormal Fayre in Glastonbury, to now cooking three days a week with Amy, it had all happened so quickly and smoothly as if it was meant to be.

"You know, you're not bad for a blow-in."

"Thanks. What's a blow-in?"

"It's an Irish expression. Joe's mum uses it. A newcomer."

"Right, well, I'll take that." I *was* a newcomer, but I'd never be made to feel like one. There was something very special about Peace Summerton. I went across to the table and had a quick look at the orders while Amy drank her coffee. "Are these for Megan?" I pointed to some of the containers that Amy had put to one side.

"Yes. Shall I drop them off on my way home?"

"Oh, no, it's fine. I can take them up to the farm shop and give them to Tye."

"Of course." Amy was smirking.

"Tye likes to drop them down to her himself so he can see the kids."

"Of course." Amy suddenly laughed.

"What?!" I turned and looked at her.

"You take them up to the farm shop so that you can see Tye," she said. "Willa, you and Tye are the worst kept secret in Peace Summerton!"

"There's nothing secret about us," I protested. "We're just friends."

Amy was trying hard not to laugh again. She straightened her face and said, "Right. Which is why he can't take his eyes off you when he's with you."

"He can't?" I felt a warm flush of pleasure wash over me.

"No and you sparkle like a disco ball every time he's around."

"I do?"

"Yes! And Angelica is convinced that she put a spell on you both and it worked."

"Oh."

Amy finished her coffee and rinsed the mug. She was heartily amused by the whole conversation, and I could see her grinning as she dried her mug and put it away.

"Do you need me to stay and help Angelica load up?

"No, it's fine." I glanced at the station clock that Maud had above the door. It kept perfect time, and it showed just after twelve. We started our cooking sessions promptly at nine a.m. straight after school drop off and finished usually by midday. "You get off Aims. We're all done, and you'll be home in time to get Joe some lunch."

"Like the good 1950's housewife that I am." She rolled her eyes, took off her apron and hairnet and put them both in her bag. "See you tomorrow."

"For fish pie," I said. "Cici is expecting the ingredients delivery this afternoon so Tye will drop all the food down to me tonight." I bundled up a tea towel and threw it at her. "Stop laughing in that dirty way." She caught it and threw it back to me then pulled on her parker and headed for the door. "We're just friends," she mimicked, as she left. "Who see each other every spare minute of the day..." She banged the door shut and I smiled. Amy was more than just a colleague. She was a mate, and it was a long time since I'd had one of those.

THIRTY-NINE

TYE

Cici was on the phone when I came into the farm shop. She was organising delivery of the fresh fish for that afternoon. I checked my watch; it was lunchtime, and I couldn't work in the office past twelve p.m., not when I knew that Willa would be dropping Megan's food up to the shop at some point in that hour between twelve and one. I constantly told myself that it was good business relations to make sure that suppliers were happy, and Willa was a supplier, but that was bullshit. I couldn't wait to see her. I took any excuse I had to go to the Lodge or call her up to the farm shop on some errand. And when she wore those dungarees, the same ones she'd worn that first night we were together, all I wanted to do was peel them down in the same way she'd done that night and pull her astride me. Fuck, it was both agony and ecstasy.

"Hey."

Cici waved at me as she finished up her call. I checked the stock in the freezer in the shop and then went into the back to check the luxury Mac and Cheese that Angelica had delivered half an hour earlier. We fast froze it and then it was ready for delivery to the cafés and for sale in the farm shop the following day. Not that it lasted long; we had so many pre-orders for Willa's food that we could barely keep up. I did the stock check, made a note on my phone, and went back into the shop.

"All good?" I asked.

"Yup. They just needed to let us know that they're replacing the haddock with line caught cod. I said that was fine, they're doing the same price."

"Good."

"Did you ask Willa about the food for Megan yet?"

"What about the food for Megan?" Willa came into the shop. She carried a bag with Megan's Mac and Cheese in and placed it on the counter. "Shall I put these straight into the fridge?"

Cici jumped up. "No, I'll do it," she said, grinning. "I'm going to pop into the house to see Mum and Basil for five minutes anyway. Angelica's in there with them."

She winked at me on her way past and as soon as she'd left the shop I reached for Willa and pulled her in close. Fuck, just the sight of her, even in an apron and hairnet gave me a hard-on. I lifted her up and turned her round to sit her on the counter. She wrapped her legs round my waist and her mouth found mine instantly.

"Love the hairnet," I murmured between kisses.

"Oops!" She pulled it off and shook her hair free. She pulled back. "What did you want to ask me about the food for Megan?"

I put a little distance between her groin and mine. I couldn't talk seriously with Willa pressing her vulva into my pulsing cock. I cleared my throat.

"Megan was telling one of the nurses at the hospital,

when she went for her check-up yesterday, that you make meals for the family a couple of times a week, to give Alfie a break so that he doesn't have to cook, and the nurse thought that was amazing. Anyway, the nurse, Suzie something, I think she said Suzie Wight... rang the office this morning and she's got another family who are struggling, and she wondered if we'd do meals for them too?"

Willa's face changed. She lost that soft look that turned me on so much. She frowned, thinking it through.

"How many?"

"Four. Dad's a single parent, three kids. He's having treatment for cancer, and his daughter who's younger than Alfie, does lots of stuff at home. Cooking and cleaning, but mainly she gets dinner ready most nights and it's not very healthy apparently, you know, frozen chicken nuggets, chips, and it's expensive. Suzie said it would be nice to give the daughter a bit of a break. She's in year 7 at the same academy as Alfie."

Willa jumped down off the counter. She went through to the fridge at the back. Moments later she returned. "We've got eight extra meals today, the luxury Mac and Cheese. Amy said we had a few spare but I didn't realise it was that much. Could we use those? If it affects the margins, then I'd be happy to pay for them?"

My heart swelled. It kept doing that, filling with love or happiness or whatever the fuck the romantics called it. "You absolutely will not pay for them, and it won't affect the margins at all. We can manage to supply a few extra meals without it making a dent in our business model."

"Oooh, our business model, eh? I love it when you talk technical."

Willa came across to me and put her arms round my neck. She pulled me in to a long kiss. I walked her back and pressed her up against the wall, moving my head down to her neck.

"HmmHmm."

We jumped apart.

Angelica stood in the entrance to the farm shop. Shit, we were going to have to be more discreet. "I am going to have to bottle that spell!" She announced. "And sell it as LOVE POTION!"

She came into the shop, grinning.

"I've come for today's deliveries."

She went round the back of the counter and bent to retrieve a stack of paper carrier bags. I gave them to the cafés to put our food in when people bought it; they had the classy Peace Summerton House logo on them, and it was good advertising.

"And I've got my leaflets, Tye." She held up a stack of printed sheets. "Hot off the press! Are you sure you don't mind me side hustling like this?"

I grinned. I wasn't sure what the market was for white witches and personalised magic, but I loved her inventiveness. "If the cafés are happy to hand them out then of course not. I hope you get some business out of it."

"I'm sure I will. Who doesn't love a bit of magic in their lives?" She went through to the back to begin loading the freezer bags with the frozen food Willa and Amy had made yesterday.

I glanced at Willa and smiled. She was right; a bit of magic in our lives was what we all needed. Willa was mine.

"Here, I'll give you a hand," I said.

"Me too."

We each took a bag of frozen meals to Angelica's car. She was highly organised and loaded the car with the bags in order of delivery route. She closed the boot with a bang and a rattle, and I winced.

"Not sure how that thing keeps passing it's MOT," I said. Angelica drove a beaten-up old VW Polo, scratched, dented and rusting at the seams.

She laughed. "Doh... Magic of course!"

"Oh yes, of course! I should have known."

"Thanks Tye," Angelica said, climbing into the car, "I'll message when I'm all done."

I waved and turned to Willa.

"Delivery," I said. "Angelica's round just reminded me. How are we going to get the meals to this dad and his kids?"

"Actually, I've been thinking," Willa said. She had this gorgeous little crease that appeared just above her top lip when she was concentrating. "Do you think there are other kids in the area, in Peace Summerton, or around us, who have to cook for their families? And probably do the washing, cleaning and all the rest of it as well? I read an article a while ago about young carers. They're kids like Alfie who take responsibility because their parents can't."

"I'm sure there are. Why?"

"Well..." she took a breath. "It's just an idea, but I was wondering if there *were* kids like Alfie then maybe we could set up a small meal delivery service for them?"

I stared at her. Her face was serious, earnest, but her eyes were excited, sparkling.

"A charity?"

"No, not really, just helping the community. I mean, Amy and I could easily do an extra twenty or thirty meals a couple of times a week and we could get some people to deliver..." She chewed her nail and stared at me. "What do you think?"

I thought that for a young woman with two kids and

now a busy demanding catering job, it was fucking incredible. And fucking mad. But mostly fucking incredible.

"Do you think it has legs Tye or is it a crazy idea?"

"It's not a crazy idea Willa, it's..." I stopped. "It's generous and kind and..." I reached for her hand. "Let's go into the shop and start making some notes. We need to see how many people in the area would want meals, how much it would cost and how we'd get the meals to them. We could start with Ellie Blackmore and see if she knows of any families in the school or the academy who'd like help? What do you think?"

Willa took my hand and gave it a squeeze.

"I think," she said, "That if anyone was going to make this work, it would be you."

FORTY

WILLA

Tye made everything work, he was that sort of person. I knew, as soon as I mentioned the idea to him, that if there was a need, he'd find a way to meet it. And I was sure there was a need.

Walking back to the lodge with Basil, I thought about Lexi. I thought about the day she came home with her diagnosis, about the weeks and the months that followed. God, what I would have done for someone to cook us a meal. I know I wasn't a kid, but I hadn't got a clue. I burnt food, served it raw, jiggled Teddy on my hip with Esme round my legs while I made lumpy cheese sauce and congealed pasta. I was seventeen, I'd dropped out of sixth form college to look after Lexi and the kids, and I was sad, frightened and exhausted. And I was a terrible cook.

I dug my hands in my pocket and felt the hand warmer that Amy had given me the first day I met her. I used it all the time and it kept my hands toasty warm.

That's how I felt here, all the time, toasty warm, even on the coldest of days. Inside and out. It was nearly the end of

November, thanksgiving in America, and the trees were bare, often laced with ice, but my heart was warm. I was happy in Peace Summerton; it was a place of friendship, community and kindness and it was home to the man that I loved. I suddenly stopped in my tracks. Loved? Basil stopped beside me and looked up at me.

"I know," I said aloud. "I think, only think mind you, that I might love him."

Basil tilted his head to one side.

"I know, who'd have thought, eh?" I bent and patted him. "Well, you obviously, because I know that you think he's wonderful, don't you Bas?"

I glanced up at the sky. "Yeah, I know Lexi, he's not gonna answer me."

Then I glanced back down the drive to the old Georgian stone Manor House where Tye, Eadie and Cici lived, and I knew with certainty that I loved him. I loved them all. And that was quite a revelation for a loner like me.

I *was* a loner. I'd only ever loved Lexi. She'd brought me up. She was older than me by twelve years. I was an accident, apparently, after a one-night stand with a bloke our mum had met at a concert, and I proved too much for a free spirit like her. She left when I was four. She was a flake, Lexi said, a waste of space and she just kind of wandered off into the sunset. She didn't come to Lexi's funeral. I didn't know where to reach her and honestly, I didn't care. You can't miss what you've never had, I guess.

My dad had never been around either. So, we were on our own, Lexi and me. Lexi's father had died young, Lexi never mentioned him and mine worked in New Guinea, in the rain forest, saving Gorillas or something equally worthy. I'd never met him. Funny that, caring so much about animals and not giving a fig about your own child. And not funny ha-ha either, funny peculiar. Weird. Our parents were simply names on a birth certificate.

Lexi always said she had no idea how I'd turned out so balanced, with the flake and the absentee. *I* did. I knew it was Lexi. She was solid, my sister. Always there, always loving, even when Syd came on the scene - and went off the scene again when they split up a few years later - even when she and Syd had Esme and Teddy. Until one day she wasn't. Although it wasn't one day, it was half a year of being sick and waiting to die.

I suddenly felt sad. Whenever I thought about Lexi, I felt sad. It never goes away, that feeling of loss. It eases, and sometimes I don't think of Lexi for a whole afternoon, but it's always there; I carry her in my heart. No wonder there hadn't been room for anyone else before, Lexi took up a lot of space. Perhaps that's what *'larger than life means?'* She was certainly that.

I started walking again, briskly, to ward off the cold and my melancholy and within minutes I was down the drive and through the woods to the Lodge. Maud's home and now ours. Maud had tried hard when Lexi died, but she was eccentric and unreliable even though she meant well. Two peas in a pod, Maud and her sister, our mum. Still, she'd saved us now. I thought briefly of Syd and all the things that Harry had told me she was planning. Yup, Maud had saved us, and more than that, she'd made life possible again.

FORTY-ONE

TYE

I should have turned the lights on. I could barely see what I was doing, and I'd got chocolate sauce everywhere. Fuck. I wiped the rim of the plate with a paper towel and sponged the work surface, then I washed my hands and tried to sponge the chocolate sauce off my shirt cuff.

"Are you OK Tye?"

Willa was at the table. The kitchen was lit entirely by candles, and I was determined not to spoil the romantic atmosphere. More fool me. Trying to drizzle chocolate sauce in a pattern over the cheesecake I'd made was impossible in the dark. It was probably impossible even in bright light for someone of my limited culinary talents, but for some insane reason I'd decided to have a go. I should have stuck to ice cream. That's what Eadie suggested, and I thought I knew better. I wanted to impress Willa, especially tonight.

"I'm fine," I answered, slightly distractedly. I'd just seen a globule of chocolate sauce on my crotch. How the fuck did

I manage to dribble it down there? Shit, if I sponged that off it was going to look like I'd wet myself.

"Dessert is almost ready." I'd given up on the idea of piping a raspberry coulis into the words *I love you*. That was way beyond my skillset. But that *was* the whole point of tonight; to tell Willa that I loved her. That I was *in love* with her and that over the past six weeks, she had completely changed my life.

"Where did Eadie go this evening?" Willa called over to me. "Cici mentioned something about Sam?"

Eadie was giving us space, and when she'd mentioned it in passing to Sam, he'd offered to take her out.

"Cinema," I said.

"Oooh." I could hear the smile in Willa's voice.

"There's nothing in it," I said quickly. "They're just friends."

"Still, he's handsome, for a man over sixty, and he's got all his own hair and teeth."

I brought the two plates over to the table. "As far as we know," I said, smiling. "They can do great things with wigs and dentures nowadays."

I placed the desserts on the table and pulled my chair out.

"This looks lovely Tye," Willa said, "Thank you."

We both stared down at our plates. It looked like a dog's dinner. The cheesecake had collapsed when I'd cut it, the biscuit base was burnt, the chocolate sauce was all over the place, (including me) and the raspberry coulis sat in blood like blobs around the plate.

"Well... it doesn't look quite like the picture in the recipe book..." I said.

Willa started to giggle, "That's a relief," she said, "If it looked like this in the book there'd be a problem." She snorted, trying to bring her giggles under control.

"Hey," I said, grinning, "I'm sure it tastes good..." I took a mouthful. It did not taste good. It was terrible. As Willa went to eat a mouthful, I quickly knocked her arm to distract her. The cheesecake on her spoon shot off, onto her chest. It landed with a plop.

"Oi!" She stared at it then me for a moment, then she took another spoonful and flicked it at me. It hit me on the cheek. She laughed.

"You..." I flicked a forkful back. It landed in her hair.

Suddenly Willa jumped up, grabbed a fist full of cheesecake and lunged at me, smearing it all over my face. I tried to fight her off, but I couldn't. I managed to grab myself a handful and splattered it into her neck. She jumped back, ran to the work surface, and took the plate up.

"Willa..." I warned, "Willa, don't you dare..."

She did. The whole cheesecake left the plate and came flying across the room. It hit me square in the chest. I burst out laughing, then I dived for her and caught her round the waist as she attempted to run off.

"Right!" I announced. I lifted her up and threw her over my shoulder. "You, young lady, are in big trouble." I smacked her lightly on her beautifully rounded bum.

"I'm not letting you down until you apologise and promise not to throw anything else at me!"

"I promise," she waited, upside down, "I'm sorry and I promise not to throw anything else."

"Right." I plonked her back on her feet and as she spun round, she grabbed the jug of chocolate sauce and tipped the last of it over my head.

"You said throw," she cried, dodging quickly back. "Not pour! You didn't mention not pouring anything!" Snorting with laughter, she darted out of the kitchen and headed for the hallway and the stairs. I went after her. She was fast, but my legs and strides were longer and I caught her halfway up the staircase. I grabbed her round the waist, we wrestled for a moment and then as swiftly as the food fight had started, it stopped. She suddenly kissed me, her tongue finding mine and my desire flared instantly. I pulled her down onto the stairs and moved over her. She wore nothing under her dress, just a pair of stockings and my fingers found her wetness instantly. She moaned and kissed me harder.

"Here?" I murmured.

"Yes, here. Now."

I moved back and she half sat, pulling the dress over her head. She lay back on the stairs, her thighs sheathed in sheer black, the rest of her naked and wanting me. I yanked my shirt off while she unfastened my jeans and freed my cock, then sitting forward she ran her hot, wet tongue over it, taking the tip of me into her mouth and then the whole of me.

"Oh God, Willa..." She moved her mouth, up and down, moving my cock in and out of her mouth, slowly at first, then faster, her hands cupping my balls.

"Willa, slow down, I..." She was moving too fast, I wanted to taste her, to feel myself inside her. She drew back and smiled at me.

"I literally had you in the palm of my hand," she breathed. Smiling, I bent my head and kissed her. Hot *and* funny.

"Fuck me," she murmured.

I reached behind me for my jeans, and she caught my wrist to stop me. "No," she said, "Just fuck me." Willa never swore and the word hung between us. It was so fucking sexy.

I looked at her. "You mean, not use...?"

She smiled and raised an eyebrow. "If you want..."

Oh God, to be inside Willa, to feel her tighten and shudder and come, with nothing but her muscle and wetness wrapped around my cock. God, yes, I wanted to.

"Are you sure? I mean..."

"I have the pill and I don't have any STDs."

I smiled again. Only Willa would feel the need to reassure me of that.

"Me neither..."

She opened her thighs under me and took me in her hand, guiding me towards that hot, tight place where I knew I would lose myself and never want to be found. I raised my hips and thrust into her. She cried out and wrapped her legs even tighter round my waist. I began to move and as I did Willa seemed to melt underneath me. She moved with me, lifting her hips, gripping my back, pulling me down deeper and harder into her until it felt as if we were one person, both moving towards that mounting, flooding, ecstatic moment.

She moaned and called my name as her climax began to tremble inside her. I thrust every inch of my cock, fast and deep as one wave after another of orgasm washed over her. She cried out as I came with her, exploding with a force I'd never felt before.

It took some time before I was able to speak. I could feel her heart fluttering beneath me, feel the damp of sweat on her skin. She ran her fingers over my back, gently, caressingly, until reality began to claw again at the edges of perfection. I wanted to say I love you. I wanted to whisper it over and over again into her hair, her neck, her ear. But I didn't. It felt wrong to say it after fucking her like that. It felt as if it might be something I thought I *had* to say.

I opened my eyes and moved my face so that I could see her.

"You OK?"

"Yes. Very OK."

I moved to sit up. "I think we're both covered in chocolate sauce," I said. "Would you like a bath?"

"Hmmm, sounds lovely."

I stood and took her hands. I had a suite of rooms and a bathroom at the top of the house and I led Willa up the main staircase and along to the back staircase and the entrance to my apartment. Once there, I wrapped a big soft blanket round her shoulders and ran the taps for a hot bath.

"I'll grab our clothes," I said. "Are you warm enough?"

The small sitting room that I had housed a fireplace with a wood burning stove. It kept the apartment warm and I'd stacked it earlier, hoping that I might bring Willa up here.

"Toasty," she said and then she smiled at herself, as if she'd said something that she found amusing.

"Good. I'll be back in a moment." I stopped at the door. "I'll grab your phone too." Cici was babysitting Esme and Teddy, and I knew that Willa liked her phone nearby in case the kids needed her.

"Thanks," she said. She blew me a kiss and flashed her tits at me. I laughed as I went downstairs.

I collected our clothes from the staircase and followed the trail of chocolate sauce into the kitchen to find Willa's phone. I'd have to clear that up before Eadie came back.

Willa's phone was on the table, she always had it close at hand, and as I picked it up, I saw that she'd had a text message from Harry. Harry? She'd never mentioned anyone called Harry to me. I glanced at the message, and it started with '*Willa darling.*' I felt an odd sense of apprehension. I couldn't see any more of the message, Willa's phone was locked, and I wouldn't have looked at it even if I could have. But one thing was clear to me, and that one thing filled me with unease. Whoever Harry was, there was a blue heart emoji next to his name and he was clearly someone important to Willa.

FORTY-TWO

WILLA

There was something fateful about tonight, I just knew it. And there was I naively thinking that after nearly two months here in Peace Summerton, and weeks of bliss with Tye, it was going to be something to do with that. How wrong was I?

As soon as I saw the screen I panicked. I was in the bath, thinking about Tye and how nice it would be if he slipped in there with me when he passed me my phone. He didn't look at me, which, with soapy foam all over my breasts, was a bit of a surprise. I took it and glanced up at him. His face was closed as he turned away.

"You've got a message," he said, "from someone called Harry."

My heart stopped.

"Right," I murmured. Tye left the bathroom.

Unlocking my phone, I opened the message.

Willa darling, things seriously bad. Call me urgently. Xxx

I closed the message, my fingers trembling and stood up.

Reaching for a towel, I dried myself hurriedly and saw that Tye had left my clothes on the side. I dressed, let the water out of the bath and went into the sitting room. Tye was staring at the fire.

"I have to go," I said. "Harry's an old friend and he's asked me to call him."

"You can call from here if you want?"

"Thanks, but it may take a while and I really should get back to the kids." God only knew what Harry had to say. *Things seriously bad.* What the hell did that mean? My stomach was in knots.

"Fine."

It clearly wasn't fine. Tye's face was tense, and he didn't look up.

"I'm really sorry," I said, "I hope you're not mad at me?" There was nothing I could do if he was and honestly, Tye's feelings were the last thing on my mind right then.

"No, it's fine Willa." He stood and turned to me, and his face softened again. He looked at me with longing and what felt like love. "Can I help? Is there anything you need from me?"

My heart suddenly ached, and I felt the sharp prick of tears in my eyes.

"No, but..." I looked right back at him. "Thank you, Tye."

"I'll see you out."

"OK."

We made our way down the stairs in a very different mood to the way we'd gone up. I grabbed my coat from the kitchen and stood awkwardly for a moment. I wanted to kiss him, I wanted him to hold me close and tell me it was all fine, that it was all going to be OK, but Tye knew nothing about Syd and Harry and the whole awful mess, and I wasn't about to start telling him now.

"I should go."

"Yes."

He made no move towards me, nor I towards him. I opened the back door, waved at him and hurried down the steps to the van. I was going to sort this out and make sure my life here was secure. So why, as I drove away and left Peace Summerton House behind, did I feel like I might never come back here again?

CICI WAS SURPRISED to see me when I rang the bell and then let myself into the Lodge. She was watching TV with Basil and had a plate of the now famous chocolate and hazelnut biscuits by her side.

"Hey! You're back early?" she said. "Everything OK?" She looked momentarily worried, like I'd missed something important.

"Yes, sort of, and no. A mate just called, and I need to give him a ring. I think he's in trouble, so I came home to do it. It might take some time on the phone."

"Oh, right, I see. I'll get myself off then." She stood and looked quizzically at me for a few moments.

"Am I delivering to the families tomorrow?" she asked, taking her coat off the sofa next to her and pulling it on. "Or is Nellie?"

"I think you're on the rota," I said. I swallowed down a sudden lump that rose in my throat. We had four families in Peace Summerton who all had kids that cared for their parents and now, twice a week, we took meals to them. We took the sort of meals that I would have given my right arm for when Lexi was dying. Delicious, home-made, healthy meals to pop in the oven, made and delivered with love. It was one of the things that I felt I'd done right since I arrived; one of the things I was proud of.

"Good," Cici said, still looking at me. I blew my nose and turned away.

"Is everything OK Willa?" she asked as she made her way to the front door. She touched my arm in that gentle, unassuming way she had and again tears threatened to spill.

"Yup," I said. "Just need a bit of time to talk to my friend."

"OK. Shout if you need me."

I knew she meant it. She opened the front door, rattling the keys for the Land Rover and waved briefly as she climbed into it. I waited for her to drive away, then I called Harry immediately.

"Yo."

"Harry?! What's going on?"

"I'm at Peace Summerton station. God this place is dead. Quaint, but dead. I'm getting a taxi to you now."

"You're what?!!" My stomach lurched.

"Hang on a minute Willa... Peace Summerton Lodge please. Yeah, that's right, she does."

I head the slam of a car door. "Seems like you're well known in these parts. Nice work Willow Tree."

That was his pet name for me and it annoyed the life out of me. It always had and this certainly wasn't the time for pet names.

"Harry," I said crossly. 'What's going on?"

"You're in big shit Willa, that's what's going on. Syd is on her way to Peace Summerton."

"Syd? Here?"

"Yup. But don't worry. You're lucky I'm ahead of her. I've got a plan. See you in five."

And with that he ended the call.

I WAS PACING the floor by the time he arrived. I opened the door, thankful that Sam was out with Eadie, and it was a driver I hadn't seen before.

"Community cook, eh?" Harry said, walking straight into Maud's house and dumping his overnight bag on the floor. "Apparently you're the saviour of young carers." Harry turned and smirked. "Saint Willa. Makes up for all the terrible things you've done."

"What? What are you talking about?!"

Basil suddenly appeared in the hallway and growled, loudly.

"Hey Bas!" Harry knelt expecting Basil to trot over, but Basil stayed where he was by my side which was odd as Basil was a terrible flirt; he loved attention, from anyone. Harry stood again.

"Syd's on her way here to take the kids back," he said. "She's got legal papers to prove that you're unreliable and that she should have custody."

My legs gave way, and I slumped down onto the chair in the hallway. I put my head in my hands. "What legal papers?"

"I have no idea, but she's hired a top barrister and a firm of lawyers, and she means business Willa."

I felt a sob rise in my throat. Basil put his head on my lap and I stroked him. Syd couldn't do this. She could not take Esme and Teddy away from me. I had looked after them since Lexi was ill, I'd been everything to them; Mum, Dad, Aunt. Everything. All Syd had ever done was hand over a monthly sum, which the courts enforced, and insist on sending them to a posh private school that made Teddy wet the bed and Esme cry herself to sleep. What did she think she was going to achieve, taking them away from me, from all they'd ever known?

"Willa?"

I looked up. Harry handed me a crumpled tissue.

"She can't take them away from you if you're not here," he said.

I blew my nose and then stood and went into the kitchen for the box of Kleenex I kept there. I blew my nose several times and wiped my face. Harry followed me in.

"I've found an Airbnb," he said. "It's about a two-hour drive from here, in the middle of nowhere and we can hole up there for a while."

I looked at him aghast. "I can't do that! The kids have school and I have work and..." And there's Tye, I thought. Oh God, what about Tye?

Harry came across to me as I began to pace the floor again and he stopped me, holding my arms.

"Yes, you can! Syd will stay, what two days, three, maximum? She's got a business to run, she won't hang around if she can't find you. And besides, if you clear out of here and make it look as if you're never coming back, then why would she stay?"

"Clear out of here? What tonight?" I shook my head. "Harry, you're mad."

"No, I'm not Willa. Just think about it. If we start now, you can pack as much as you can into the van, all your valuables, some food. Put the rest into cupboards, so it looks like you've gone. It'll take a couple of hours, tops. Then you get the kids, put them to bed in the van and off we go. I've got the place booked. For a week. We can be there by midnight and you, and the kids would be safe."

I moved away from him and chewed my nail, thinking

hard, trying to weigh it up. If Syd had legal papers, then she could take the kids immediately, tonight, or whenever she arrived and then I'd have to fight legally to get them back. That would cost me thousands and I didn't have that kind of money. But if we weren't here, if we'd disappeared again then...

"What about if she comes back," I said. "A few months down the line when we've come back to the Lodge?"

"Why would she? If she thinks you've moved on, why would she come back?"

I narrowed my eyes. It did make sense.

"Why are you here helping us, Harry? Why are you getting involved?"

Harry shrugged then he moved close to me.

"I've missed you, Willa. You know they say you never know what you've got until its gone." He took a breath, visibly upset. "Look, I know we weren't anything more than a fling back in the day, but you are a good person Willa, a really good person. You were the one that got me the job at the café in the first place, remember? And I owe you. Besides, when I first overheard what Syd was up to, planning to get custody of the kids, I knew I had to tell you about it."

I looked closely at his face, and I saw sincerity there.

"And you made the right decision. You moved and you're happy here. You love those kids; Lexi asked you to care for them and that's what you've done, and I don't see why some entitled bitch with money thinks she can come along and mess that up. Just because she's met someone who wants a family."

"Daisy?!" Daisy was Syd's new partner. "You think that's what's behind all this?"

"Yes. Daisy wants a family and Syd has one."

"But they're Lexi's children. Her eggs, she carried them."

"I think Syd sees them as hers."

I nodded. "Because she pays towards their keep?"

"Yes. And didn't she fund the sperm donation too?"

I nodded again. I could see exactly how this would stack up in court. I took a big breath then I looked at Harry.

"I'm helping you because you deserve it, Willa. Besides, I was the one who warned you about Syd last time and look how well that turned out."

He was right. I'd trusted him before, and it *had* worked. I made my mind up there and then.

"Thank you," I said. "I think you're right. I think we need to leave, at least for a few days."

I looked around the kitchen. "Right. Let's start down here. You start packing the van and I'll get the place downstairs looking like we've left for good."

Harry nodded. He came across to me. "Hug?"

I thought about Tye suddenly. "I should ring Tye," I said. "Let him know what I'm doing."

"Tye?"

Harry shook his head. "Oh no, that's not a good idea. I don't know who Tye is, but ring no one, say nothing. The less anyone knows, the harder it will be to find you. Syd will pester and bully if she thinks someone knows where you are."

"But Harry, I can't just..."

"Yes you can, and you MUST."

"What, just disappear?"

"Yes."

I took another big breath. I had a heavy weight of sadness on my chest, pressing down, making it hard for me to breathe.

"It'll be OK, Willa. As long as you've got the kids."

"And Basil,"

"Yes, and Basil, that's all that matters, right?"

"Yes."

But was it? For the first time in years, I wasn't quite sure.

FORTY-THREE

TYE

I hadn't slept well. I'd laid awake thinking about Willa, longing to have her in my bed, imagining her next to me, and then having that image ruined by thinking about Harry, whoever the fuck Harry was! *Willa darling?* What was that supposed to mean? Why had she never mentioned Harry if she was such a darling to him? And why was she in such a rush to leave? The erotic images of Willa and the confusing thoughts of Harry jarred in my head until I fell into a fitful sleep around three a.m.

I woke again at five a.m. and sat bolt upright in a state of panic. There was a loud and persistent banging on the main door. I went to the window and looked down at the drive, in front of the house. There was a white four-wheel Porsche Cayenne parked up. Who the hell was that?

I pulled on some sweatpants and a jumper and hurried downstairs. The banging continued.

"All right," I called out, "Stop banging, you'll wake the whole house! I'm coming!" Fear gnawed at my gut. Peace

Summerton House was not a place that people just dropped in to, especially not at five a.m.

I unbolted, turned on the porch and hallway lights and opened the door.

"Can I help you?" I snapped.

A woman turned. She was in her late thirties I'd have thought, tall, dressed in jeans and a long sweater, with high heeled boots. She had an expensive coat thrown over her shoulders, its collar turned up. Her hair was dark and cut short. I was no expert on women, but I could see immediately that this one was high maintenance.

"I'm looking for Willa Hart," the woman said. "She's living at Peace Summerton Lodge, which I think belongs to this house?"

Her voice was assertive, but sharp. There was an edge of anger to it.

"Yes, she is and yes, it does. Sorry, why are you here? At five in the morning?"

"I just said," she replied curtly. "I'm looking for Willa Hart." Her voice had that tone that I'm guessing she reserved for idiots.

"She lives at the Lodge," I said. "We've established that."

"And she's not there."

"Sorry, what?"

"She's not there. I called into the Lodge first." She raised an eyebrow at me. "Obviously."

"She is there," I insisted. "She lives there. Perhaps she's asleep? It is five a.m." I remained outwardly calm but inside I was beginning to freak out. I knew something was wrong. Willa was usually up by five. She liked to organise the kitchen before the kids went to school, get it ready for the morning's cooking with Amy which started right after school drop-off.

"She's not there," the woman said. "Her van's gone, and the house looks empty. Daisy and I had a good look in, from outside that is. Have you got keys, to check?"

"Wait, let me get this clear? You want me to open the house that belongs to one of my tenants so that you can have a good look round. And why is that exactly? Who are you, who the hell is Daisy, and what the fuck are you doing here?"

She took a step backwards and rolled her shoulders up and back, standing a few centimetres taller, as if preparing for battle. "I'm Syd," she said, "Daisy is my partner and I'm Esme and Teddy's mother." She stared me down. "Willa Hart has abducted my children."

BY THE TIME I got back from the Lodge, Eadie and Cici were both up. They were in the kitchen. I'd directed Syd and Daisy to the pub in the village that they'd booked to stay in and rung Jimmy the landlord to warn him that they were super-early. I should have asked them back to the house, but I was in shock. Syd was right. Willa had gone. No van, no kids, no food in the fridge, nothing. She'd cleared out and gone. Just disappeared. Without a word.

Plus, I'd taken an instant dislike to Syd, and I didn't want to spend any longer in her company than I had to. There was something domineering about her, something mean. She was assertive, but I liked assertive people, people who were straight and sincere. Syd's assertiveness seemed to be about winning, about taking the advantage and I didn't like that.

As I came into the kitchen Eadie and Cici looked up, as if I'd caught them talking about me, which I probably had.

"I've made tea," Eadie said. "Sit down, I'll get you a cup."

I pulled out a chair, sat and put my head in my hands. I felt Eadie behind me. She put her hands on my shoulder and very gently squeezed.

"It'll be OK Tye," she said softly.

I shook my head. "Will it? She's gone. Just upped and left. And if what Syd says is right then she's on the run." I could feel myself choke up. "She's taken those poor kids and she's on the run to somewhere else and God only knows where..."

"No," Cici said firmly. 'That's just not true Tye. I don't believe it. I don't believe Syd and I don't believe for one moment that Willa would be doing anything to hurt Esme and Teddy and that includes taking them away from their '*mother*.'"

Cici did little air quotes with her hands when she said the word mother, to show that she didn't give any credence to that idea. To be fair, I couldn't see Syd as a mother either.

"But she said that Willa can't be trusted and that she's got proof of that."

"How?" Cici was indignant. "How can't Willa be trusted?"

"I don't know, she didn't say. She wanted to get to their B&B to have a rest; they'd been driving all night apparently. She's asked me to meet later so that she can tell me more."

"Do you need to know any more?" Eadie brought tea over and placed it in front of me.

"Mum's right Tye. I trust Willa, she's a good person. Look at the young carer work, and how much people have warmed to her. Whatever she's done, she'll have done with the right intentions."

"You think?"

"Yes, I think!" Cici looked hard at me. "You don't have to listen to Syd, and honestly, I'm surprised that you'd want to."

"Well maybe some of the things that Syd is saying make sense. Willa's always said very little about home or what she left behind. None of us know very much about her, her past. Plus, she got a message last night from someone called Harry and as soon as she did, she left. It was all a bit odd."

"Harry?" Cici looked surprised and a little knocked off guard. "Willa mentioned Harry when she first arrived. She said that he was the one who told her about Syd wanting custody."

"Look," Eadie said, "I am sure that there is a perfectly reasonable explanation for all of this, and that Willa is going to breeze in the door at some point soon and give it to us." She pulled her dressing gown tight around her. "And all of us sitting here worrying and chewing it over in the meantime is not very helpful. I would suggest that you hear Syd out, not least because it will give you a chance to defend Willa, but most of all Tye, try to not worry!" She headed for the door. "There's not much I can do, so I'm going back to bed for a couple of hours. It's six a.m. and I don't have to be up until eight. I'll see you both later. Call me if you need me."

Eadie left and Cici stood as well.

"You don't really believe Syd, do you Tye?"

I shrugged. I didn't know who or what to believe. What Eadie and Cici seemed to be forgetting was that we'd only known Willa for a few months. That wasn't very long. And last night, when I thought that we were so close, when I was just about to tell her that I loved her, she got a message on her phone and left abruptly, without an explanation or even a kiss goodbye. This morning, after not answering my text last night, she had disappeared. Were those the actions of someone we could trust?

"Follow your gut Tye," Cici said. "You're a good judge of character." She bent and kissed my cheek then went upstairs to get dressed. A good judge of character? Was I? Percy and I had been friends, I trusted him, and look what happened there. A secret affair with Cici behind my back when she was sixteen and when she wouldn't sleep with him because she realised that she preferred girls, he threatened to tell everyone she knew, message all her friends, expose her to the whole world, unless I paid him off. She was distraught. She wasn't ready to come out and the fear of exposure nearly destroyed her. I paid him off. Obviously. There was never any question that I would and at least he'd had the foresight to take himself off round the world for a few years. If he'd stayed here, I think I would have killed him. A good judge of character? I don't think so.

I stood to make myself more tea. Placing the kettle on the hot plate of the Aga I thought back to last night, to what we'd said, what we'd done, searching for any clues in Willa's behaviour for what was to come. I couldn't see any, but perhaps that was me. Perhaps I was so desperate for love that I was blinded by it when it came along, and I couldn't see the truth. Or perhaps I just ignored it. Whatever it was, I think I'd made a massive mistake and I felt foolish, angry, but mostly, I felt incredibly sad.

FORTY-FOUR

WILLA

We slept late, or at least it felt late. I'd left my phone in my bag by the front door, so I had no idea what the actual time was, only that it was light, and it usually got light around seven fifteen a.m. I was surprised I hadn't heard Esme and Teddy or Basil. I'd let Basil out just before I got to bed about two a.m., so he'd probably be crossing his legs by now.

I felt Teddy stir, then roll onto his side and stare at my face. He pinched my cheek.

"Willa?" He whispered loudly. "Are you awake?"

"I am now," I said. I pulled him into a hug, but he wriggled free.

"Can we go and explore?" he asked, poking Esme.

"Ouch! Get offfa." Esme kicked him under the duvet. She was not a morning person.

"There's not much to see Ted," I told him. Harry had rented a one bedroomed place, sparsely furnished, with a sitting room and kitchen combined, where he was asleep now on the sofa bed. We were in the bedroom, squished into a small double bed, with Basil sleeping by the window. I'd told the kids we'd come away for a mini break, but I'm not sure how that was going to stand up when they realised where we were. From what I could see last night, this was a tiny outhouse conversion in the middle of a field, miles from anywhere in deepest, darkest Cornwall.

"How about I let Basil out and you stay here. We can read for a short while and then get up and have some breakfast?"

"OK."

"Right," I said. "The books are in the van, so I'll let Bas out for a you know what and pop out to get them. I can bring some hot chocolate back to bed as well. How does that sound?"

Esme opened one eye. The way to her heart had always been through her stomach.

"With marshmallows?"

"Don't push your luck," I said. Hot chocolate in bed was a treat enough. I stood, pulled on a sweater and some socks, and then realised that this was supposed to be a mini break, so I said, "with marshmallows if I can find them. OK?"

"Yay!" Esme sat up as I quietly prised the bedroom door open. "Come on Basil,"

I let Bas out first and followed him into the living area.

The curtains were open. The sofa was still a sofa and not a bed.

"Harry?"

The place was empty. Deserted. I opened the door to let Bas out. Outside, the van had gone. *My van* had gone. My stomach lurched. I looked at the front door, no bag. My bag had gone. No bag meant no phone, no purse, no laptop, nothing and outside there was no van. No van meant everything we owned of any value was gone.

I turned and crossed to the fridge. I had stupidly left all the food in the van last night. It was cold out, it was late and I reckoned I could leave the chilled stuff where it was and transfer it in the morning. Maybe Harry had popped out for some more supplies and brought the food in before he'd gone. I opened the fridge. There was a pint of milk in there, a bottle of water and a bottle of white wine, all left by the AirB&B landlady. There was nothing else.

I staggered back and slumped down onto a chair. Where the hell was Harry?

Harry. I dropped my head into my hands. This was surely not what it looked like. It couldn't be. A mixture of panic and despair rose in my chest and a snippet of a past conversation, like a bolt from the blue, shot into my head.

But theft Harry?

It's bollocks. Have you read all the messages Willa?

No, but...

Don't bother...

I thought hard, trying to remember what we'd said. He'd left the café, dismissed Syd's accusations of theft, explained them away and told me not to worry. Then last night...

I stood up and began pacing the floor. I was making a habit of this.

Last night he'd insisted we left immediately and bring everything of any value. Had he convinced me to leave it all in the van so he could make off with it? I racked my brains.

Shall I just bring the bags in?

No, leave them. We can do it in the morning.

Have you seen my bag?

It's by the door. Go on Willa, get to bed! It's late. You don't need your bag, just get yourself off to bed. Go!

But Harry wouldn't do that to me, would he? No. No, he wouldn't. I was sure he wouldn't. I glanced across at the time on the microwave. It was eleven a.m. Eleven a.m.?! If he hadn't left, then where the hell *was* he? I began searching the place for a note, for any sign that he might be coming back. There was nothing. It was as if he'd never been there. What the hell was going on? Why would Harry do this?

"Because Willa," I said aloud, "if he really is in trouble, if he's been stealing from the café, then he's done a runner with your stuff. He can sell it all - your phone, your laptop and your van and make a run for it with the cash." I was catastrophising and my imagination was running away with me. "And he'll be long gone before you can even raise the alarm." I started to panic again. We were in the middle of nowhere with no food, no clothes, no phone. We had nothing and no way of getting help.

"Shit, shit, shit!" This was bad. I rarely swore and I needed to calm down, at least for the kids. The kids!

I stopped pacing as Esme appeared in the doorway in her pyjamas.

Oh God. Oh, dear God no! I had carried Esme and Teddy into the van last night and let them sleep on the two-hour drive and then carried them from the van to the bed here when we arrived. They were in their pyjamas, no shoes, no coats, no clothes. I'd left everything in the van. If I walked to get help, I'd have to carry them.

"Oh Jesus, Harry, you..."

"Willa, who are you talking to?"

"No one sweetheart."

Esme came in and took a long look round the empty room.

"Willa, if I tell you something, will you promise not to be cross."

I went to Esme and knelt, opening my arms for her to step into my hug. I kissed her hair.

"I won't be cross," I said. "I promise." How on earth could I ever be cross when *I* had made such a monumental mess of everything. Perhaps Syd was right, perhaps I was unreliable and the kids would be better off settled with her and Daisy.

"Don't cry," Esme said. I released her and wiped my face on my sleeve. "I'm not crying, I just have a nasty cold at the moment." I faced her. "Now, what did you want to tell me?"

She disappeared into the bedroom and came back a few moments later with something in her hand.

"When we got in the van last night I couldn't sleep and I know you said never to touch your phone, but I did, and I took it out of your bag so I could watch Dragons with the volume off." She hung her head. "Here," she held my phone out to me. "I'm sorry Willa. I shouldn't have taken it without asking."

I swallowed down the lump that rose in my throat. "That's OK," I said. "Thank you for being so honest. I love you Esme. I love you and Teddy more than anything in the world. Remember that, will you? Always." I held my breath and looked at the screen. My phone was on low power mode and I had two percent of battery left. I unlocked it and called Harry. Number unavailable. My heart sunk to my boots. I called Tye. He picked up instantly.

"I don't have much battery," I said. "And I don't know exactly where we are. The last signpost was Little Mudderton in Cornwall, so we're about twenty miles from there. It's an AirBnB. Harry's gone. He's gone off with my van and all our things..." A sob caught in my throat. "I'm so sorry Tye. Please can you come and get us?"

FORTY-FIVE

TYE

I was sitting with Syd when the call came through and it felt as if my whole body stopped for a nanosecond. I snatched the phone up and the moment I heard her voice a huge wave of relief washed over me. Then anger. I was suddenly so angry I couldn't speak. I took a breath.

"Yes," I said tightly. "I'll come now..." I stood and moved away from Syd. "For the kids, I'll come because of the kids." I said and I ended the call.

Syd was up on her feet as I turned back. "Where the hell is she?"

"Miles away," I answered. Even though Syd had been wronged and Willa had been stealing from the café, it didn't mean I liked her. She was here for vengeance and not because she cared. Syd might have had evidence and legal papers, but I had the feeling that she didn't have a kind bone in her body.

"I'm going to get her," I said, "And I'm going on my own."

"Why do you have to go and get her? What's happened?"

"Some bloke went off with all their stuff. He's taken the van."

Syd threw her hands up. "Well that's just great!" she cried. "And how do I know that you'll bring her back?"

I scowled at her. "Really?" I snapped.

She chewed on that for a few moments. "OK," she finally said. "I'll go back and wait with Daisy at the pub. I suppose the upside is that we won't have to pack anything up for the kids when we leave. Doesn't sound as if they've got anything left to pack."

I felt a stone of sadness settle in my chest. The idea of Esme and Teddy leaving was bad enough but the idea of them leaving with Syd floored me. I made for the door.

"What bloke?" Syd called after me.

"Someone called Harry," I said. I glanced back at her.

"Harry?" Syd's face had changed, but I didn't stay to find out why. Minutes later I was outside and in the Land Rover. I dialled Cici.

"Willa called. I'm going to get her."

"Oh, thank God for that Tye!" I could hear the genuine relief and love in her voice, and it made me angry all over again. How could one person fool so many of us?

"Can you look up Airbnb for me Cici? Willa is in an Airbnb rental somewhere in Cornwall. She said it's about twenty miles from Little Mudderton. Can you find out what rentals are around there? I don't need an exact address, I'm sure I'll find it if I ask around. I just need an idea of the area, whether its north or south of Little Mudderton."

"OK, I'll do that now. Are Esme and Teddy OK?"

"I didn't ask."

I could hear Cici weighing up the tone of my voice. "I'll message you when I find something," she said.

"Thanks."

"And Tye?"

"What?!" I was trying hard not to be snappy, but the last thing I needed was advice.

"Don't make your mind up until you've heard everything. OK?"

I didn't answer her.

"OK?" she insisted.

"Fine." I growled. I ended the call and put the jeep into gear. Minutes later, I was headed on the main A road towards the next county.

FORTY-SIX

WILLA

Finally, just after two p.m. Tye arrived, and he was furious. But, even in his fury he'd stopped for milk, hot chocolate powder, dog food and a small bag of provisions.

When he pulled up outside the rental in the Land Rover, Teddy dashed out in bare feet and pyjamas and Tye scooped him up into a hug. Basil barked enthusiastically and nearly knocked Esme over with his wagging tail. Tye pulled his coat round Ted to keep him warm and carried him into the house. He bent and hugged Esme and gave Basil a dog treat he must have been keeping in his pocket. My heart swelled. Then I saw his face.

"You two must be starving," he said. "Who wants hot chocolate and a banana sandwich with sugar on top?"

Teddy was jumping up and down trying to see what was in the carrier bag, Esme had gone back to sitting on the sofa with the duvet from the bed wrapped round her, sucking her thumb. She hadn't done that for years.

"Basil first though. Esme will you open the can of dog food for me? I really need your help."

Tye threw me a curt nod and helped Esme with Basil's food. As Basil nuzzled her legs waiting for his breakfast she began to giggle. When she put the bowl on the floor, he barked twice and started hoofing it down. Tye grinned at her.

"Well done, Esme! You've just saved a dog's life," he said, and she smiled up at him. He moved on to making them something to eat and five minutes later he had Teddy and Esme sitting at the small table with a drink and a sandwich. He didn't look at me once.

When they'd finished eating, Tye cleared away and went to the jeep for some blankets.

I'll give you both a piggyback to the Land Rover," he said, wrapping a blanket round each of them, ready for the journey. "Who's going first?"

"ME!" They both shouted together.

"I think I can manage two," Tye said, "but it'll be a piggy-hip, one on each side."

I smiled. "A piggy-hip," I said, "Nice one."

There was no reply.

As Tye settled the kids into the car, I checked the rental for anything we might have missed. It was a pointless action. We had nothing but the clothes we stood up in and a mobile phone, out of battery. I closed the door behind us and wondered how long Harry had rented the place for. Probably just the one night. I climbed into the front seat of the Land Rover and Tye shifted into gear to drive off.

"Tye, I..." He looked at me then and his eyes were so hard and angry that I didn't finish. There was no point. I looked out of the window as we silently started the long journey back to Peace Summerton.

FORTY-SEVEN

TYE

I saw Syd's car parked at the Lodge as we pulled into the drive.

"Look," I heard Willa say, her voice unnaturally bright. "It's other Muma's car. She's come to visit! Isn't that nice?"

Esme and Teddy said nothing. The front door opened and Syd came out. She must have heard the jeep.

"How did Syd...?" Willa asked.

"I let her in," I said. I stopped and pulled on the handbrake, leaving the engine running. Syd opened the back passenger door.

"Hey you two bozos. How are you doing?"

Still Esme and Teddy said nothing.

Willa went to get out, but Syd stopped her. Willa seemed to slump, as if all her strength and energy had deserted her. I couldn't bear to look at her face.

"We've got this Willa," Syd said. She reached in for Teddy and Daisy came to the other door for Esme. In a matter of moments Esme and Teddy were lifted out of the Land Rover and taken inside. My heart sank.

"Tye?"

We were alone and I knew Willa wanted to explain, but I just didn't want to hear it.

"Tye, I know you're angry that I left without saying anything, and I'm not surprised. It was awful and Tye I'm so sorry, I really am... I thought I was doing the right thing, I..."

I held up my hand to silence her, staring straight ahead. "Save it," I said. "I know that you've been stealing from the café and that you ran off with the kids, with Syd's children." I could barely get the words out I was so angry.

"I've what?" For a moment she seemed completely dumbfounded. "Stealing?!" Her voice came out as a squeak.

I finally turned to her. I could see that her face was on the verge of collapse, but I couldn't let that get to me, not this time, not now. "Don't bother Willa. It's over. And you know what's the worst thing? The worst thing is I honestly don't know why you had to create such an elaborate lie, with the catering business and me, letting me think that I could be in love with you...."

"A lie? Is that what you think I've done? Lied to you?"

"Yes. Or did I get that wrong? Have you always been completely honest and up front with me Willa?"

"Yes! Yes, I..." Her voice trailed off. "I don't know," she said.

"I thought so." She didn't need to say any more. I hadn't ever pushed her to give me answers about her past and she'd never offered them up. She may never have told me a direct lie, but she had certainly avoided the truth, that much was clear. She couldn't be trusted.

I shifted into gear. I was too angry to register the look of devastation on her face, too angry to recognise what I was saying.

"Don't let me keep you," I snapped.

She didn't answer me. What more was there to say?

FORTY-EIGHT

WILLA

Tye sat there, the engine ticked over and all the happiness I'd once imagined evaporated. It simply vanished into thin air. He'd asked me if I'd lied. No, I hadn't. But he also asked me if I had always been completely honest with him and the answer to that was also no. There were so many things that I should have told him, that I should have said.

It's over...

I climbed down and slammed the door after me. I was angry and hurt and disappointed.

Letting me think that I could be in love with you...

You either are, or you aren't in love with someone in my mind. And if you are, that should be a feeling that wild horses couldn't drag you from. Without looking back, I went into the Lodge and Tyler Malloy drove off and out of my life.

THE LODGE WAS LIT up inside like a Christmas tree; Syd and Daisy had all the lights on. They clearly wanted to see the truth. Esme and Teddy were in the snug, watching TV with a plate of biscuits by their side. There were two big wheely bags by the front door.

I went into the kitchen. Daisy and Syd were in there, Daisy seated at the table, Syd standing by the window. But Cici and Angelica were there as well, along with Percy who was lifting a singing kettle off the hot plate.

"I'm just about to make tea," he said. "We're all gasping. Would you like some?"

I stood in the doorway, bamboozled by them all, and unbidden tears streamed down my face. These people that I'd come to know, and to love, were now all against me. I was completely alone.

"Oh my god, Willa, please don't cry!" Cici was on her feet with her arms round me in seconds. Angelica joined her and they surrounded me. The thought of losing this was too much and I sobbed.

"Willa," Syd said loudly. "Willa, pull yourself together. There really is absolutely no reason to cry!"

Cici stood back. "She's right Willa, there really is nothing to cry about, I promise. Come on, sit down." She glanced at Angelica. "A bit of magic please Nellie, to help Willa feel better."

Angelica put her hands on my head and said something under her breath. Then she took my hand and led me to a chair.

I sat and strangely, I did feel a bit better.

"Have some tea," Syd commanded. "It'll do you good."

Percy brought the pot over and a fist full of mugs. He plonked them all down on the table and started pouring. He cracked a joke with Daisy about magic and she laughed. Angelica elbowed him, Cici smiled at me, and Syd began handing round mugs of tea. The atmosphere was not at all what I was expecting. Cici poured some milk into a mug and loaded several spoons of sugar into it. She handed me a mug of hot, milky, sugary tea.

"It's good for shock," she said, "And you've had a shock."

"We all have," Syd said, "Courtesy of Mr. Harry Lyme."

"What do you mean?" I asked.

"When Tye mentioned that Harry had run off and left you in the lurch, I felt decidedly uncomfortable," Syd said. "There were certain things that he'd said to me over the past few months, things that I'd believed and acted on that I suddenly worried might not be true."

"Which is where we come in," Angelica said. "Cici and I were convinced that you couldn't ever have stolen anything or run off, so we came down here to speak to Syd."

I was trying to keep up, but I must have looked confused at that point because Syd said, "Tye let us into the Lodge so that we could wait for you here and also so we could pack anything up that you might have left behind."

"I see." My eyes filled with tears again. That explained the bags in the hall by the front door.

"When Cici and Angelica arrived, I was already going through the bank accounts to see if things didn't add up and well... to be honest they didn't. I had always thought it was you, stealing..."

A sob escaped me.

"Oh, for goodness sake Willa. Please stop snivelling." Syd said sharply.

Daisy passed me a tissue from the box I kept on the side and glared at Syd.

"Why don't you start at the beginning *darling*," she said pointedly. "You're upsetting Willa and quite honestly, I think she's been upset enough for one day."

I looked up and Daisy smiled reassuringly at me.

Syd continued. "Harry came to me about ten weeks ago and said that he suspected that you were stealing from the café. He said that you'd been going on about not having enough money for the kids. I was angry and I told him to tell you to come and see me and that all you had to do was ask. You didn't come. He told me he'd relayed my message and that your response was that you were taking what was rightfully yours as you ran the café."

At this point Daisy harrumphed and Syd looked at her. "And Daisy told me not to believe him but to talk to you directly."

"Which you didn't do."

"Which I didn't do."

I blew my nose. "I lost my bank card for the café about three months ago. Harry told me he'd asked you to organise another one and that it was all in hand."

"He did not." Syd had the grace to look momentarily embarrassed. "But that explains a lot. Each week, a couple of times a week, after he spoke to me about theft, there were cash withdrawals from the business account, always up to the daily limit of two hundred and fifty pounds. I thought it was you. I spoke to Harry again to say that I was going to expose you and that your dishonesty made me doubt your suitability to parent the children."

"I disagreed."

"All right, thank you Daisy."

"No, I'm sorry Syd, but I think it's important to establish that. I've never doubted Willa's role as a mum. She's bloody good at it."

I welled up again and had to blow my nose once more. The tissue was quickly disintegrating. Angelica passed me the box.

"Why didn't you just stop the card Syd?" I asked. "Why did you let it go on?"

"Because I was worried that you needed the money, and you were guardian to Esme and Teddy. I didn't want to cut you off. I was waiting and hoping that you'd come to your senses. But the theft continued and then you left. And I was convinced that you were guilty and irresponsible, disappearing without a word."

"But Harry convinced me it was the right thing to do."

"Yes, we know that now." Syd frowned. "Anyway, we finally worked out where you might be and having seen a solicitor and a barrister, we came after you. But you'd disappeared again. When you rang Tye, we were waiting here to take the kids and that's when Cici and Angelica arrived. They defended you so vehemently that I had to tell them you'd been stealing, even after you left, but they asked me to prove it..."

"Which is where I come in," Percy interjected.

My head was swimming. What on earth was going on? This was like trying to follow the thread in a badly written whodunnit book.

"Syd had been going over the business account and she showed us where you'd taken money out. Some of the cashpoint withdrawals were out of London and could potentially have been you, so Angelica asked me to check the postal register. None of them are anywhere around here, so they weren't you."

"Plus," Angelica said, "One of the withdrawals is for the night you were decorating Megan's house. And another, which was done quite near here, was the day you and Percy delivered biscuits to the cafes."

"Nellie wanted to check with me that we were together the whole time and that you couldn't have possibly slipped away to withdraw cash." He looked triumphant. "Which you couldn't, because we were."

"But I've never made a cash withdrawal on that card," I said. "Ever."

"Well, we know that now! None of those could have been you, not the ones after you left, which threw doubt on all of them."

"Sorry, what did you mean by cash from a cashpoint quite near here?"

"We think that Harry probably came here, checked you out and worked on the best way to extricate himself from the situation," Percy offered.

I took a breath. "So, Harry was withdrawing cash and blaming it on me and he told me that you planned to take the kids away. He said you wanted full custody, and you wanted the house back. Was that true?"

"When I thought you'd been stealing, yes. I didn't think you could be trusted. But I'm sure now that he planned the whole thing, to take the card, use it, blame you and when you'd disappeared, to keep stealing. When I found out about your Aunt Maud he suddenly resigned and left the café. I guess he had to find a way to keep me off his tail, so he came down here and convinced you to run away again."

"Only he didn't reckon on us," Percy said. "Coming to your rescue."

"That was Tye," Cici said sharply.

"Why?" I looked at Syd. "Why did he do all that? I trusted him."

Syd shrugged. "Gambling debts? Drugs? I'm certain that he owed money somewhere Willa. People can do terrible things if they have to." She raised an eyebrow. "Look at your disappearance without a word because I wanted custody of the kids."

I took a large gulp of my tea and the sugar hit the back of my throat.

"And do you?" I asked. My voice trembled. "Still want custody of the kids?"

Daisy looked at Syd and Syd took a deep breath.

"We'd like to be more involved Willa if you'd let us. To try to be closer to you all." Syd looked pained. Daisy coughed.

"But no, we are not going to seek custody."

"What about the bags in the hall?"

"They're empty," Syd said. Suddenly she smiled. "You left all the crap behind Willa and we weren't going to clutter our lovely home up with all that shit."

And more from relief than humour, I suddenly burst out laughing.

FORTY-NINE

TYE

I was waiting in the kitchen for Cici to come home. I'd messaged her a few times, but she'd not replied. Very unlike Cici. I was worried about her and about Willa and try as I might to dismiss the way I'd behaved today as righteous because I was wounded, I felt terrible. Actually, I felt fucking terrible, and I didn't know what to do.

I heard the cab pull up and went to the door. Cici climbed out and waved to Sam, weaving her way up to the kitchen, a little unsteady on her feet. Crap.

"Are you OK?" I asked as she came into the house.

"I am fine," she said, "I am a few margaritas and a Chinese takeaway fine. Thank you."

She unwound her scarf and threw off her coat.

"You, however, are not fine." She stood and faced me, her arms folded across her chest. "You, Tyler Malloy, are a fucking dick."

I took a step back. "Whoa! Where did that come from? What the hell did I do to deserve that?"

Cici swayed slightly on her feet and stared at me.

"Harry was stealing from the café where he and Willa worked. The café that Syd owned. And he told Syd that it was Willa who was stealing." Cici continued to stare at me with an unstinting glare. "He told Willa that Syd was planning to try and get custody of Esme and Teddy, her sister's children, the sister who died of cancer at thirty-eight and who wanted Willa to take care of them."

Bam, there it was. Her words punched me right in the gut and I felt suddenly winded.

"Wait, Esme and Teddy are her sister's children?"

"Yes. Lexi, her sister, was Syd's partner. They'd broken up by the time Lexi got sick and Willa dropped out of college to look after her. She's been caring for those kids since she was seventeen years old Tye. And Harry, fucking Harry Lyme, nearly ruined her life."

Cici was upset, her eyes glinted with tears. "She couldn't bear to give up Esme and Teddy and anyway they wouldn't have gone, they love Willa..." Her voice trailed off for a moment. She took a breath. "And I thought you did too," she said. "I thought you loved Willa..."

She walked across to the tap, ran it, and filled a glass with water. She drank it down then turned back to me.

"I was wrong." She shook her head. "You are such a dick..."

She wasn't making exact sense, too much Tequila, but I got the gist of it. And she was right, I *was* a dick. I sat down and dropped my head into my hands.

"I should go and see her," I said. "I'll go now."

Cici was headed for the door. "I wouldn't bother," she shot back. "We had a good night with Syd and Daisy, Nellie and Percy. Nellie and I left him at Willa's. Just the two of them." She looked at me one last time.

"You had your chance Tye, and you blew it."

Then she walked out of the kitchen and made her way up to bed.

OKAY, it was stupid, and I knew I shouldn't have done it... but I just couldn't help myself. I grabbed my coat and walked out of the door, down the drive and through the woods to the Lodge. I was contrite, angry and jealous, and all sorts of other shitty feelings I couldn't name. Together they made a tornado of emotion that swirled around my head in a way I'd never experienced before. I walked across the front lawn and stood on the drive, suddenly torn between knocking, and going home. The kitchen lights were on, I could see that much, but the rest of the house was in darkness. I stood where I was, paralysed with indecision. Hamlet, eat your fucking heart out.

Suddenly the main bedroom light went on and I glanced up at the window. I wish I hadn't. Percy stood there. He looked down into the garden and for one awful, terrible, long instant, our eyes met. He smiled. The bastard actually smiled at me. Then he closed the curtains and the lights went off. Tormented by my own stupidity, I turned on my heel and walked away.

I'd said it myself.

It was over.

Cici was right, I was a fucking dick.

BUT AS I got to the woods, I stopped. There was something in Percy's manner at that window, something gloating, but also something dishonest. I knew that I couldn't trust him as far as I could throw him. He wanted me to think he was in Willa's bedroom for a reason, which almost certainly meant he wasn't. I retraced my footsteps and stood at the edge of the garden. It was fucking freezing, and my legs were numb, but I held my ground and half an hour later, as I thought he might, Percy emerged from the house, pulling on his hat and gloves.

"Percy."

I stepped out of the woods onto the drive and barred his way. He started.

"Fuck! Tye! Have you taken to stalking Willa like some thwarted weirdo boyfriend?"

"Shut the fuck up Percy." I growled. I was not in the mood for his snarky remarks.

"What were you doing in Willa's bedroom?"

I watched his face. I knew his compulsion to lie, and I noticed a flicker of amusement in his eyes. I moved a bit closer to him threateningly and it disappeared.

"Willa had too much to drink," he said. "I helped her upstairs and put her to bed."

"How much to drink?"

He pulled a face. "How the fuck do I know? I wasn't counting!"

"You must know how drunk she was."

"OK, she was pretty out of it. Why? Why d'you want to know?"

"Because you have to go back in and look after her."

"No mate, not me. I'm going home. I've got work tomorrow."

"Yes mate. You. She needs someone to sit with her in case she's sick, or falls over if she gets up. And it can't be me, so it's got to be you." I was raising my voice and Percy backed away.

"I'm not going back in," he said. "I told you; I'm going home. You can fuck off Tye."

Without thinking, I grabbed his collar and pulled it in tight around his neck. I lifted him slightly off his feet. "You *are* going back in. I have keys and I'm going to let you back in and you are going to sit with Willa to make sure she's OK." I said it slowly, squeezing his collar as I spoke. "All night." His eyes bulged as he stared at me. "Have you got that Percy?"

He said nothing.

"Have you got that?" I repeated.

Finally, he nodded. "Good."

I released him and he stumbled a few paces back.

"I'm going to get the Land Rover now and I'm going to sit out here to make sure you stay in there."

"You're fucking mad Tye." He rubbed his neck. "You can't leave it alone, can you?"

"Nope."

"You have to be in control."

"Yup."

I walked across to the front door and opened it for him.

"Get upstairs and keep an eye on her like any decent person would do if their friend was out of it. Have a bit of integrity Percy. Fucking man-up."

He went inside and I closed the door. I waited a while to make sure he'd done what I'd asked him to do then I jogged back up to the house to collect the car. I was going to freeze my bollocks off sitting out there all night, but I deserved it. As long as Willa was OK. That was all that mattered.

FIFTY

WILLA

"Oh God..." The throb in my brain hit me before I'd even opened my eyes. I had a pounding on the inside of my head as if someone with a huge baseball bat was thwacking against my skull, trying to get out.

"Oh God..." I rolled onto my side and a wave of nausea rose up into my throat. I opened my eyes, leaned over the side of the bed, and threw up into the bowl someone had left there.

"Ouch," Amy came in to the bedroom.

"Amy?!!" I lay on my back and squinted at her. "What are you doing here?"

"I heard you were a bit the worse for wear last night and so I thought I'd pop over with my lot and help you get the kids ready for school. Or, as it now appears, give you some paracetamol and leave you to sleep while I get them ready for school myself." She laughed. "Here." She held out a glass of water and two tablets.

I took them, swallowed, and wondered how long I'd keep them down. I felt absolutely wretched.

"Oh God..." That seemed all I was capable of saying. I pulled the duvet up to my chin and gritted my teeth.

"That'll teach ya," Percy called from the doorway.

"Percy?"

"He stayed last night," Amy said, "to make sure you didn't choke on your own vomit."

"Oh God... was I that bad?"

"No," Percy said, "But you're not a drinker Willa Hart. You barely had to sniff the Tequila and you were off your face."

I felt sick again and rolled back onto my side to hang my head towards the bowl.

"I must get on," Amy said, "It's seven a.m. and not a child in the house washed." She smiled, gave my leg a squeeze through the duvet and disappeared.

"You'll feel fine once the paracetamol kicks in," Percy said. He came in and took a blanket and his jacket off the armchair in the corner of the room.

"Where did you sleep last night?" I had an awful vision of him lying next to me on the bed while I snored my way through the night.

"There."

I rolled over and sat up. "God Percy, that is so nice of you. It must have been really uncomfortable."

"Yup."

"Did you get much sleep?"

"No."

"Oh God..."

He pulled his jacket on. He did look pretty tired.

"Thank you." I rolled onto my side again to stop the wave of nausea reaching my throat.

"It's fine. I'm off to work. See you later?"

"Oh erm..." No was what I wanted to say, but he had

just spent the night watching a drunk woman snore and probably fart her way through the early hours. "Sure" I said. I closed my eyes.

"See ya," Percy called.

I tried to wave but even my arms felt hungover.

I WAS up by the time Amy came back from the school run. I was showered and dressed, and I had managed to keep a coffee down along with a dose of ibuprofen. I think I remember Esme and Teddy coming in to poke me, but the memory was fuzzy. I had clearly been out for the count.

"I've made you some fresh coffee," I said, trying to look brighter than I felt, "And I owe you one. Thank you, Amy."

"You look a little less green," she said, taking her coat off and pulling on her hairnet and apron. "I've missed you. It was a shit load of work yesterday on my own."

I felt the tears well up. Oh, my Lord, what was wrong with me?! I'd spent the last six years stealing myself not to cry and now it seemed I couldn't stop.

"I'm really sorry Amy," I said, "for running off like that. I panicked, I thought..."

Amy came across to me and swept me into a bear hug. "You do not need to apologise." I'd told Amy on the phone last night what had happened and now she rubbed my back as if I was a child. That made me cry even more. I sniffed and she released me.

"Tissue," she said, handing me the box. "I do not want snot on my shoulder." She smiled. "I'm just glad you're back." She went to the sink to wash her hands. She had prepped everything before she took the kids to school and the kitchen was ready for action.

"Chicken pie," she said. "Tye delivered the chicken a bit earlier and left it in the big fridge in the shed."

"Tye?" So, he hadn't come in. He'd sent me a message very early this morning; *sorry, can we talk*? But that was all. He was a coward; he hadn't thought to come in and see if I was all right.

"Yup." She looked uncomfortable for a moment and busied herself getting the pans out from the boxes under the trestle tables. "I saw him..." She stopped suddenly.

"You saw him when?"

"Oh, we passed as I left for school," she said brightly, loading up the kitchen table with everything we needed to cook with.

"Did Percy call you to come over? He stayed last night to look after me."

"Hmmm?" She had her back to me and was sorting through the bags, looking for carrots and onions.

"Percy's been really lovely," I said.

Amy turned. "Percy is really lovely when there is something in it for Percy," she said brusquely. "Now, Willa - drunk on two shots, throwing up on three - Hart. We've got seventy-five chicken pies to make for the farm shop and fifteen for our young carer families." She grinned. "So, stop ya snivelling girl and let's get to work!"

FIFTY-ONE

TYE

"Hey." Cici came into the kitchen and across to the table where I had my laptop open and was working. She pulled out a chair and sat down opposite me.

I nodded.

"I saw Amy this morning on my run. She was pulling into the Lodge drive about six thirty a.m., just as you were pulling out." She stared pointedly at me. "Tye?"

I sighed.

"What's going on?"

I looked up at her. She was persistent, always had been and I doubted if I could fob her off with a lame excuse.

"Ok, if you must know..."

"I must."

"Willa was apparently very drunk last night so I told Percy to stay with her to make sure she was OK, and I rang Amy early this morning to ask her to go over and help get the kids ready for school."

"And you were there why?"

"I was there in case I was needed in the night."

Cici shook her head. "Let me get this straight. You slept in the car all night, in the freezing cold in case you were needed?! What the fuck Tye?"

"I was worried about Willa. She barely drinks and I was worried that she'd have a bad reaction, I..." I stopped. "Willa knows nothing about this, so don't say anything. I've fucked up Ci and if I can't make it right then at least I can try..."

Cici stood. "To be less of a dick and look out for her. OK, I get it." She moved to stand behind me so that she could see what I was doing on screen.

"Customer research?"

I had Google Maps up.

"No. I'm going to try and find the van and get Willa's things back." I glanced behind me at Cici. Her reaction was important. She was a good sounding board and if she thought I was on the wrong track, then she'd tell me.

"OK. And how do you plan to do that?"

"I've been looking at car dealerships fifty miles each way from that Airbnb he left them in. I'm guessing that Harry will try and sell the van and he'll have to do it somewhere reasonably close by because he's going to be low on gas. I don't think he'll have the cash to refill the tank."

"Nice work Miss Marple. Then?"

"I'll ring round and see if any of the dealerships have been approached."

"Ah, right."

"And then I'll go and get the van and return it to Willa."

Cici narrowed her eyes. "You know she's going to go back North at Christmas, don't you? When the kids finish school next week."

I swallowed down a lump that unexpectedly rose in my throat.

"You should talk to her Tye."

I shook my head. "I sent a message. No response. And I don't blame her. I didn't trust her Cici, and I let her down when she needed me the most."

"But you went and got her from the back of beyond."

"And I told her that it was over."

Cici sat down again. "Oh." She reached out and put her hand on my arm. "Shit. That makes sense now, that's why she's leaving."

"Is that what she said?"

"No, but Syd said it was up to Willa, wherever she decided to settle they'd support her and that's when she said she'd go home, back to the café. I was surprised, I thought she'd been happy here and well, when you two..." She stopped suddenly. "Sorry."

I closed my eyes. I had well and truly fucked up.

"Tye, is it worth going down to see her now? Before this gets any worse? At least you can try and explain?"

"I don't know." But I did know; there wasn't any point. Willa was a strong person and if she'd made up her mind to leave then that's what she would do. "I think..." I took a breath.

"I think that I've made a massive mistake and that she won't forgive me. So, the best thing I can do, the only thing I can do, is try to make Willa's life a little bit happier. I'll find her van and return it and then at least she won't feel that she's leaving here with nothing."

I stood up and went across to make myself another cup of tea. I'd drunk endless cups of tea this morning, it was the only thing that made me feel any better.

"I'd better open the shop," Cici said. "Can I do anything to help?"

"No." There wasn't anything anyone could do to help. I

was miserable, it was my own stupid, fucking fault, and I was just going to have to sit with it.

FIFTY-TWO

TYE

Tanya hadn't changed. She waved and smiled at me with the same enthusiasm she'd had as a teenager. I'd always loved that about her. I waved back and crossed the café to her table. She stood and we hugged.

"Tye, you handsome devil!"

"Tanya, you gorgeous gal!" It was an old routine and one we'd been playing since school. For some reason we'd thought it was hilarious back then to greet each other like we were in a nineteen fifties Hollywood movie. It wasn't hilarious anymore, but we still laughed.

I pulled out a chair and sat, carrying it on. "So, how you been?"

"Oh, you know, so so." Tanya settled back down on the sofa. She grinned. "Your American accent is still shocking."

"But nice to know that some things never change, right?"

"Right. It's good to see you Tye. How are you and how's Peace Summerton?"

"Yeah, OK. We're both OK."

"Hmm, that doesn't sound very convincing." She raised an eyebrow.

I shrugged. "How are you? How's the force?"

"Yes, I'm good, very good. Force is as it always was. Had a promotion, as you know, got another cat, so you're looking at a senior ranking cat lady."

I smiled.

"So, what's up and what can I help with?" She picked up her coffee cup and readied for my narrative. That was another thing I'd always liked about Tanya. No bullshit, straight to the point.

"A friend of mine has been ripped off by a guy called Harry Lyme. He was stealing from their workplace and implicated her to cover up his theft, and then he ran off with her camper van and all her belongings."

"Ouch. That's the abridged version I'm guessing?"

"Yup."

"And you want to find this Harry Lyme?"

"Yeah, and the van. After this I'm headed down to Cornwall where he was last and I'm going to try the local dealerships, see if he's tried to flog it. I've rung a couple, but nothing has shown up yet."

"Nice work detective. When did he disappear?"

"Yesterday. Well, technically, about 36 hours ago."

"Right. And are the workplace pressing charges?"

"They will, if we can find him."

"How old is the van? Will he have sold it to be shipped to Europe d'you think?"

"No, it's ancient, held together with string."

Tanya smiled.

"OK." She replaced her coffee cup on the table. "So, from what you've told me, my guess is the same as yours, he'll have tried to off load the van as quickly as possible for cash. If it was a newer model, I might suggest that he's got contacts and it's gone abroad already, so you'd be wasting your time with dealerships. But it sounds like what you're doing is a good plan of action."

"And Harry Lyme?"

"Well..." Tanya thought for a few moments. "It is a matter for the police of course. But having said that, a prosecution is unlikely. If he's got a criminal record already you've got more chance of finding him, but if he's a new offender, then I think it'll be like trying to find a needle in a haystack." She shook her head. "What would you do, if it was you?"

"I'd look at the stuff I'd gone off with, realise that it wasn't worth anything and flog the van as quickly as I could. Then I'd probably go to ground."

"Exactly."

"So, you're saying don't bother trying to find him?"

"What's more important, the van or finding Harry?"

"The van."

"Then focus on that. Do you need any help? It sounds as if you've got it covered. Have you?" Tanya looked at me in the searching way she looked at most things, as if seeing something there that wasn't apparent to everyone else.

"Most of it, DS Crossly."

"Detective Inspector Crossly, thank you." She grinned. "Well, whoever owns the van is a very lucky girl." She looked at her watch. "Tye, I'm sorry, but would you mind if I cut this short? New job, new workload, new boss breathing down my neck."

"No problem. I need to get off on my travels anyway."

"Thanks. The role of DI comes at a price." She finished her coffee and stood. I stood as well and realised that I hadn't even ordered a drink. She pulled her jacket on, and we hugged.

"Are you going my way?"

"I'm going to grab a takeaway," I said, "For the journey."

"Good luck with the van," Tanya said. 'And good luck with the owner." She smiled and winked. "Not that you've ever needed luck in that department. Heart breaker Malloy." She laughed and headed towards the door. "See you later," she called over her shoulder, "Take care." And she was gone before I had even got to the queue.

I'D INPUTTED ALL the dealership numbers into my phone before I left and so I rang them one by one on my way back to the Land Rover after coffee. I was parked on the edge of Kimberton town, so I had plenty of time as I walked. Mostly I left messages to call me back if anything came up. I only hoped that this was going to pay off and that I wouldn't have to trawl the countryside looking for the van.

And, as I set off on the A39, what I'd hoped for came through. A garage on the north coast called me, about seventy miles from the Airbnb. I pulled into a layby and took the call.

The garage owner described Harry and the details of their conversation. He had bought the van off Harry for just five thousand pounds because it needed so much work and Harry was desperate. I could have it for seven thousand. Nice fucking work if you could get it. The garage owner went on...

"He'd done what?" Harry had left all the windows in the van open, to get rid of the smell of dog, apparently. Overnight.

"How wet and damp was it?" It had rained and all the

stuff in the van was soaked. I sighed. "Yeah, it is really upsetting. No, no please don't throw anything out. I'll take it exactly as it is."

I got my wallet out of my jeans. I had savings, I could use them. Let's face it, what else did I have to spend my money on?

"Yes, yes that's fine. We can pick it up tomorrow. Oh, really, when could you deliver and how much would it be?" I calculated the cost of Cici and me taking the morning off to drive to collect the van, closing the farm shop, no food deliveries to cafés, time off from the estate. The owner quoted me a price. "Yes, that's fine. Yeah, I've got my card now. If you could deliver tonight that would be great, thanks." I read the card number out, gave him my address and postcode and finished the call. I sat in the Land Rover and then called Cici.

"I've got the van," I said, "but before I give it to Willa, I'm going to need your help."

FIFTY-THREE

WILLA

If it hadn't been for Amy, Percy, and the young carer families we cooked for, I think I would have left before school was out. I'd have gone as soon as things with Tye were over. I was miserable. No, more than that, I was bereft. I was too sad to even talk to Lexi.

After the Harry debacle, Tye had messaged me; I messaged back. I was curt and to the point. What more was there for me to say? He hadn't trusted me. He hadn't trusted his own feelings. So, how could we ever build a relationship on that foundation? That's what I'd told him. He hadn't disagreed. Of course I meant it, but he hadn't tried to change my mind or argue his case or even ask me to forgive him. Not that I would have, but I would have liked him to ask. Percy had told me that once Tye makes up his mind about someone, he doesn't change it back. So that was it.

But a failed fling was one thing, the atmosphere at Peace Summerton House was quite another. Tye avoided me. He was never there when I was and that hurt. Cici seemed distant, preoccupied, always busy, always disappearing into the house, and it was as if she was upset on Tye's account. Perhaps I was oversensitive, but I felt that under the surface something was going on.

Thankfully though, today was Friday, the last day of the school Christmas term and we were leaving on Sunday. I was relieved to be going. It wasn't that I wanted to leave, but more that I felt I had to. Syd was arriving that afternoon and after our goodbye drinks tonight at Peace Summerton - which Cici insisted on and which I really didn't want to go to - we were heading back North first thing on Sunday morning.

BY THE TIME I arrived at the farm shop with our batch cook that lunchtime, I was sad, frustrated and altogether frazzled. I'd had a rotten morning. Teddy was playing up. He didn't want to leave Peace Summerton and every time I tried to pack something - not that we had much left - he unpacked it and threw it across the room. We had a whole hour of it before school and I felt like a wet dishcloth when we started cooking.

Then Amy was quiet, so quiet and so unlike Amy that I wondered if something was seriously amiss. It was our last cook together, but we'd agreed she would take the catering business over and she was happy to do so. I had no idea what the problem was and when I asked her, she was all cagey and odd and that made me feel even worse. What was wrong with everyone? More importantly, what was wrong with me?

As I came into the shop I saw Megan, which was a surprise. More of Cici avoiding me?

"Hey. How are you? I didn't know you were here today?" Megan usually helped Cici on a Thursday.

"Hi Willa, yes, I..." Megan stopped halfway through her sentence, as if she'd remembered not to say something. She paused then said, "Cici asked me. She said she's got a lot on today."

"Ah, all right." But it wasn't all right. In the past Cici would have asked me to help if she needed someone extra and I felt hurt. I couldn't help it.

Megan came across to help me with the food. She took a couple of bags off me, and we carried them into the back. We unpacked them and stacked some of the cartons into the fridge and some into the freezer.

"That smells good, even in the cartons," she said.

'Thanks." That made me feel sad.

"If you weren't leaving, I'd ask for cooking lessons."

"Oh Megan, I would have loved to help you learn to cook!" My voice faltered. I was close to tears. Yet again. "That is a great compliment."

I cleared my throat and reached into my pocket for a tissue.

"Here."

I turned to see a clean white handkerchief held out. I took it and blew my nose. I held the hankie and sniffed. Weird, but it smelled of him and then the tears spilled over. Oh God, now I looked pathetic.

"Thanks," I croaked.

Tye was staring at me.

"Onions," I said.

He smiled. God, I'd missed that smile; his eyes crinkled at the side and his smile was slightly lopsided, not in a strange way, but in a way that made him look as if he was secretly amused by something.

I offered the hankie back and he smiled again. "Keep it," he said. "You could start a small collection."

My cheeks felt suddenly hot and I put my hand up to them.

"Look Willa, I owe you an apology," he said. "I've not been around much the past week and I know it's your last one and I'm sad about that. I had something that I had to do that was really important, and it's taken up all my time."

I nodded, but I couldn't look at him. I stared down at the ground and twisted the hankie in my fingers. Why did I keep wanting to weep?

"And Cici's been helping me, so she's been preoccupied too. You must have thought we were ignoring you." He waited for me to look up. "So, I hope you're coming tonight as then we can have a chance to talk and catch up. You are coming, aren't you?"

I stopped twisting the hankie like a dingbat and looked directly at him. I was a grown up, I was an independent woman with my own vibrator, I had two children, and I could fix an engine and change a tyre. I was not going to wobble like a schoolgirl.

"Yes, I'm coming. I..." I couldn't say I was looking forward to it. I wasn't.

"I'll be there on time," I said. Then I cringed as he looked at me oddly for a second. *I'll be there on time?* Oh, dear God, what was that?

"Good, so will I." He laughed. "We'll both be there bang on seven."

He headed for the door. 'See you later Willa."

"Yes. See you later."

When I looked round Megan was staring at me and smiling.

"What?!"

She shook her head and walked back to where she had been stacking jams onto the shelf. "Nothing," she said.

"What is up with today?" I said aloud and then I went in search of Basil to take him home.

FIFTY-FOUR

TYE

Cici was right, as always. There *were* things to be said, things that I *should* have said, before it was too late. I knew that as soon as I handed Willa my handkerchief. I'd been a coward, hiding behind my pride and a false sense of right and wrong. What it boiled down to was Love. I loved Willa. Simple as that. And yet I'd let all sorts of fears - of losing her, of being left, of having my heart broken - get in the way of that. What a fucking idiot. I'd had my heart broken once, I'd lost the two most important people in my life, in one night, and I'd survived. Why hadn't I focused on that? Instead of being terrified of what giving my heart away meant.

I walked into the barn across the yard from the farm shop and kicked the tyres on the camper van, which was fine because they were new. I'd replaced them this week.

Fuck.

I hadn't seen Willa since the day I'd rescued her, well, not really *rescued* her because I didn't act like Prince Charming. I was more the wicked stepmother, seeing only my own reflection in the mirror. But I'd avoided her, put all my energy into fixing the van and so just now, when I saw her again, it was like seeing her for the first time. Wild hair and DMs, self-assured innocence, sassy, and kind, and all of that was just so fucking sexy. My heart stopped, did a somersault, and then started beating again. Yes, I loved Willa Hart. I just hadn't had the balls to face up to it.

Not that I'd come to all this self-realisation myself. No, I wasn't that enlightened. It was Sam mostly, who drove the taxi. Overalls on, under the VW, replacing the engine with a reconditioned one I'd found. It's easy to talk when you're doing something and the past week restoring the camper van with Sam had made a lot of sense. Yup, Sam had told me a thing or two about love, as well as being one of the best car mechanics I'd ever met.

"So how are we going to play this?" Cici asked. She was carrying a small vase of flowers and a diffuser from Neal's Yard – just the sort of thing that Willa would love, all herbal, organic and floral.

"I'm just going to pop these in the van, but I think we should leave the bags until just before she's due to arrive. I don't want the kids' stuff to get cold and damp."

Cici and Eadie had been washing and ironing, rummaging the charity shops for replacement games and Cici had been sewing new curtains and cushion covers. The van had been revamped, put back to its original condition before the rain damage, with a few improvements that meant it would last Willa another good ten years. I asked Sam to make sure of that.

"I think we should leave the van at the front of the house so that she sees it when she drives up with Syd. What time is everyone arriving?"

"I told them six thirty and not to be late as it's a surprise.

Sam's doing a lot of the ferrying and so is Eadie, so we know the families will be here on time. Do you think she suspects?"

I thought about Willa's face, how unhappy she looked, and I felt a pang of distress. "No," I said, and I wished that she did.

Cici came across to me. She stood in front of me, head on and said,

"Don't let her go Tye."

I could smell the diffuser, geranium and rose and it reminded me of Willa. "It's not up to me," I answered, but as soon as I said it, I knew I was wrong. It might not be my decision but that didn't mean I couldn't try to persuade her.

"I won't bother to respond to that," Cici said. "Keys?"

I dug in my pocket for the keys to the van and handed them over.

"Thanks." She moved across the barn to the van.

"Nice job by the way," she said as she opened the door. "Just missing the new dog bed for Basil?"

"On its way."

"Great. Tye, you've thought of everything."

Except how to tell Willa that I loved her and couldn't let her go. The most important thing was the one thing that escaped me.

FIFTY-FIVE

WILLA

Groundhog Day! I came downstairs ready for the drinks and Esme took one look and shook her head.

"You can't go in jeans Willa," she said, "not to a party!"

Oh God, we'd been here before, but the dress I'd worn all those weeks ago was gone, vamoosed with the rest of our things on that fateful night. Harry-gate had a lot to answer for.

"Well, I've nothing else," I said. There was a knock on the door.

"That's Syd, so let her in and I'll get our coats. You look lovely by the way. Where did that dress come from?"

"What?" Esme said, moving towards the door. She was stalling; I knew a stalling tactic when I saw one.

"Esme?!"

She opened the door and Amy stood there. Esme grinned. "Just in time," she said, "she was going to go like that."

Amy held something in dry cleaning cellophane draped over her arm.

"Here," she said. "Esme rang me, so I popped up to get it."

I took what she held out. "What? Sorry? Popped up where? Esme?" I was going to say I told you not to go near my phone, but I stopped myself. That phrase didn't hold much sway now.

"What's this Amy?" I looked at the hanger and what was beneath the cellophane. "Amy, is this?"

"Yes, your velvet dress. Don't ask me any more questions please Willa! Just get dressed and I'll see you up at..."

"See me up at?" I was bewildered. What on earth was going on.

"Nowhere, I mean just get dressed Willa. Put it on, please? Now!"

A car pulled up into the drive.

"That's Syd. I should go." She backed away and then ran to her car which was parked haphazardly in the drive. I turned.

"Esme, what is going on?"

Esme shook her head. "You know as much as I do," she said. Seriously? That? My own words right back at me.

"No young lady, that's not good enough..."

"What's not good enough?" Syd asked, walking right in.

"There is something going on and I have no idea what it is, but Lexi's dress has mysteriously appeared out of nowhere, a dress I thought we'd lost forever, and Esme is involved and..." My voice faltered.

"And it's five to seven Willa! We're due at Peace Summerton House at seven." Syd tapped her watch. "Daisy is in the car. Just put the dress on and let's go." She threw me a look.

"There is nothing to cry about!"

That's what you think, I wanted to say, but I didn't. I felt miserable and now I also felt very unnerved. I pulled my jumper over my head, took the dress out of the cellophane and slipped it over my head. I undid my boots, yanked them off, peeled my jeans off and put my boots back on. I was ready and I stood in Lexi's dress, the flowing folds of deep blue velvet falling over my hips and swirling down to the floor. Syd looked me over and I saw, for one fleeting moment, a glimpse of sorrow. Then it was gone and replaced with determination before I could blink.

"Right, all out and into the car," she said.

"Teddy?!" I called.

Teddy came down the stairs. He was wearing a pair of swimming shorts, a tee-shirt, sunglasses and flipflops. The whole outfit was finished with a Santa hat and behind him, wearing a dog version of the same hat trailed Basil. I glanced at Esme. "Amy?"

She nodded.

"You'll need a coat over that," I said. "It's cold out."

"Won't."

"OK." I was beyond arguing. If he was cold, then so be it.

We squidged into the back of Syd's car, which wasn't really a squidge as you could have held a small cocktail party in there it was so roomy. Syd peered at her watch again as a message came through.

"Right," she said, glancing sidelong at Daisy. "Everything's ready. Let's go."

Everything's ready? What did she mean by that? We headed off, out onto the main road and then immediately right into the drive of Peace Summerton House.

"Wow!" Esme gasped as we drove slowly – not at all

Syd's style – up the drive. The trees had been hung with small, twinkling lanterns and in between each tree that lined the drive, a flare had been lit. It was magical. Wow indeed.

As we approached the house it too was lit up. The windows glowed, the trees either side of the front door were garlanded in white lights and there, right in front of the steps, wreathed in fairy lights and wrapped in a huge red bow was a VW camper van. I blinked. I saw the number plate. It was *my VW camper van*! I gasped. I actually gasped, like they do in the movies, and Syd pulled to a stop. I climbed out and went across to the van.

"How on earth?"

I felt a little hand reach for mine. I took it and squeezed.

"Did you know about this?" I looked down into Esme's shining face and she nodded.

"But you are hopeless at secrets! How did this happen? And how did you keep it quiet?"

"It wasn't easy," Cici said, coming down the steps of the house. She hugged me. "Look inside."

I opened the door and inside the van were our bags, but not packed in the higgledy-piggledy way that they had been, and thrown into the van, but laid out and open to show all the clothes we owned neatly stacked and folded. I sniffed the air.

"Lenor," I said. "Did you...?"

Cici laughed. "You are not an easy person to hide from Willa. I'm so sorry that I was always avoiding you. Eadie and I washed everything. It had got very damp when Tye found the van."

"Tye?" I turned. He had come down the steps to join us.

"I went after Harry and found the van. Not him unfortunately..."

"Or fortunately," Eadie added. "I think we'd all have had something to say to that scumbag!"

"Mum!"

"Sorry Cici, but there's no other word for him."

I had begun to walk around the van. The body work had been done and not just 'done', but beautifully filled, repaired and resprayed... the same colour. I looked at the tyres. New. The trim work, polished.

"There's a reconditioned engine as well. Would you like to see it?"

I think my mouth dropped open. Not a great look. "Oh Goodness, yes! Would I?!"

He went into the driver's side and popped the bonnet.

I bent and peered inside. "Oh my God!" This was overwhelming. "And a new battery and starter motor?"

"Yup."

I straightened. "Tye, you did all this?" I glanced round, but everyone had gone inside. We were alone. Me in my velvet dress, with Tye, in the dark, looking at an engine. Like I said, Groundhog Day.

"Sam helped." He smiled and I knew that I loved that smile. He did all this. For me.

"Actually, Sam did most of it. I just farted about a bit and looked pretty."

"I don't believe that!"

"What the farting about bit or the looked pretty bit?"

I laughed.

"I didn't want you to go without..." He stopped and swallowed hard. I saw him hesitate in that way that he had; being thoughtful, considering his words. Then he said,

"I don't want you to go."

He stepped closer and took my hands. "I thought I was

doing this as a goodbye gift, but I wasn't. I was doing this to show you how much I love you."

I held my breath as my stomach did double back flips and my heart practised the samba.

"I fucked up Willa, I was frightened of losing my heart, which was stupid because it had already gone. I lost it the first time we stood in the barn, and you smiled at me. And..."

He dug in his pocket and handed me another clean handkerchief. I blew my nose and wiped my face.

"And I know it's only been a few months..."

"Two... and a half..." I stammered.

He smiled and everything stopped for a moment.

"Two and a half, but I also know, completely and wholeheartedly, that I don't want to be without you." He put my hand up to his mouth and kissed it. "Will you forgive me?"

I stared at him. I'd been so angry, so let down and betrayed by his lack of loyalty, but I had also wanted him to fight for me and I thought he hadn't. He had. This was Tye's fight; something practical that took time and patience and love.

"If you say no, then I understand and I'm glad that I've been able to do something for you so that you leave here knowing that we all cared. That you changed our lives..."

I blew my nose again and from out of his other pocket he produced another clean white handkerchief. He was the hankie elf.

"That one was meant for me, for if you say no."

I laughed, let out another sob and hiccupped all at the same time. "I won't... I won't say no..."

He moved a tiny step closer.

"Willa, will you stay?"

I could feel his warmth and see the pulse in his neck beating fast.

"Will you stay with me, and the kids, at Peace Summerton House, as a family?" He stopped and took a big breath. "Will you marry me?"

Suddenly shocked, I stared down at the ground. Was he serious? He kept hold of my hand tightly in his and I could feel him looking at me, willing me to love him right back. But, he didn't need to will it, it had already happened. I took a breath, almost as big as his had been and then I nodded.

"If you promise to always supply me with clean hankies." My voice was wobbly.

"I promise. Is that a yes, you'll stay?"

"Yes. Yes, I'll stay. With you."

He put his arms around me and for the first time since Lexi died, I knew that I was no longer alone. He released me and looked towards the house.

"Shall we go in?"

He led me up the steps and into Peace Summerton House.

"Welcome home," he said. "This is where you belong."

He flung open the doors.

And inside the hall a huge cheer went up and Basil broke into a peal of barks. There were people and candles and fairy lights. There was holly and roses and champagne. And everywhere I looked there was someone I knew and someone I loved. Even the young carer families we cooked for had come. I saw Amy, Angelica, Cici and Eadie and I even spotted Percy in a corner with Syd and Daisy; Lord knows what he was up to. Esme was on Cici's shoulders, Eadie held Teddy aloft and as we entered, I heard Tye shout above the noise.

"Willa is going to stay" he called out, "And she said YES!"

Someone popped a champagne cork and the cheer escalated.

He was right. This is where I belonged. I blew a kiss to Esme and Ted. It was where we all belonged.

EPILOGUE

SIX MONTHS LATER

It is a perfect English summer's day, light cloud, a golden sun in a pale blue sky and a tender cool breeze – kissing skin and gently flapping the silk skirts of dresses and brims of straw hats. It's a poet's English summer day. In a field on the Peace Summerton Estate, the one that looks out over the whole valley, a cream tepee marquee, festooned with floral linen bunting and roses from the garden, stands proudly welcoming the small crowd gathered on the grass outside it.

The occasion is a wedding. Nothing extravagant or showy; a simple celebration, where the bride has cooked the food herself and walked to the church holding hands with two small children, seven and nine, followed by a scruffy dog in a pink diamanté collar. The dog looks very pleased with himself.

Now, at the celebration, they stand together with the groom, and they make a striking sight.

The little girl wears a net skirt in fluorescent pink, a silver sequinned tee-shirt and a pair of orange trainers with stars on and the small boy wears what he always wears on special occasions, flip flops, swim shorts, a tee-shirt, and sunglasses. The bride is radiant in midnight blue velvet, a dress that means she was married with her sister there, the memory of her stitched into every perfect seam of the dress. The groom cannot stop smiling – something he is not famous for – he smiles at everyone and everything because he never believed he could be so happy.

Over in the corner a young woman with flame red hair is organising the bar, and waving a gnarled stick over all the glasses as they are set out, murmuring something under her breath. She is dressed in a long turquoise gown decorated with silver stars and moons. The bar is going to be staffed by a handsome blond man and members of his band. But for now, he stands, leaning against a tent pole, drinking a beer, and scanning the crowd. He gives off a bad-boy aura, but he's too attractive for anyone to take any notice of that. Little do they know the amount of trouble he will cause in the future.

The guests begin to filter in, a tall woman with her arms around a smaller, very beautiful girlfriend, a family of four children with their mother, who sends the young ones off to find the play area and immediately goes to the bar with the older boy for some trays of champagne to hand round. There's another family chatting shyly to a woman in a pink straw hat and matching dress. She is clearly someone important, although you'd never know because she treats everyone, especially the children, with the upmost kindness and respect.

The afternoon moves on, the marquee fills with friends and the newly married couple finally enter to huge cheers from their friends and community. They are both much loved.

Behind them the two children, the boy now wearing his flip flops on his hands and walking barefoot, and a striking woman in her sixties who holds hands with a younger woman who seems to radiate sunshine as she moves, smiling and laughing and waving at all the people she loves. This young woman has found her sense of self and is not afraid to be who she really is at last.

It is a grand day. A day of joy and laughter, and light. It is the sort of day that is taken home in every heart and when remembered, brings a smile. It is their day, but it also belongs to everyone there.

You see, love has the power to do that; to embrace and enfold, and to spread, like small ripples on a still lake, further and wider than you could ever imagine possible.

COMING SOON...

Next in the Peace Summerton Series...

WHAT WE'D ALWAYS WANTED

There's another wedding at Peace Summerton House, only this time it's a big, expensive, grand affair and it will put the house and the estate - now a new, stylish wedding venue - on the map. Willa will oversee catering, and Cici has planned an event that will not only enthral the guests but will also provide stunning photographs for the magazines and on-line celebrity sites that have negotiated a hefty sum for them.

All things being well – and with a little bit of Angelica's magic - this celebration looks set to be the wedding of the year!

Only sometimes things don't go quite as well as we'd hoped, and they certainly don't if Percy Dunston has anything to do with it. An old rival of Tyler Malloy, what starts out for Percy as a petty revenge - a bit of meddling and messing - quickly escalates to fever pitch and puts everything; weddings, love, Peace Summerton House itself and whole lives in jeopardy.

Printed in Great Britain
by Amazon

46304358R00165